OKOBOJI

Editor: Marilyn Lund

Graphic Design: Debbie Wilson

Front Cover Photo: Cynthia Frederick

Back Cover Photo: Susie Jensen

Thanks to my wife, Bev, sons Les and Chris, and friends, George, Mike, Nancy, Keith, Bob, and Barb for your interest in this book and for your encouragement. *– Peter Davidson*

OKOBOJI

Peter Davidson

SWEET MEMORIES PUBLISHING

A Division of Sweet Memories, Inc.

sweetmemories@mchsi.com

This novel is a work of fiction. Although several real people have cameo roles in the story, all of the main characters are fictitious and any resemblance of these fictitious characters to real persons is purely coincidental. When persons are mentioned by their real names, they are represented in fictitious situations and the reader should not infer that these events or dialogue actually occurred. Some events in the story may be based upon events that actually happened, but the portrayal of these events are the product of the author's imagination and are not intended to represent those events as they may have occurred.

ISBN: 0-9762718-0-X
LCCN: 2004098381

First printing July, 2005

Published by Sweet Memories Publishing, Sweet Memories, Inc.,
P.O. Box 497, Arnolds Park, IA 51331-0497

PRINTED IN THE UNITED STATES OF AMERICA

10   9   8   7 6   5   4   3   2   1

Dedication Number One

To all those who have spent a day, weekend, month, or lifetime in Okoboji and have fallen in love with it. I am proud to say that I am one of you.

Dedication Number Two

To all of you who loaned me your names, personalities, and traits for this book. It is you, and others like you, who make Okoboji the fun, exciting, crazy, wonderful place that it is. I am glad to know you.

Dedication Number Three

To those who will soon visit Okoboji for the first time. The people named in this book are real, and they are unreal. Stop and say hello to them and sit and visit for a spell. I have told a few stories about Okoboji in this book – they have many more to tell. And, once you have been to Okoboji, you will be one of us - and we hope that you will come back again and again.

Peter Davidson

1

The sound was coming from over there, beyond the tall wrought iron fence and thick hedgerow. It sounded like muttering punctuated by shouting. The muttering was inaudible, but the shouting was almost recognizable. It sounded like "beeswax" or "camshaft" or something like that.

The house sat in the middle of a lush bent grass lawn shaded by towering palm trees. Actually, even in Beverly Hills, house isn't the right term to use – mansion is more appropriate. Any house with ten bedrooms and twelve bathrooms deserves to be called a mansion. The grounds were carefully manicured and were large enough to easily accommodate the putting green, tennis court with basketball hoop at each end, and Olympic-size pool.

He was a handsome man, more than six feet tall, with shaggy blonde hair, a mustache, and a month's stubble on his face. He was stomping back and forth in his den, back and forth, back and forth. He was reading from a floppy manual that he held in his left hand. He would read a few words in a fairly normal tone and volume – that would be the muttering. Then, he would thrust his right hand into the air, and, starting at a shout and building to a scream, he would holler, "This is a bunch of bullshit." Then, some more muttering as he read from the manual and then it came again, "This is a bunch of bullshit."

Finally, apparently having had enough of this bullshit, he threw the manual on the floor and jumped up and down on it screaming "Bullshit, Bullshit."

Perhaps he would have had a heart attack right there, or at least might have blown a gasket of some sort, if the phone hadn't rung.

He walked over to the phone sitting on top of the desk and took a couple of deep breaths. He placed the fingertips of his outstretched hand on his forehead and slowly pulled his hand down across his face until the fingertips reached the bottom of his chin. His face was instantly transformed from a twisted, snarling ball of rage into a vision as calm, serene, and stoic as the face of an undertaker.

He calmly picked up the phone and answered in a smooth, melodic voice that belied the anger that was present only a moment before.

"Hello."

"H-e-l-l-l-o-o-o…"

"Charlie," he interrupted, "I'm glad you called."

The smooth, melodic voice was replaced by one filled with urgency and pain. "This new script you sent me is nothing but a bunch of bullshit – hang on a minute."

He walked over and picked up the manual from the floor where he had tried to stomp the life out of it. He cradled the phone between his chin and shoulder as he thumbed through the pages.

"Here, listen to this," he said reading from the manual. "'Your smile is like a happy face and your eyes remind me of a deer.' For God's sake, Charlie, I could write better than that when I was in the third grade. Can't you get me a script with some meat to it – a little substance? I mean, I'm not asking to do Shakespeare, I just want a part where I can act – I mean really *act*."

"You're not an actor," Charlie replied, "you're a movie star –

there's a difference, you know."

"But, I want to *act*. I want a part – I mean a *real part*," he argued.

"Face it," Charlie answered, "you're the Bunny Boy…"

"Don't call me that, Charlie. I've warned you before – don't call me that."

"Okay, okay, Alex," Charlie said. "But you've got to face the facts – we've had eight Bunny movies and they've all been box office smashes. I agree, they're a piece of crap, but they sell. The public is begging for more – let's give it to them."

"But…"

"Besides, the Bunny movies have made you rich and famous and have provided you with a fabulous lifestyle – let's show a little appreciation."

"Okay, Charlie, okay," Alex said, "but I can't take this Bunny Boy bullshit much longer. Will you at least *try* to find me a role that I can sink my teeth into?"

"I'll try, trust me, I'll try," Charlie agreed, happy to have survived this latest tirade from his star client.

"Oh, by the way," Charlie said, changing the topic, "the reason I called is to remind you that you're escorting Heather Devreaux to the Save The Universe banquet Thursday night. The limo will pick you up at five-thirty."

"Charlie, please, I'm begging you," Alex said, "can you get me out of this, somehow? I just can't spend another evening with that airheaded bimbo. Once was enough to last me a lifetime."

"Alex, are you insane?" Charlie asked. "Heather is one of the most beautiful women in the world – according to *Glamour* she's *the* most beautiful woman in the world. Get a grip, man, get a grip. You're losing it."

"She's pretty – beautiful – I'll grant you that," Alex agreed, "and she's built, but she's an idiot, Charlie, a blooming idiot. Her idea of a stimulating conversation is to discuss the number of

3

flavors that bubble gum comes in. Do you know how many, Charlie, do you know how many flavors bubble gum comes in? Thirty-nine. According to Heather, the genius, thirty-nine."

"Alex, I'm not asking you to marry her, I'm just asking you to be seen with her. When you escorted her to the Academy Awards, your picture appeared on the cover of forty-eight magazines, and there were stories in three hundred more. We can't buy promo like that - it's priceless. Just escort her this one last time, Alex, for me. Do it for me. And, next time I'll find you an ugly horse with an IQ of 200 if that's what you want."

"All right, Charlie, okay. I'll think about it."

"Good boy! I knew I could count on you. Remember, limo at five-thirty."

Alex hung up the phone and slumped down into the leather recliner sitting next to the desk. He rested his face in his hands and shook his head back and forth.

"What I need is a vacation," Alex muttered offhandedly.

Slowly, Alex pulled his hands from his face and gazed off into space, a small smile starting to pull at his lips. "Why not?" he said aloud. "Why not take a vacation? What's stopping me? I can come and go as I want. I don't have to answer to Charlie. After all, he works for me – I don't work for him. Ya, a little vacation, a little break – that's what I need. Maybe a trip to the mountains, maybe the desert, maybe the gulf coast – somewhere where they don't know me. Fat chance. Everybody knows the Bunny Boy, thanks to Charlie. Well, I'll just let fate decide."

Alex rose and took an atlas from the magazine rack sitting next to the recliner. He paged through it until he came to a map of the United States. He ripped the map out and walked over to his desk. He opened a drawer and scrounged around until he found a couple of thumbtacks. He walked across the room and removed three darts from the dartboard hanging on the wall. Then, using the thumbtacks, he attached the map to the dartboard.

4

"That ought to do it," Alex said as he turned and walked across the room. He positioned himself in front of the desk, about twenty feet from the dartboard. Alex launched a dart in one smooth motion. The dart stuck a little above the middle of the map.

"And, that's where I'll take my vacation," Alex said as he approached the map.

Alex removed the dart and scrutinized the location that the dart had pinpointed. "Oko... Okah...Ojabokee - hell, I'm not going somewhere I can't even pronounce," Alex said, further analyzing the map, "not in Iowa, anyway. I'll try again, but to be fair I'll shut my eyes this time. And, wherever the dart lands is where I'll go, regardless of where it is. I promise."

Alex again positioned himself across the room from the dartboard, and as he'd promised himself, he closed his eyes. To make it even fairer, he turned around three times, so he would be taking a totally unprejudiced shot at the map.

Alex reared back and let the dart fly. Suddenly, there was a loud crash from busting glass. Alex instinctively dove to the floor and covered his head with his hands. When the glass finally stopped falling, Alex rose and took a look. With all of his fancy spinning around before throwing the dart, he'd gotten himself backwards and had thrown the dart through the window next to the sliding glass door on the wall opposite the dartboard.

"Okay, okay," Alex conceded. "I'll go where fate wants me to go – I'll go to Ojobokee or whatever it's called. I'll go."

The window had imploded and most of the glass had fallen inside the house, but a few pieces landed outside on the cement patio. Alex reached through the opening where a window once had been and picked up the pieces of glass and threw them back inside onto the floor.

"Ouch!" Alex moaned as a piece of glass sliced his ring finger.

Blood dripped from his finger onto the busted glass and onto the carpet as Alex quickly made his way to the desk for a tissue to press against the wound. Alex held the tissue tightly against his finger as he made his way to the bathroom and found an adhesive bandage. "Bled like hell for a small cut like that," Alex said as he taped the bandage in place.

"Now for the rest of the plan," Alex said as he opened a cabinet next to the shower and removed a canvass backpack. Alex removed the contents from the bag – makeup, hair dye, brushes, and other tools of the makeup artist.

Alex was glad that through the hundreds, or perhaps thousands, of hours that he had been the object of makeup artists he had been an inquisitive subject. The makeup artists were thrilled that they finally had a star who appreciated their craft and was interested in it, so they had shared with him all of the secrets of their trade. Alex had long felt that he was fully capable of applying his own makeup for his movies, but he enjoyed the camaraderie with the makeup artists, so he never brought it up. Finally, he would have a chance to apply what he had learned.

Alex studied several bottles of hair dye and finally settled on a jet black. "It worked for Elvis," he said aloud.

Alex rinsed the dye into his hair and blow-dried it. He stood back and admired his work in the mirror. "Not too bad," he said, "but, could use a little trim."

Alex removed a scissors from the backpack and began trimming. Puffs of coal black hair fell into the sink. Finally, when more than an inch had been trimmed from all sides, Alex peered into the mirror. "Perfect," he said.

Alex carefully wiped up the hair with a tissue and flushed it down the stool. Then, he carefully washed the remaining strands down the drain of the sink.

Next, Alex took a can of shaving cream from the cabinet above the sink and shook it vigorously. He studied his face in the mirror and stroked his stubble. He smiled a thin smile and said, "It's gotta go."

Alex moistened his beard with a warm, wet towel for a few moments and then lathered up. He held the razor up to the right side of his face near his ear and hesitated for a moment. This was, after all, the beard that had started the scruffy, unshaven look that drove women wild and that men around the world had copied. Alex had created the look quite by accident, showing up for makeup for the start of his second Bunny Boy movie with a month's growth. The director, Otto Luscombe, took one look at him and screamed, "That's it, that's it — that's the look I've been looking for for twenty years. I'll kill any makeup artist who shaves even one whisker without my approval." And, as they say, the rest is history.

Gillette had offered Alex ten million dollars to shave off his trademark beard for a television commercial, but, following Charlie's advice, he had turned it down. Charlie had thought it might cost a whole lot more than that in lost movie ticket sales, and eventually, in Alex's fee per movie, since his female fans absolutely adored his beard. Alex had agreed. And now, here he was, shaving it off for free so he could escape those very fans who adored him.

Suddenly, he did it. He whacked and hacked until the beard and the mustache were nothing but a memory being washed down the drain.

Alex took a good look in the mirror. It had been seven years since he had seen his clean-shaven face. He tilted his head from side to side and stroked his face with both hands. He liked what he saw. "So that's what you look like," he said with a smile.

Alex fished a plastic container from the backpack and opened it. More than a dozen different colors of cosmetic contact lenses appeared before him. He selected a dark brown, almost black, and held it up next to his newly colored black hair. They looked like they were made for each other. Besides his scruffy beard, the other thing that drove Alex's female fans insane was his trademark baby blues, which had been described by one columnist as being "Paul Newman's eyes with a touch of moonglow and a dash of the rainbow." Alex didn't know what the hell she had meant by that, but the definition had stuck.

Alex inserted a contact lens over his left eye and studied the contrast between his left and right eye. He smiled and inserted the lens over his right eye.

As a final touch, Alex jammed a set of slightly discolored and somewhat crooked tooth caps over his perfect pearly whites.

Alex stood back and observed himself in the mirror. "The Maaaaaster of Disguise. The Maaaaaster of Disguise," he said in his best Vincent Price impersonation. "Heck, even my own mother, rest her soul, wouldn't recognize me."

Alex carefully returned all of the makeup materials to the backpack. "This," he said, "is going with me."

Alex returned to the den and approached a picture hanging on the wall. He pulled on the left edge of the frame and the picture swung out from the wall on a hinge, revealing a wall safe. "Just like in the movies," Alex chuckled.

Alex spun the dial to the right, then left, and then right again. He pulled on the door's handle and reached inside. He removed several stacks of bills and stuffed them inside the pockets of his jeans. "This should hold me for a couple of weeks," he said as he closed the safe, gave the dial a twirl, and swung the picture back in place.

Alex took a look around the room. Had he overlooked anything? No. He had it all covered.

"Oh," he suddenly said aloud, snapping his fingers as he remembered something. He walked to the kitchen, opened a drawer and pulled out a box of puppy chow. He filled a dish to overflowing and filled the adjacent dish with water.

"George," he yelled, "George."

A fluffy-haired poodle raced into the room at the sound of Alex's voice and came to a screeching halt four feet in front of Alex. The dog stared at Alex for a moment and then cut loose with a high-pitched mournful wail as it back peddled and finally turned and ran in the opposite direction.

"Wow!" Alex said, "I'm a better makeup artist than I thought."

Alex called in the direction that the dog had retreated, "See you in a couple of weeks, George. Harriet will be here in a day or two to take care of you – and to clean up the broken glass, too. Be a good dog."

Alex returned to the den and took one last look around. He walked over to a well-worn guitar resting against the wall. He dropped his backpack on the floor, picked up the guitar, and strummed a few chords. He set the guitar back down and patted it on the top of the neck a couple of times. Alex picked up his backpack and slipped his arms through its straps as he walked towards the sliding glass door. He opened the sliding glass door, walked out, and closed it behind him.

About ten seconds later, Alex returned. He walked over to the dartboard, removed the thumbtacks, and stuffed the map into his pocket. He threw the thumbtacks on his desk as he walked by and continued on to the sliding glass door, which he locked from the inside. He squeezed himself through the opening where a window once had been, and, adding a little slouch to his posture and a shuffle to his gait, left his fabulous, but flaky, life behind for a two-week vacation in Ojobokee, or Okoboji, or whatever it's called.

2

Alex slouched down at the end of a wood bench directly across from the ticket booths, his eyes peeping over the newspaper he held in front of his face, darting around the room. Nobody seemed to be paying him any attention, being too engrossed in their own lives, plans, and problems. So far, so good.

Alex had taken a circuitous route from his home to this, the jumping off point of his vacation getaway. He had simply walked out of the side gate of his mansion security fence, walked to the corner, turned right, walked two blocks, turned left, walked three blocks, and hailed a cab.

Along the way, he had met two teenage girls on the sidewalk who had looked him over curiously but apparently didn't recognize him – at least his clothes had remained intact and he didn't need to run for his life.

The real clincher, though, that his disguise actually might be working, was when a Celebrity Homes Tour Bus slowly rolled by. All twelve of the blue hairs on his side of the bus had leaned out the windows gawking at him hoping, praying, that he would turn out to be a celebrity. Then, in unison, they had turned away in disappointment without a single one of them clicking a shutter.

Still, Alex had switched cabs three times, just in case. In case of what, he really didn't know, but it seemed like the right thing to do. After the third cab switch, Alex had to laugh at himself – perhaps he'd been watching too many spy movies.

And all that had brought Alex here, without a single incident. Without a single Bunny Boy sighting. Even if the rest of the trip turned out to be a bust, it already had been worth the trouble. This was the first time in five or six years that Alex had gone out in public without creating a mob scene or getting his clothes ripped off. Actually, getting his clothes ripped to shreds didn't bother Alex so much, but when they started grabbing handfuls of hair, he went into semi-seclusion. In fact, it had been at least six years since Alex had been able to come and go like a normal person. Oh, he went places and did things, but always to private parties, fundraisers, banquets, and the like where there was security and the Bunny Boy Bunnies, as they were called, couldn't get at him.

Yes, this was great, sitting here on a wood bench in a bus depot and being anonymous. This was living, really living.

Alex thought back to the last time that he had been in this same bus depot. That was a little over eleven years ago and he was coming instead of going.

Alex grew up military. His father was air force, but he wasn't a pilot. He was in supply – commissary. The first twelve years of Alex's life, through the seventh grade, were pretty stable. Just two moves that Alex could remember – when he was five moving to Dyess Air Force Base in Abilene, Texas, and when he was seven, moving to Ellsworth Air Force Base in Rapid City, South Dakota, where they stayed for nearly five years. But then The Kaiser, as everyone called Alex's dad for his tendency to run his professional and personal life like a dictator, got on the fast track and got promoted every year or so. After seventh grade, school was a blur for Alex as his father moved to Moody AFB in Georgia, to Keesler AFB in Mississippi, to Barksdale AFB in

Louisiana, to Warren AFB in Wyoming, to Seymour Johnson AFB in North Carolina, and to Langley AFB in Virginia. Finally, The Kaiser stopped long enough at Nellis Air Force Base just outside of Las Vegas for Alex to graduate from Green Valley High School in Henderson, a suburb of Las Vegas.

After the first few moves, in eighth and ninth grades, Alex had tried to make friends, and he did. But then, as soon as he made a great new friend or two, he was off to a new base and a new school. Parting from his new friends had been painful for Alex, so after the first couple of moves he just resigned himself to the fact that he'd be moving on soon and he didn't bother to make friends. Acquaintances, yes. Friends, no.

When Alex finally graduated from Green Valley High School, it was a relief for everybody. Alex was finally free from The Kaiser's forced march crisscrossing America. Alex's mother was free, too, from the guilt of dragging her only child from one school to another with no semblance of a normal upbringing. And, The Kaiser was free, too. Free from seeing the disappointment in Alex's eyes every time he announced that they were "breaking camp." Oh, Alex had been a good soldier, never complaining the last three or four moves and accepting it. But, The Kaiser knew Alex didn't complain because it wouldn't do any good anyway. Not with The Kaiser.

Mostly, though, The Kaiser would be free from the damned bitching and complaining from his wife every time they broke camp. She was concerned about moving Alex from school to school once or twice a year, sure. But, The Kaiser secretly believed what really upset her was that she had to find new bridge partners and locate new liquor stores way too often. After Alex graduated, they would probably continue to break camp every year or so, The Kaiser figured, but at least she couldn't use Alex as the lightning rod for her bitching and moaning any longer.

13

For as famous as Alex had become in the past half dozen years, not a single person had ever come forward to claim that they had known Alex in high school, as was common when someone went from being "one of the boys" to being a star – or, in this case, a superstar. That was because in high school, in addition to being in and out of the school so fast that it resembled a fire drill, Alex was invisible while he was there. Vanilla. Nondescript.

Most likely, not a single person who attended high school with Alex at any of his schools even knew that they had brushed shoulders with the Bunny Boy. Part of the reason for this was that Alex didn't cultivate close friendships. The other part of the reason was that Alex didn't grow into his handsome good looks until about a year after he graduated from Green Valley. He had been a late bloomer. In grade school, he had been gawky, with arms and legs too long for his body and ears and a nose that didn't seem to fit with the rest of his face.

Alex was a good athlete in high school, but never got to play varsity sports because he was never in a school long enough to become eligible or he knew he'd be moving before the season was over, so why bother.

It broke the hearts of three or four basketball coaches to find out that the best player in school was a guy who wasn't even out for the team and was playing intramurals.

There were two constants in Alex's life in high school – playing the acoustic guitar and working in the school's audio-visual department.

When Alex was thirteen years old, he had saved up $75 to buy a beginner's guitar. He went to a music store in Bossier City, Louisiana, to buy that guitar, but the slick salesman talked Alex into buying a ukulele instead. He said that for $75 you could either get a poor quality guitar or a high quality ukulele. And, he recommended the ukulele. Since a ukulele had only four strings and a guitar had six, he said, the ukulele was much easier to learn to play. Why, Alex would be playing complete songs within an hour or two. Great songs like "Row, Row, Row Your Boat," and "Mary Had A Little Lamb." And, in no time at all, Alex would be playing at a level that would rival those two legendary ukulele players, Arthur Godfrey and Tiny Tim. Besides, judging from the dust on the ukulele, it had been in the store for a while and a dumb thirteen-year-old seemed like the perfect sucker.

It only took The Kaiser a moment to size up the situation after taking a glance at the ukulele and hearing Alex strum a few off-key chords. The Kaiser marched down to that music store in battle mode and when he got done with that salesman, Alex was the proud owner of a brand new Epiphone guitar, and one worth a whole lot more than $75. The guitar became Alex's new friend. A friend that he could count on day and night and a friend who would move with him whenever they broke camp.

In every new school, the first thing Alex did after enrolling was to seek out the audio-visual director. Usually, the A-V director was a full-time teacher who got a small stipend of $500-$1,000 a year to keep the school's VCR's, video cameras, tape players, DVD players, projectors, and the like in some form of working order. Normally, the A-V director got little assistance, or sympathy, from anyone and was often the source of ridicule and the butt of the blame when a teacher couldn't get a piece of equipment to work. So, when Alex showed up to volunteer to work in the audio-visual department, the A-V director welcomed him like a gift from God.

Alex enjoyed puttering with the equipment to keep it running and he took pride in being able to help some mechanically challenged teacher learn how to operate a DVD player or digital camera.

What Alex really enjoyed, though, was videotaping activities around the school. Every A-V director at every school that Alex attended was swamped with requests for videotaping. The coaches wanted practices and games taped. The speech teacher wanted speeches taped. The play director wanted rehearsals and performances taped. The science teacher wanted the stars and the moon taped. The list went on and on. And, Alex was the man behind the camera. When requested, Alex would even edit the tape for them, adding headings, captions, and background music.

When Alex moved on to a new school, the weeping that was heard coming from the school that he left was from the basketball coach who had just lost his new star before he had even played one game. But, the wailing that could be heard was from the A-V director who had just lost his right hand, his left hand, and his new son.

Three weeks after graduating from high school, Alex left home with his guitar, a cardboard suitcase stuffed with clothes, $450 cash, and a bus ticket to Los Angeles. He was off to begin a career in the movie business - not as an actor, to be sure, but as a cameraman.

Alex's journey had brought him to this very same bus depot, arriving on June 23. He was young, naïve, green, dumb – add a few, if you want. But, he had been around a bit and had youthful optimism and boundless energy as his allies.

Even though Alex's goal was only to work his way to the middle of the movie industry, it went a lot slower than he had expected. He applied for jobs at all the major studios as soon as he arrived in Hollywood, but the only job he could land was as a gaff. Basically, he was a roustabout – an errand boy – and he'd often go a week or two without even seeing a movie camera. And, the job paid peanuts.

To help support himself, Alex also worked four hours an evening as a telemarketer, calling Midwest and east coast residents conducting polls about people's movie viewing interests and habits. After his first month on the job, Alex received three awards from the telemarketing company. The first was for showing up for work every day, the second was for showing up for work on time, and the third was for actually meeting his quota of polls completed. Most of the other telemarketers showed up for work if they wanted and when they wanted. And, usually, they just phoned their friends and completed bogus polls while they chatted about last night's party or the one that was about to begin.

After two years, Alex had been promoted to supervisor at the telemarketing company, but he was still a long way from reaching his goal of becoming a movie cameraman. Then, suddenly, a break came that, in a roundabout way, changed his life forever.

A friend told Alex about a cushy job that was fun and exciting and that paid good money and fabulous tips. The job was in transportation at MGM. Transportation meant driving a limousine to escort movie stars, directors, producers and other bigwigs around town. It sounded great to Alex so he applied and was hired on the spot.

Alex came in contact with many big stars including Matt Damon, Brad Pitt, Jennifer Aniston, Julia Roberts, Kevin Costner, Russell Crowe, Denzel Washington, Robin Williams, Gweneth Paltrow, Tom Cruise, Harrison Ford, Meg Ryan, Drew Barrymore, Jim Carey, Tom Hanks, John Travolta, and Ashley Judd, just to name a few. It was a great study in human nature as Alex was variously ignored, appreciated, insulted, complimented, mocked, praised, scorned, and flattered. Regardless of how the stars treated him, though, they almost always tipped very, very generously. Nobody wanted the MGM limo driver telling future passengers what a tightwad so and so was, you see.

It was easy, it was fun, it was profitable. And, it was a long way from the goal that had burned inside of Alex ever since he

17

arrived in Hollywood. Alex was starting to think seriously about giving it up and making an all-out attempt to become a cameraman. That is, until one day he was instructed to pick up a talent agent named Charlie Waller and take him to a meeting with an MGM producer.

Charlie had about a dozen actors and actresses as clients, but none of them had ever appeared in anything above a B-movie. Charlie dreamed of finding that one big star that would catapult him into the big time, but with hundreds of talent agencies in town, even Charlie knew that it was only a pipe dream. Besides that, Charlie had never even had a client receive serious consideration for a role of any kind, other than being part of a crowd scene, in a major movie.

Maybe he was mired in B-movies, Charlie mused to himself, but life could be a whole lot worse. After all, here he was, riding in an MGM limo being squired to a producer's meeting at the Polo Lounge. Not too bad.

Charlie struck up a conversation with the handsome young driver and was instantly captivated by his engaging smile and down-home, unassuming charm and honesty. No, the young man had no intentions of being an actor. Yes, he loved the movie industry. Yes, he had goals – he wanted to be a cameraman.

Alex dropped Charlie off at the Polo Lounge and headed back to the MGM motor pool for his next assignment.

As it turned out, Charlie's production meeting was about a new movie that was destined to be a B-movie if there ever was one – right up Charlie's alley. *Beach Bunny* was the name of the movie and it would feature a beautiful young woman romping on the beach with a handsome young man.

The producer, Halbert Tandy, thought this movie had the potential to be a big hit with the right casting.

"No shit, Halbert," Charlie had thought to himself. He'd heard that statement from every B-movie producer that ever lived. Of course it would be a big hit if you got big names, Halbert, but last he'd heard Marilyn Monroe was dead and Tom Cruise and Julia Roberts were busy.

Then, Halbert dropped the bombshell that got Charlie's wheels spinning. He had already signed Shanna LaDue to play the female lead in *Beach Bunny*. Shanna was a hot young star on the rise. She had starred in three mediocre movies that had become substantial box office successes, largely because of Shanna. Oh, she wasn't much of an actress, but who gave a damn, anyway. She had the physical attributes that made men of all ages drool and, at the same time, she was perceived as a role model for young women. How the hell the studio was able to cultivate two polar images like that was a mystery, but somehow they had done it.

Anyway, Shanna insisted on an unknown male lead, rather than a known star, so she wouldn't have to share the spotlight with anyone. She even had his description – around six foot one, blonde hair, blue eyes, muscular, but not muscle bound, and a non-smoker. And, he had to have a brilliant smile and be a genuinely nice guy besides. The description could have fit any one of a thousand hopefuls in the San Fernando Valley, until she got to that last requirement – that really threw a clinker in the works. And, that was why Halbert wanted to talk to Charlie, to see if any of his clients, all basically unknowns, could fit the description.

Charlie's mind was already racing. He had met the perfect male lead only an hour ago – he had driven him to this very meeting, but Charlie wasn't going to tell Halbert that.

"I've got exactly what you're looking for," Charlie had told Halbert, "but he's very choosy about his parts. I'll have to talk to him about it."

"If he doesn't want to audition for this part he isn't choosy, he's insane," Halbert had replied. "I did say Shanna LaDue, didn't I?

19

Or was I dreaming?"

Charlie had walked out of the meeting slowly, casually – like it was just another day at the office. But, when he was out of Halbert's sight, he broke into a sprint, charging onto the street to hail a taxi.

At first, Alex had no interest in auditioning for the part. He was, after all, not an actor. He wanted to be a cameraman, he had reminded Charlie. Eventually, though, Charlie wore him down and he conceded, reluctantly, to give it a try, just as a lark.

Shanna LaDue was the one and only casting director for the male lead of *Beach Bunny*. She had total and final say – it was in her contract. Shanna had interviewed over two hundred hopefuls and none of them seemed to have that right spark – that magic.

And then Alex walked into the room and Boom! She anointed him before he finished reading three lines of the script.

As everyone knows by now, *Beach Bunny* was a huge box office success and it spawned a whole rash of sequels. And, it thrust its two stars, Shanna and Alex, into the stratosphere of stardom, making them instant superstars.

After two Bunny movies with Alex, Shanna had wisely moved on to other roles, not wanting to become typecast as the Bunny Girl. She had major roles in several critically acclaimed movies that were also box office smashes, including *Land Baron* and *Birthright*. Alex, under the guidance of Charlie, had stayed with the Bunny movies and had, in fact, become typecast as the Bunny Boy. Shanna LaDue was wise beyond her years.

Alex lowered the newspaper and looked around. The bus depot hadn't changed a bit in eleven years. Same wood benches, same tile and carpet on the floor, same ceiling fans. Hell, even the people looked the same, dressed in jeans, khakis, and t-shirts. Not a suit in the bunch. The suits were all boarding airplanes and the common people were boarding the bus. Alex was glad to be among the common people. Besides, if Charlie tried to find him, he'd never think of the bus. Perfect.

The voice over the loudspeaker made the announcement Alex had been waiting for: "Now departing at Gate 15 to Palm Springs, Indio, and Blythe, California, and Quartzsite, Buckeye, Tempe, and Phoenix, Arizona."

Alex stood and looked around to see if anyone was watching him – they weren't. He joined the line at gate 15, gave the agent his ticket, and got on board.

Alex was overwhelmed by a feeling of relief and with euphoria. "This must be the way a bank robber feels when he knows he's gotten away clean," Alex thought to himself as he settled into a window seat in the fifth row from the front. Alex thought back – he hadn't felt this excited since his first movie seven years ago when he had actually kissed the most beautiful and sexy starlet of the day, Shanna LaDue. Or, more accurately, since the time he had made love to Shanna LaDue in a gazebo after the wrap party for *Beach Bunny*. Twice. That was a rush to be sure.

The bus backed out and slowly moved away from the depot, out onto the street. Alex pushed the seat's recline button and tilted the backrest back a couple of notches. He laid his head back against the seat and a thin smile appeared on his lips as he said to himself, "Okoboji, here I come!"

3

It had been a little over eleven years since Alex's last long-range bus ride. Back then, he had been a teenager full of adrenaline, piss, and vinegar. He would have ridden a camel to Los Angeles or would have walked to get there. Since then, Alex had become accustomed to traveling via expensive sports cars, chauffeured limousines, and privately owned jets. He had totally forgotten what a bitch traveling by bus can be. The four hundred-mile bus ride took over eight hours, including six stops along the way to drop off and pick up passengers.

The parade of ever-changing traveling companions, though, more than made up for the inconveniences of bus travel. There was the 75-year-old widow, for instance, with six children, fifteen grandchildren and nine great-grandchildren who confessed that she still enjoyed sex with her former mailman two or three times a month. There was the sixteen-year-old runaway who looked like she was twenty that Alex had convinced to at least call her parents to let them know that she was alive and okay. Alex had even monitored the call at the pay phone to make sure she called. And, after the call, she'd decided to get back on the bus going in the opposite direction and go back home.

Another memorable traveling companion was a 52-year-old former lawyer. His wife had divorced him and run off with a judge she'd been having an affair with for over five years. Bud, as he preferred to be called, had closed his law practice, sold all of his worldly possessions, and purchased one of those "Travel-anywhere-you-want-by-bus-in-180-days" tickets for $229. Bud had been on the road for 118 days, so far, and didn't know where he had been, where he was at the moment, or where he was going. Perhaps his quart of gin a day diet led to his nonchalance. And, he was planning on buying another 180-day ticket when this one ran out.

Then, there was Jennifer. Around midnight she proudly announced to Alex that she was a whore. To prove it, she invited Alex to join her in the bus's restroom for "a little action," as she put it. Alex kindly refused her offer, but a nineteen-year-old college student sitting behind them overheard the conversation and volunteered to take Alex's place. The banging, kicking, and moaning coming from the back of the bus reminded Alex of the time he and Shanna LaDue had tried to do it standing up in a hammock in his back yard. Thank God for the college student.

And then, there was Preacher Smith, as he called himself. He was self-ordained, he'd confessed, so he wasn't a real preacher. But, he had been called to spread the word where regular preachers didn't, couldn't, or wouldn't. His parish was the bus depots, the buses, and the bars. And, his mission for the next seventy-five miles was to exorcise the hell out of Alex. When the bus reached Preacher Smith's destination, he jumped out of his seat, held both hands firmly over Alex's head and shouted, "Heal this miserable sinner – heal!" He also healed the bus driver before departing in search of other sinners.

There were others, too – Henderson, Gomez, Carrington, and Wilson, but they were all pretty normal – pretty boring.

Whoever they were, wherever they came from, wherever they were going, and whatever their story was, Alex was glad to have met them. It had been a long time since Alex had talked to real, honest-to-goodness people, especially in a setting where they didn't know he was a celebrity. Although he was stiff, sore, tired, and hungry when he reached the bus depot in Phoenix, Alex was sorry to see this part of his journey end. Not sorry enough, however, to buy another bus ticket for the remainder of his journey.

Alex took a cab from the Phoenix bus depot to the airport and booked a flight to Sioux Falls, South Dakota, with a plane change in Minneapolis. Sioux Falls was the nearest city to Okoboji with major airline service. And, having spent some of the happiest years of his youth in Rapid City, from third grade into seventh grade, Alex was looking forward to placing his feet back on South Dakota soil.

Alex was self-conscious when he entered Sky Harbor International Airport in Phoenix, expecting to set off a mob scene with fans attacking him, ripping off his clothes, and chasing him down the concourse. But, it didn't happen. Nothing. He was totally ignored, and it felt good.

To continue with his masquerade, Alex flew coach. He took a window seat where he would be less visible. Again, it didn't matter because nobody gave him even a second glance. The guy sitting next to him was in management with a telecommunications company, and he was stone sober. How boring. Alex preferred his bus-riding buddies.

Alex had forgotten how handy small airports could be. Within five minutes of walking off the plane in Sioux Falls, Alex was sitting in a taxi heading for a truck stop for the next part of his adventure.

Alex slouched down in the back seat of the taxi and recalled what he knew about the state of South Dakota. That information would be vital for his "cover" in Okoboji.

In many ways, South Dakotans consider South Dakota to be two separate states – East River and West River. The Missouri River, running north and south, dissects the state in about the middle. The state is sparsely populated with only two cities of any size and impact – Rapid City and Sioux Falls. Rapid City, on the west, is about thirty-five miles from the Wyoming border. About 400 miles to the east of Rapid City is Sioux Falls, about a dozen miles from the eastern border of South Dakota. Basically, the East River folks don't give a damn about West River South Dakota and the West River folks don't give a hoot about East River South Dakota.

Rapid City, in the heart of the Black Hills, thrives from the tourist trade generated by Mount Rushmore, the Crazy Horse monument, the annual Sturgis motorcycle rally and, sixty miles to the east, Wall Drug. Sioux Falls, on the other hand, is more urban and is a booming retail, manufacturing, and financial center that is one of the fastest growing cities in America.

Alex had been a West River youth and recalled school trips to Mount Rushmore, Deadwood, and other historic sites in The Hills, as locals called the area. Alex had three good friends back in those days, Ken Horner, Willie Heil, and Keith Wells. He thought of them as the plane flew over South Dakota and vowed that one day he'd track them down – maybe on next year's vacation.

The taxi driver dropped Alex off at a truck stop at the intersection of Cliff Avenue and Interstate 90. Alex had to ask only five truckers to find one who was heading east to Iowa. In fact, the driver was heading to Spirit Lake, just four miles from Okoboji.

The ninety-five mile trip from Sioux Falls to Spirit Lake flew by as the trucker, who often spent weekends in Okoboji, filled Alex in on the background and history of the area. Alex was an eager student, bent on learning all that he could so he wouldn't stick out like a sore thumb – or more accurately, like a movie star in a cornfield.

The trucker explained that Okoboji was a quaint resort area

26

about ten miles south of the Minnesota border. Even though there was a town named Okoboji and there were two lakes named East Lake Okoboji and West Lake Okoboji, the term, "Okoboji," had evolved into a broader meaning to encompass the entire resort area.

At the north end of the region is the town of Spirit Lake, which borders on a lake of the same name. Four miles to the south is the town of Okoboji, which borders on both of the Okoboji lakes, referred to simply as East Lake and West Lake by the locals. Across the bridge, a stone's throw south of Okoboji is the town of Arnolds Park, which borders on five lakes - East Lake, West Lake, Minnewasta, Upper Gar, and Lower Gar.

To cloud the confusion even further, the trucker explained, most of the shops, restaurants, lodging, bars, and entertainment attractions are in Arnolds Park. So, when tourists talk about going to Okoboji, they're usually talking about going to Arnolds Park.

Rounding out the towns in the Okoboji area is Milford, about four miles south of Arnolds Park. All four of the towns in "Okoboji," Spirit Lake, Okoboji, Arnolds Park, and Milford, are along a twelve-mile stretch of Highway 71. Years ago, each of these four towns was geographically separated from the others. Progress had come to Okoboji, however, and now there's hardly a bare spot along the strip as businesses have sprung up all along the stretch from Spirit Lake to Milford.

In the days before air-conditioning, many wealthy families from several hundred miles around moved to their cottages in Okoboji for the summer to take advantage of the cool lake breezes. The trend continues to this day, the trucker said, with many families moving to their cottages or condos in Okoboji for the summer or coming up just for the weekends. In addition to the summertime residents, tens of thousands of vacationers and tourists pack the motels and campsites all summer long. On the three major summer holidays, Memorial Day, Fourth of July, and Labor Day, Okoboji is overrun with well over a hundred thousand vacationers and tourists, in addition to the year-round residents and summer residents.

There was more to tell, the trucker had said, but Al, as Alex was now calling himself, would need to learn that on his own since they were at Alex's – uh, Al's, destination. Alex shook hands with the trucker, thanked him, and jumped down from the truck at the four-way stop.

It was a beautiful day – bright sunshine, maybe eighty degrees. Alex checked his watch – it had taken almost twenty-four hours of hard traveling to get here. Well, he had wanted an out-of-the-way place for a little rest and relaxation out of the glare of the public eye and it looked like he had found it.

Alex looked around. He was at the intersection of Highway 9, running east and west and Highway 71, running north and south. Across the road on one corner was a convenience store. On the other corner were a pizza place and a drug store, and, farther down the frontage road, Wal-Mart. Behind Alex was the Polaris manufacturing plant with a sign proudly proclaiming that they made ATV's and that this was the only plant in the world that manufactured the Polaris Victory motorcycle.

The business across the road on the remaining corner really caught Alex's attention – a used car lot. Perhaps he could rent a car for the next ten days or so. A big sign with a great big yellow lemon painted in the middle loomed over the car lot. "Lyin' Louie's Lemon Lot," the sign proclaimed.

Alex studied the cars as he approached the lemon lot. There must have been a hundred of them – a mixture of cars, pickups, and SUV's, ranging from nearly new to maybe twenty years old.

Alex had barely set foot on the lot when he was approached by a wiry bald-headed guy wearing a bright yellow suit with even brighter yellow lemons painted all over it. The man started talking at a machine gun pace when he was about ten feet from Alex.

"Good afternoon, young man, beautiful day isn't it – great day to buy a car – young man like you should be on the beach on a day like this – why I can have you in a beautiful car and out of here in fifteen minutes - you can be on the beach in twenty minutes – Lyin' Louie's my name and this here's my lemon lot – every car's guaranteed to run – at least until you get it off the lot."

Lyin' Louie grabbed Alex's right hand and pumped it vigorously while he slipped his left arm around Alex's shoulder, just as if they'd been buddies for years. Alex had the sudden urge to check if his wad of cash was missing, but dismissed the thought.

"I'm Al," Alex said, "and I'm looking for a car to rent for about ten days."

"W-e-l-l," Louie said slowly, stroking his chin, "I don't have any rentals, but, I've got a very, very, special deal that will be just perfect for you. Come with me."

Louie led Alex past rows of cars and around the corner of his building and there it sat in all it's glory – a 1965 Pontiac Bonneville convertible – a bright orange one with it's top down, breathing fire.

"This is you, Al, my pal," Louie said. "It's got a 421 V-8, automatic transmission, and power steering – and it comes with a stick to chase the women away."

Alex slowly walked around the car, inspecting it inside and out. It must have been twenty-five feet long and was built like a tank. It wasn't just orange, it was bright orange, about the shade of the vests highway workers wear to make sure motorists see them. But, Alex was partial to convertibles. In fact, at this very moment, there were eight cars in his garage in Beverly Hills and six of them were convertibles including a Mercedes, a Jaguar, a

29

BMW, a Lexus, a Cadillac XLR, and an Aston Martin.

Louie got in the car and turned the key. The motor groaned and choked a couple of times before it finally started. Louie gunned the motor and a puff of black smoke belched out of the tailpipe. After that, it settled down and actually ran pretty smooth.

"Got any other convertibles?" Alex asked.

"Nope, just can't keep 'em on the lot," Louie answered.

"How much?" Alex asked.

"Special price today," Louie answered, "thirty-five hundred."

Alex reached in his pocket and produced the wad of bills he had taken from the wall safe in his den. "I'll give you three thousand, cash," Alex said.

"Cash? Did you say cash?" Louie asked eyeing the roll in Alex's hand. "Hell, I'll take twenty-eight hundred, cash."

And in less than ten minutes Alex was now the proud owner of nine cars, seven of which were convertibles.

Alex pulled out of the Lemon Lot onto Highway 71. There was a small dip in the road where the Lemon Lot joined the highway and as the rear wheels bounced through the dip Alex heard a loud clank. Alex took a quick look in the mirror and there in the middle of the road laid his rear bumper. He quickly spun the car around, jumped out, and threw the heavy chrome bumper into the back seat of the car.

Alex pulled back into the Lemon Lot to seek assistance in putting the bumper back on. Lyin' Louie saw Alex coming and ran toward him. Before Alex could mutter a word, Louie pointed to the exit with his outstretched arm and yelled "Get that piece of junk out off my lot – you're making the place look shabby." And then he burst out laughing and turned and walked away. Apparently he wasn't kidding about the car being guaranteed only until it left the lot.

It was no big deal, Alex figured, so he turned the car around, entered Highway 71 and headed south as he waved goodbye to Lyin' Louie with his middle finger. The only difference between Lyin' Louie and a Los Angeles car dealer, Alex decided, is that Louie told you he was going to screw you before he did it to you. And, when he did it, you almost enjoyed it.

4

Alex headed south on Highway 71. Much to Alex's surprise, the Orange Blossom Special, as Lyin' Louie had called it, ran like a top. The hot sun felt good on his skin and he tilted his head back to enjoy the full effect of the wind blowing through his hair. You just couldn't beat driving a convertible on a day like this.

The trucker had done a good job of painting word pictures of the four-mile stretch along Highway 71 from Spirit Lake to Okoboji. Businesses, small shops, and a few homes filled most of the space on both sides of the four lanes. Alex watched for some of the landmarks the trucker had mentioned. There on his right was Forbes Liquor Locker and on his left was the hospital. Then came Dowden-Hinn Realty, Ferguson's Floral, and Lakes Rental. If Alex remembered correctly, the Lakes Art Center should be coming up soon, and sure enough, there it was.

Alex had expected some huge sign with flashing lights to mark the city limits of Okoboji, but there was just a small green highway sign along the road just before the Lakes Art Center. Alex was officially in Okoboji.

The trucker had warned Alex that the traffic would get heavy when he got into the town of Okoboji, and he was right. But, what they called heavy traffic here in Okoboji would be considered light traffic or no traffic at all in L.A.

Alex glanced from side to side looking for more landmarks. On his left was the Okoboji Town Hall, on his right was Arrowwood Resort and then Brooks Golf Course.

The Kum & Go Convenience store was coming up on the right and Alex instinctively glanced down at the fuel tank gauge. It was a quarter inch below empty – he was driving on the fumes. Good ol' Louie. Alex pulled into Kum & Go and filled up. The Orange Blossom Special took a big drink. Alex went inside and paid cash and was soon back on the highway, looking for more landmarks that the trucker had told him to watch for. Ah, there was Tweeter's restaurant – he was on the right track.

Alex passed a big sign that said, "Welcome To the University of Okoboji." The trucker had raved about The University and had made Alex promise that one of the first things he'd do when he got to Okoboji would be to go take a look at the campus, which he described as being one of the most beautiful in the world. Although Alex had never heard of the University of Okoboji, he'd promised. "Just ask anybody," the trucker had said, "everybody knows where The University is." And, so, Alex made a mental note to make an excursion to the campus of the University of Okoboji one of the first things on his list.

The Orange Blossom Special crested a small hill and Alex got his first glimpse of the lakes, just beyond Mau Marine and The Wharf restaurant.

About three minutes ago Alex had entered the town of Okoboji and now he was already exiting it as he approached the bridge separating East Lake on his left and West Lake on his right. It was a beautiful sight with dozens of boats slowly crossing under the bridge going from one lake to another.

Alex could see the shoreline of each lake and recalled that the trucker had said both East Lake and West Lake were long and narrow. Boats of all sizes, some seeming oversized for the relatively small lakes, cruised the glistening waters in all directions as far as Alex could see. Alex made another mental note, this time to rent a boat and to do a little cruising himself.

Alex was leaning back, basking in the sun, taking in the sights as he approached the big wooden sign that said "Welcome To Arnolds Park." All of a sudden there was a big SPLAT and what seemed like fifty gallons of water or some other liquid hit the windshield of the Orange Blossom Special and sprayed all over Alex.

Alex's first reaction was, "Oh my God, cows *can* fly."

Alex fumbled with the knobs on the dash, trying in vain to find the windshield wiper. There was a small parking lot to the right, overlooking the beach just before the Arnolds Park city sign, and Alex pulled off and slammed on the brakes. Alex jumped out of the car and looked all around – left, right, up, down – there didn't seem to be any flying cows.

"Cease fire, cease fire, fifteen degrees west," someone down on the beach yelled.

Before Alex could figure out what the guy was yelling about, SPLAT, it hit him squarely in the face this time. The liquid ran down his face and onto his shirt and pants like someone had thrown a bucket of water on him. Alex wiped the liquid from his eyes and face and tried to brush it off his shirt with his hands.

"Sorry, real sorry," the voice said.

Through bleary eyes Alex saw a form running toward him. Alex wiped the liquid out of his eyes and got a clearer look. Approaching was a man with white hair and a white beard and mustache. He was wearing white shorts and a white cap and white shirt with some type of nautical markings on them.

The man tried to brush the liquid off of Alex's clothes. "Sorry, real sorry," he said again.

Just then, it happened again, SPLAT. This time it hit about four feet from where Alex and Whitey were standing.

35

"Stop, you old coots, stop," Whitey yelled to someone out on the lake as he waved his arms back and forth.

Alex peered out onto the lake. About fifty yards off shore was a pontoon with five guys of the same vintage as Whitey, all wearing white outfits identical to Whitey's. One guy was driving the pontoon, two were holding the ends of a giant water balloon launcher, another was pulling back the business end of the launcher and another was loading a water-filled balloon for launching when Whitey finally got them stopped. A stack of maybe fifty water-filled balloons rested on the deck of the pontoon.

"Aren't you boys a little old to be playing games like this?" Alex asked with a smile.

"Playing?" Whitey said. "This is serious – we're on maneuvers. We're preparing for battle with…"

Whitey suddenly stopped in mid-sentence and stared intently at Alex's face. "I'll be damned," he said. "I'm eighty-four years old and you're only the second guy I've ever met who had one blue eye and one brown eye – the other was a guy named 'Wild-Eyed Eddie,' back in '38 or '39. What's your name?"

"I'm Al," Alex said as he grabbed Whitey's outstretched hand for a shake.

"Wild-Eyed Al," Whitey said. "You're not Wild-Eyed Eddie's son are ya – or grandson?"

"No," Alex replied, "my father's name was – was Kaiser."

Alex got back into the Orange Blossom Special and checked out his eyes in the rear view mirror. Sure enough, the head-on blast had washed away one of his brown contact lenses. Alex unzipped his backpack and withdrew the container of lenses. He carefully replaced the missing lens and checked himself out in the mirror – no more wild eyes.

Alex pulled back onto the highway. Behind him he heard a voice yell, "Nice meeting you, Wild-Eyed Al – love your car."

Just beyond the Arnolds Park sign was the Water's Edge Condos and across the street was The Ritz bar – a good place, the trucker had said.

The trucker had recommended that Alex stay at the Four Seasons Resort, which was right next to the Water's Edge Condos. Alex pulled into the parking lot and parked in front of the office. It was a two-story Ma and Pa motel with maybe fifty rooms - and it was on the beach - just what Alex was looking for.

A man, maybe in his fifties, looked up from his newspaper as Alex walked in the door.

"Got any rooms available?" Alex asked.

"What happened to you – been swimming with your clothes on?" the man asked without answering Alex's question as he inspected Alex's soggy appearance.

"Some guys down on the lake are launching water balloons – I got hit by a couple of them," Alex replied.

The man behind the counter grinned. "A bunch of older guys wearing white uniforms?" he asked.

"Right," Alex answered.

"That would be the commodores of The Iowa Navy," he said, grinning again.

"The Iowa Navy?" Alex asked.

"During World War II," he explained, "the U.S. Navy was afraid that if they did all of their training in the ocean they were too vulnerable to enemy attacks. So, they did a lot of their training inland where they would be safe. The Iowa Navy trained right out here on West Lake Okoboji and the Nebraska Navy trained on Lake McConaughy in Nebraska. Fortunately for them, neither the Iowa Navy nor the Nebraska Navy ever saw combat action – probably would have been a disaster. But, an intense debate continued for years between the Iowa and Nebraska navies, over who had the better navy.

"Every year during the last week in July we have the Summer Games here in Okoboji," he continued. "There's all sorts of rowing, canoeing, swimming, tennis, golf, basketball, soccer, rugby, bicycling and running events. But, the highlight of the summer games is when the Iowa Navy and the Nebraska Navy square off and do battle with each other. They each get a half dozen guys on a pontoon, right out here in front of the motel on Smith's Bay, and launch water balloons at each other. These guys are all about eighty years old and it's quite a show. It's this coming weekend – you'll have to take it in."

"I'll look forward to it, but in the meantime, got any rooms?" Alex asked for the second time.

"Nope, we're full up," the man replied.

"Any motels you'd recommend that might have a room?" Alex asked.

"I'm sure everybody in Okoboji's full - Summer Games this week, you know," he replied. "Your best bet might be to check out Estherville or Spencer."

"Where are they?" Alex asked.

"Estherville's about twenty miles east and Spencer's about fifteen miles south," he said.

Alex frowned. The dartboard had said he was destined to vacation in Okoboji, not Estherville or Spencer. Alex thought fast.

"You know," Alex said, "I worked in a small motel like this one once, and we always held back one room just in case we made a mistake. You don't happen to have an extra room like that, do you?"

The man's eyes lit up and a wide grin covered his face. "We're kinda talkin' innkeeper to innkeeper here?" he asked as he checked his computer.

"Something like that," Alex replied.

"How many days are you planning on staying?"

"Ten," Alex answered.

"That might be tough."

Alex reached into his pocket and pulled out the wad of bills – it had worked wonders with Lyin' Louie. "I'll pay cash – in advance," he said.

Again the grin, even wider this time. "I think we can work something out. I'm Deano," he said, reaching out to shake hands.

"And, I'm Al," Alex said.

"Where you from?" Deano asked.

Alex had rehearsed for this in his mind. "South Dakota – West River," he said like a native.

"How far west?" Deano asked.

"The Hills – Rapid," Alex answered, realizing that saying the full names, the Black Hills and Rapid City, would make him sound like a tourist and not a local.

"I like The Hills. My lady friend, Jodell, and I go out to Deadwood on a little gambling excursion every once in a while," Deano said.

Fortunately, Deano let it lie there and didn't grill Alex on any details about the Black Hills, Rapid City, or South Dakota. It had been, after all, years since Alex had been in Rapid City or had even thought about South Dakota.

Alex completed the registration card and forked over the cash. Deano gave him a key to the room and walked outside with Alex.

"That your car?" Deano asked pointing to the orange beauty parked out front.

Alex nodded.

"Buy it from Lyin' Louie?"

"How'd you know?" Alex asked.

"Just a wild guess," Deano said, and there came the grin again. "I'll have one of the guys put the bumper back on while you put your things in the room."

Just then a biker roared out of The Ritz parking lot across the street and was barreling down the highway when he saw Alex and Deano standing in front of the motel. He made a quick right turn and headed in their direction. It was a beautiful display of chrome, custom made, reminding Alex of the chopper Peter Fonda rode in *Easy Rider*. He brought the Harley to a stop a couple of feet in front of Alex and Deano and backed off the throttle a couple of times. He might have been in his forties – old enough to have been around the block once or twice. With his long hair and beard he looked like a thousand bikers Alex had seen on the California freeways. But, it was the eyes that set him apart – that and the attitude. He didn't say a word. He just sat there sizing Alex up, looking him over with those steely eyes.

Deano didn't move an inch. Either he was petrified with fear or he knew he had nothing to be afraid of. Alex couldn't tell.

Finally, the biker switched his gaze from Alex to Deano.

"Lyle," Deano said.

"Deano," Lyle answered.

"This is Al," Deano said, nodding towards Alex.

Again Lyle looked Alex over from top to bottom and finally gave him a slight nod. Then, before Alex could respond, Lyle popped the Harley into gear and roared out of the parking lot and back onto the highway.

"He likes you," Deano said.

"How can you tell?" Alex asked.

"You're still alive, aren't you?" Deano asked, and then he grinned that famous grin.

Alex didn't know if Deano was being serious or was teasing him, but he felt he had made his first friend in Okoboji.

"I'll show you to your room," Deano said. "Let me help you carry your stuff."

"I've only got this backpack," Alex said. "I'm going to buy

40

some clothes here – in Okoboji."

"Check out The Three Sons clothing store in Milford – just four miles south. You might also want to check the shops in The Central Emporium here in Arnolds Park – it's on the lake – about six blocks that way – there's about thirty shops," Deano volunteered as he pointed past the motel.

Deano led Alex to his room and unlocked the door. It was a standard-sized motel room with the standard furnishings – a double bed, dresser with four drawers, small round table, two straight-backed chairs, recliner, television set, and a bathroom. Not as fancy as the digs Alex was accustomed to, but it would do nicely. Deano threw open the curtains revealing a sliding glass door to a patio overlooking the lake. Deano opened the sliding glass door and Alex joined him on the patio. The patio ran the width of the room and was perhaps five feet deep with a wrought iron railing on the front and on either side, separating it from the adjoining patios. Alex surveyed the view before him. Across the bay was a marina with a big sign, Okoboji Boats. The rest of the shoreline was dotted with homes ranging from small cottages to three-story jobs that were probably considered to be mansions here in Okoboji. The far shore of the lake appeared to be about five miles away, but over water it was hard to judge the distance. Boats of all sizes, filled with bikini-clad women and beer swigging men, cruised the lake in all directions and at all speeds. An occasional Jet Ski zipped across the water near the shoreline before it dumped its rider into the drink. A dozen or more sailboats, with full sail, lazily chased the breeze across the lake a mile or two from shore. It was picturesque, it was quiet, it was quaint - it would be the perfect place for Alex to relax and unwind in peace and quiet.

When Alex and Deano returned to Alex's car, the bumper had already been reattached.

"I'm going to take a little spin around the area," Alex said, get-

41

ting into the Orange Blossom Special. "Can you tell me how to find the University of Okoboji campus?"

"Oh, that's easy to find," Deano said. "Just get back on the highway and turn right at the first stoplight onto Broadway Street. Go straight about six blocks, past the big yellow building that says Maritime Museum and University of Okoboji Foundation on the front. When you see the amusement park and the roller coaster in front of you, turn right and go a few blocks – you'll run right into it."

"Thanks," Alex said as he headed for the highway.

"Nice car," Deano yelled out to him.

Alex followed Deano's directions precisely. He turned right at the stoplight and headed down Broadway, observing businesses as he went. The trucker had said that Broadway was where the action was in Okoboji. On the left was a row of bars and restaurants – Boji Nites, Kalsows, Ruebins, Captains Getaway, Smokin' Jakes, Murphys, Yesterday's, and several others covering maybe three blocks at best. "Some action," Alex thought to himself.

On the right, down the knoll, was The Central Emporium, one of the places Deano had recommended for Alex to shop for clothes. He'd stop there on the way back.

Off to the right was another gorgeous view of the lake, just beyond a grassy area of maybe ten acres. Approaching on Alex's right was the big yellow building with the Maritime Museum and University of Okoboji Foundation signs on it. And now, maybe two minutes after turning onto Broadway Street, he was at the stop sign facing the amusement park and the wooden roller coaster.

The one word that everybody seemed to use when describing Okoboji was *quaint*, and that was the first word that popped into Alex's head when he saw the amusement park – it was quaint. He couldn't see it all from where he was seated in the Orange Blossom Special, but there appeared to be a few dozen rides along with various concession stands and several buildings that housed carnival-type games. Most of the rides that Alex could see were ones that he remembered from attending carnivals and country fairs as a youth in Rapid City – Tilt-A-Whirl, log flume, Scrambler, bumper cars, Ferris wheel and, of course, a couple of merry-go-rounds. Nothing too high tech – just basic amusement rides that were, well, quaint. At any rate, the amusement park seemed overrun with kids and adults alike who appeared to be having a great time.

Alex turned right as Deano had instructed and drove about two blocks with the amusement park and the Roof Garden Ballroom on his left and a number of small shops on his right. Suddenly, Alex found himself turning around in a cul-de-sac at the edge of the lake.

Perhaps he had misunderstood Deano's directions. Most likely, though, it was simply his own inability to sense direction that had led him here, to the wrong place. When Alex's first grade teacher taught them geography, she had placed the map on the south wall of the classroom. This caused north to be south, east to be west, left to be right, up to be down, and so on. From that day forth, Alex had no sense of direction whatsoever. Locating the North Star didn't help. Watching where the sun rises or sets didn't help. Nothing helped. While most men feel that asking for directions is almost like cheating, Alex had to rely upon this tactic as his only hope of finding where he was going.

There were pedestrians everywhere, walking to and from the amusement park and the shops. About half of them were wearing shirts with University of Okoboji written on them – The University couldn't be far off.

"Can you tell me how to find the University of Okoboji Campus?" Alex asked a young couple wearing University of Okoboji T-shirts and walking hand-in-hand.

"Why, sure," the young man said. "Go down this street and

turn left at the roller coaster. Go past the big yellow building and go all the way to the stoplight. At the stoplight, go straight ahead and go about four blocks. You'll see the University of Okoboji right in front of you."

So that was it, Alex had turned right instead of left at the stoplight – but then, Deano had said to go past the yellow building and turn at the roller coaster. So, it was Deano, after all, who had screwed up the directions.

As Alex pulled out, he heard the couple giggling and laughing – it must be wonderful to be young and in love. "Love your car," the young man called out. It seemed everybody in Okoboji loved the car – but apparently not enough for any of them to have bought it themselves. Alex followed the new set of directions and soon found himself several blocks past the stoplight, staring at another lake without a college building in site.

Alex returned to the motel and walked into the office.

"Find the University of Okoboji?" Deano asked with that grin of his plastered all over his face.

And then it hit Alex. Everyone from the truck driver, who was so eager for Alex to visit the campus, to Deano, to the couple wearing University of Okoboji T-shirts, were having a little fun with him. "There isn't any University of Okoboji, is there," Alex stated, more as a fact than as a question.

"Oh sure there is. In fact, last year the University of Okoboji football team, The Fighting Phantoms, beat both Nebraska and Notre Dame – on the same day – on September 31st. Deano was really grinning now.

"So there is no University of Okoboji," Alex said.

"Well, there is and there isn't," Deano answered. "The University of Okoboji is an *attitude* - a feeling, a concept. The whole lakes region is the campus. And, every resident and every visitor is a student. And when you leave here and go back to The Hills, you'll be an alumni, forever. And, you'll come back to The

University time and time again – everyone does once they've been here."

"Do you send everybody who visits here on a wild goose chase looking for The University?" Alex asked.

"No, not at all," Deano answered, "just when we think we can get away with it, like with you." He was grinning again.

"When you go to The Three Sons clothing store in Milford, ask Herman and Emil about The University – they're the guys who started the whole thing," Deano said.

Cars lined both sides of the street and were parked around the corner and down the street for a block in either direction of The Three Sons. There was an empty spot half a block from the store and Alex eased the Orange Blossom Special in. As Alex walked towards the store, he noticed a bumper sticking out of the trunk of the car a young man was getting into. "Buy that car from Lyin' Louie?" Alex asked.

"How'd you know?" the young man asked.

"Just a wild guess," Alex said, starting to feel that he was becoming a little street smart – Okoboji street smart.

Deano, always willing to help, had filled Alex in on the history of The Three Sons and of their founding of the University of Okoboji. The Richter brothers had started their clothing career in their teens by selling windbreakers out of the back of their car down by the amusement park. When they sold a boxfull, they ordered another and sold it and did so over and over. Buoyed by this success, they decided to open a bona fide retail clothing store but the only building they could afford was an old feed store located in Milford, a block off Highway 71. Part of the building had wood floors and the back part had a dirt floor. There were holes in the side of the building, which they patched

45

with metal signs bearing names of clothing products. Instead of buying fancy shelving and display cases, they built shelves out of pine boards and two by fours. Hardly the setting for a successful career in the clothing business.

The brothers filled the store with name brand clothes and athletic shoes and capitalized on their out-of-the-way location and humble surroundings by offering a huge selection and prices that fancy stores couldn't match. A few years later, they added on a large two-story addition, and, continuing with their Spartan motif, left the rafters and insulation bats exposed and built the new shelves from pine boards and two by fours. The floor, of course, was boards – not hardwood – just boards. And they filled the new addition, from floor to ceiling, with additional name brand clothes. They became known as the one place in Iowa, South Dakota, Minnesota, and Nebraska where you could find any name brand clothes you wanted, and in your size. They became, according to Deano, one of the most successful clothing stores in the state.

Herman and Emil came up with the concept of the University of Okoboji as a way to recognize and glorify all of the recreational aspects and fun to be had in the Okoboji area. Each year, The University sponsors a variety of sporting activities, events, and tournaments that are attended by participants from several states around. Herman and Emil registered the name, University of Okoboji, and sell dozens of clothing products and souvenirs bearing the name and logo of The University.

Alex stepped into the store and was immediately greeted by a tall, athletic fellow wearing shorts and, of course, a University of Okoboji shirt. He strode toward Alex with a boyish smile that literally extended from ear to ear. "Welcome to The Three Sons – I'm Herman. What's your name?"

"I'm Al," Alex said. "I understand you founded the University of Okoboji."

"Golly, Gee," he said, "a bunch of us guys used to talk about having so much fun at 'Camp Okoboji' and the University of Okoboji concept just grew from there."

"So, are you the President of The University?" Alex asked, playing along.

"I'm the Director of Student Affairs," Herman said proudly. "If anybody's having an affair - gosh - I want to know about it." And, the 100,000-watt smile followed.

Alex looked around. The room was filled with drinking glasses, mugs, ashtrays, stickers, golf balls, post cards, and dozens of products bearing the University of Okoboji logo. They had every promotional product that a real university has.

"I need a complete summer wardrobe," Alex said. That really made Herman smile.

Herman led Alex into the main part of the store, which was exactly as Deano had described it — wood boards for floors, pine and two by four shelves, open rafters with exposed insulation bats, clothes piled high in every direction, and wall-to-wall shoppers.

For twenty minutes Alex and Herman tore through the store with Herman grabbing clothes off the pine shelves, holding them up for Alex's approval, exclaiming "Golly, gee, that looks great," and charging off to the next shelf. That big smile never left Herman's face the whole time — he was excited, he was exuberant, he loved selling clothes, he loved life, and he loved Okoboji.

When it was over, Alex had selected four pair of pants, four shorts, eight shirts, including three with University of Okoboji on them, two pair of tennis shoes, and an assortment of socks, underwear, and University of Okoboji souvenirs.

The large sign above the cash register was an enlargement of The University logo, bearing The University's slogan, "In God We Trust — Everyone Else, Cash." Alex peeled twelve hundred dollars from his wad to pay his bill and Herman didn't flinch – he was used to making cash sales – big ones. He did smile, though. He really, really smiled.

Herman shook Alex's hand vigorously – these Okoboji guys were a great bunch of handshakers, he had found – and he was still talking as Alex left the store, "Golly, gee, we appreciate your business. Tell your friends we're open on Sundays from noon to four and open nights until eight – and we've got specials on golf shoes next week and..."

Alex's next stop was The Central Emporium. He had purchased all the clothes that he needed, and more, from Herman at The Three Sons, but Deano had recommended he stop at The Emporium, as Deano called it, so here he was.

Deano had filled Alex in on the background of The Emporium. What was now The Central Emporium originally had been the elegant Central Ballroom where famous big bands of the day like Lawrence Welk, Glenn Miller, Count Bassie, Woody Herman, and Tommy Dorsey, had played. After ballroom dancing faded out, the ballroom was used for a variety of things including boat storage and a warehouse. In the late 1960's, a young, energetic, visionary bought the building and converted it into about thirty shops. The Emporium survived and thrived and became one of Okoboji's "must" shopping destinations.

The Central Emporium is a four-story structure located on a slope that drops off about thirty feet down to the lakeshore. The bottom floor is a partial floor, about one hundred twenty feet deep, which houses Whiskey Dick's, one of the snazziest bars in the state, with a deck that extends out over the lake. The second and third floors run the entire length of the building and house the shops and Gepetto's restaurant. A portion of the top, or fourth, floor was converted into a penthouse where the building owner, Dick Brown, lives.

Alex didn't need a sweatshirt, but he bought one anyway from Heather and Heidi in the first shop inside the door, Boji Funwear. Alex was enjoying doing the tourist thing – browsing through shops, buying a few things he didn't need, and just going about his business unnoticed – a member of the general public.

The Funhouse Gallery was a gift shop featuring collectibles and photos of a bygone era in Okoboji. Alex viewed the old photos, getting a sense of the history. There were photos of the Everly Brothers in concert, surrounded by fans, an old drive-in restaurant, a funhouse, a roller rink, the amusement park, boats on the lake, classic car displays, old buildings, and lots of photos of sunsets over the lake.

There were two display racks holding perhaps three hundred movie theater posters. Alex couldn't resist – he flipped through the posters, partly because he was a collector of vintage movie posters himself and partly because he was curious – maybe they had never heard of the Bunny Boy out here. That would be okay with him.

The posters were mostly genuine one-sheets with a few replicas thrown in. Most were from movies released within the past ten years or so, but there were a few older ones including *Psycho*, *Saturday Night Fever*, *The Outlaw Josie Wales*, *Rebel Without A Cause*, and *North By Northwest*. Alex was about halfway through the display when he came face to face with his own image on a *Beach Bunny* poster. Alex quickly flipped to the next poster – it was from one of his more infamous movies, *Golf Bunny*. He had had enough and quickly flipped all of the posters back before someone caught him viewing such trash.

Alex moved on to the display rack containing celebrity posters, many of which were of his friends – Ben Affleck, Johnny Depp, Gweneth Paltrow, Orlando Bloom, Tori Spelling …. He hadn't seen most of these posters and enjoyed studying

49

the poses his friends had struck for the photo shoot. He knew them well enough to recognize when a small smirk here, a wrinkle there, or a raised eyebrow meant they were mugging for the camera or were simply saying "Screw you."

And then, there it was, the inevitable – a larger-than-life poster of himself. Alex stared at the poster for a moment, trying to remember when he had posed for that particular shot and trying to figure out what message he was trying to send with that goofy look on his face.

"Bunny Boy," the voice said.

Alex froze. He had been busted. He had become too overconfident of his disguise and had become careless.

"Pardon me," Alex said, fully expecting to be attacked by the owner of the voice.

"That poster you're looking at," she said, "that's the actor, Alex Gideon – they call him the Bunny Boy."

"Uh, I know," Alex said. "A friend of mine is a big fan of his. Do you sell many of his posters?"

"Can't keep them in the shop," she answered. "Women go crazy over them – we have to reorder four or five times a summer. We're the only shop in Okoboji that has movie posters and celebrity posters."

An idea hit Alex. "How long does it take to get in a new order"? he asked.

"Oh, about ten days."

"My friend really is a big fan," Alex said. "I'll take all the celebrity posters of Alex Gideon that you've got – and all of his movie posters, too."

"I'm Cindy, but you can call me Fred," she said. "This is my shop – but my friend, Bev, owns the stuff in this room – I'll have her come over and roll up the posters for you. By the way, we have photographs of the Bunny Boy, too. Do you want them also?"

50

"Right, I'll take all of the Alex Gideon posters and photos you have," Alex said, refusing to use the name, Bunny Boy.

Bev was a gracious lady who admitted that she had never seen a Bunny Boy movie. Alex admired her taste- he wouldn't pay to see one either. She removed all of the celebrity posters, movie posters, and photos from their displays and packaged them up for Alex. There were six or seven copies of everything. Never in his wildest dreams did Alex ever expect to buy a single Bunny Boy item, and here he was buying dozens of them.

The total came to $850.00, plus tax, totaling $909.50, but it was worth it – nobody in Okoboji would be able to compare his present appearance to his likeness on a poster – out of sight, out of mind.

Without his even asking, Bev gave him a discount of $50. These Okobojians liked cash, he could see that.

The package of posters was large and heavy, so Alex left them in the Funhouse Gallery while he visited some of the other shops in The Emporium. Alex did a quick mental calculation – at the rate he was spending money in these shops, he'd go through twenty-five thousand dollars in The Emporium if he kept up this pace. But, what the hell – he could afford it and he was having a ball – he was on vacation, after all.

"Actor," Alex said to himself as he left the Funhouse Gallery. "She called me an actor – not a movie star, but an actor." He liked that Cindy Fred. She was a good judge of talent.

Alex browsed through Expressions, T-Galaxy, Mother Goose, The Animal House, Anchor Inn, The Extra Touch and a dozen other shops without buying a thing, although he was tempted. He bought a bag of chocolate covered peanuts at the Sugar Shack and stopped into the cigar store, Okostogie. He liked the name – a classic name for an Okoboji cigar store, and purchased a box of Macanudos for $225. They would make a nice peace offering for Charlie when Alex finally returned home.

51

Alex retrieved his posters from the Funhouse Gallery and loaded them into the trunk of the Orange Blossom Special. They would be safe there until he found a dumpster to deposit them in.

5

Across the street from the Four Seasons Resort was the Hollywood Bar and Grille. Alex was hungry, and he was curious, so it seemed like the logical place to get a bite. It was a rustic looking building, with a wood and stone exterior and a patio on the street side.

Alex walked in and found himself in line behind a half dozen people. Perhaps this was considered an inconvenience in Okoboji, but in L.A. it would be considered a miracle, especially without a reservation.

Alex was soon at the head of the line, next to be seated. Out of curiosity, Alex glanced behind himself to see how long the line had become. Suddenly, two college-age women let out piercing screams and charged in his direction, continuing to scream. Alex turned his back to the women, covered his head with his hands, and prepared for the collision. There was nowhere for him to run, nowhere to hide.

One of the few principles Alex remembered from his high school science class was the *Doppler Effect*. That was the e-e-e-e-e-e-e-e-o-o-o-o-o-o-o-o sound you heard when a train passed by blowing its whistle. Alex now experienced the Doppler Effect first hand as the screams approached him, getting louder and louder, and then passed him by and got softer as the sound moved into the distance, e-e-e-e-e-e-e-e-o-o-o-o-o-o-o. Alex slowly uncovered his head and looked in the direction of the screaming, which was now about ten feet in front of him. The two screaming young women were hugging another college-age woman and were jumping up and down – a reunion of sorts. He had been spared again.

The young woman who had been the object of all of the screaming and hugging turned out to be the hostess, who led Alex to a small table along the wall. It was a nice seat with a view of the stone fireplace, which wasn't lit, of course, this being summertime, and of the Four Seasons Resort and Water's Edge Condos across the street. The dining room was nearly full, mostly with couples and groups of four or six. The room was decorated in movie décor including numerous framed movie theater posters and photos of movie stars. Bev and Cindy Fred from the Funhouse Gallery must have made a mint decorating this place. Alex wondered how much of a discount they had given to the owner.

A sneaking suspicion started to creep into Alex's mind – he looked to his left, he looked to his right. He heaved a sigh of relief – there wasn't a single Bunny Boy poster in si. . . Yikes! Right in front of him on the wall, no more than eight feet away, was a framed poster of the most gawd-awful movie he had ever made, or anybody had ever made - *Rock Star Bunny*. And, right in the middle of the poster, grinning like an idiot, was that fool, Alex Gideon. Alex had indigestion, and he hadn't even ordered his meal. Alex slumped down in his chair, pulled his collar up around his neck, and raised his menu in front of his face as a shield. His disguise had proven to be effective so far, but sitting underneath the poster might be too much of a giveaway.

"My name is Pat and I'll be your server," she said. "Would you care for something to drink?"

"I'm ready to order," Alex answered, suddenly in a hurry to get out of there. "I'll have bottled water, prawns, Boston browns, and fried okra." Having lived all over the country as a youth, Alex had developed an eclectic taste in food, normally ordering a variety of foods that most people wouldn't put together in the same meal.

Pat wrote down his order and headed for the kitchen. Alex checked his watch – it was three twenty – that would be California time. That would make it five twenty here, probably. In all of his careful maneuvering to conceal his identity, he had neglected to set his watch for the Central time zone. He did it now, slowly, deliberately – anything for an excuse to turn his head away from the poster looming overhead.

The meal was delicious - fabulous, even. Alex was about midway through enjoying the dining experience, and had pretty well gotten over his paranoia about the Bunny Boy poster, when a heated discussion broke out at the table behind him. It wasn't a real argument, but clearly, the two people weren't seeing eye to eye.

"I thought we were going to eat at Gepetto's tonight," Voice Number One said.

"It was your idea to come here," Voice Number Two replied.

"My idea?" asked Voice Number One. "Where did you get that crazy idea? You're hallucinating again."

And, the conversation went steadily downhill from there.

"Are you saying I'm nuts?"

"No, I didn't say you're nuts – crazy maybe, but not nuts."

"I should get up and leave right now."

"We already ordered. I'm not going to waste money buying you a meal you don't even eat."

"It's my money, I'll waste it if I want."

"Stop acting childish."

"Oh, so now I'm a child. First I'm crazy and now I'm a child."

"I never said you were a child, I said you were acting like a child."

"Nana nana naa-naa. Sticks and bones may break my bones but words will never hurt me."

"Now you're pouting – stop it."

Fortunately for Alex, Pat brought the guest check in time to save him from any more of the bickering going on at the table behind him. The meal came to twenty-two dollars and Alex left a fifty on the table – Pat had been a good server and could probably use a few extra bucks to help with college expenses.

The nitpicking continued behind Alex as he rose from his chair and nonchalantly glanced in that direction wanting to get a glimpse of the two boneheads as he walked by. Alex did a double take and almost tripped over his own feet. There, sitting at the table was only one guy - one bonehead carrying on this conversation, back and forth, with himself. Alex smiled as he walked by and said to himself, "And they call where I live *Hollyweird.*"

"What do people do around here for excitement on a Thursday night?" Alex asked.

"Well, there's twenty-six bars within walking distance of right here – within a mile – if you're thirsty," Deano replied with a grin.

"Anything else?"

"Then, there's the movie theater in Okoboji – just about a mile north."

Going to the movies was the last thing on Alex's list. "Anything else?" He asked.

"The racquetball tournament is going on at Arrowwood Resort, if you like watching that sort of thing – might not be much fun if you don't know any of the players, though."

Deano hesitated for a moment and searched his mind for

other possibilities, "Oh," he said, "there's the play at the Okoboji Lakeside Theater. Jodell and I went last night – it was a good play. It was fun."

"What's the play?" Alex asked.

"It's called *Sisterly Love*."

"Never heard of it," Alex said.

"The director of the theater wrote the play – it's pretty good. It's way good. Every summer the theater presents a different play every week for ten straight weeks. They hire three or four professional actors who take turns playing the lead and directing the plays. They fill in the rest of the cast with theater students from several universities and a few locals are used for some of the bit parts."

Alex was skeptical. Watching a play written by an amateur and with a bunch of amateur actors might be the ultimate torture. After all, he was a professional actor. Well, in his opinion he was a professional actor – the rest of the world didn't seem to think so, but he did. At least, he got paid the big bucks for acting – that should count for something.

"That's about it on a Thursday night," Deano said. "On the weekend there'll be dozens of things to do, this being Summer Games, but it's a little slow on a Thursday night. Unless you want to go drinking – the bars are always hopping, even on a Thursday night."

Alex had only been in Okoboji a matter of a few hours and even though he wouldn't mind a cool drink or two, he wasn't about to go bar hopping all by himself. From the likes of the characters he'd met around Okoboji, that could prove to be dangerous.

Of all the options Deano had mentioned, the play was sounding better all the time. "What time does the play start?" Alex asked.

"Seven o'clock – in about an hour," Deano said as he checked his watch. "If you're going to go you'd better get moving, the place fills up pretty fast."

"Where's the theater?" Alex asked.

Deano grinned. "You know where the University of Okoboji is, right?"

"You mean that cul-de-sac along the lake by the amusement park?" Alex replied.

"That's it – well, the theater's about a half block from there, right along the lakeshore," Deano said.

"Well, I might think about going," Alex said, still hesitant to put up with a group of amateurs for a couple of hours.

"Tell you what, Al, if you don't enjoy the play, I'll reimburse you the price of the ticket and buy you a couple of drinks to boot," Deano said. "Stop in at the Dry Dock after the play and let me know what you think," he continued, pointing at the bar connected to the motel.

That was the clincher. Alex headed for his room to change into some of his new clothes for a night at the theater – Okoboji style.

6

The Okoboji Lakeside Theater was an old wood structure, sitting on the shore of West Lake Okoboji. There were three glass double doors in the front and Alex chose the middle one. There were about a dozen people milling around the entry foyer and a half dozen more were at the concession stand. Alex headed for the ticket booth right in the middle of the room.

"One, please," Alex said.

"For what night?" she asked.

"Tonight," he said.

"We're all sold out for tonight," she said. "Have been for a couple of weeks. All sold out for the rest of the week, too. We do have some tickets for next Tuesday and Wednesday, though."

"I was only interested in tonight," Alex said, thinking that perhaps it was divine intervention that had spared him from amateur night here at the Okoboji Lakeside Theater.

"I have an extra ticket if you don't mind joining me," a raspy voice behind Alex said.

Alex turned to greet a striking woman with gray hair and perhaps a smidgen too much makeup. Her dress was a swirl of red, orange, yellow, pink, and green. There were two oversized diamond rings on her left hand and three on her right and she had four or five gold and diamond bracelets on her right wrist.

"My husband got tied up on business in Des Moines and won't make it to Okoboji until Saturday, so I've got an extra ticket. I would be honored if you would join me as my guest," she said.

"I would be delighted to," Alex said graciously, "but I insist on paying for the ticket."

She slipped her arm through Alex's and steered him toward the theater entrance. "Personally, I think my husband is back in Des Moines screwing his secretary," she said as a matter of fact, "so the least the old goat can do is pay for the ticket."

And that was that.

Martha, as her name turned out to be, had the best seats in the house – right on the center aisle twelve rows back. Close enough to feel a part of the action but not so close that you'd get a crook in your neck from looking up at the stage. She had seen almost every play at the theater for the past forty-five years, she said.

"George C. Scott performed here for a full month – oh, quite a few years ago when he was first getting into acting, you know," she said proudly. "He was such a handsome man and, oh, what an actor! And he was such a gentleman… and that's probably all I'd better say about that," she said abruptly as she closed her eyes, sighed, and smiled.

Alex gazed around the theater. There were two aisles, with about a dozen seats in the middle section and six seats in each of the two outer sections. The theater was twenty-five or thirty rows deep, which meant it held maybe six or seven hundred people – no wonder they were sold out every night. The seats were large and they were elevated so that every seat had a perfect view of the raised stage. The stage ran nearly the entire width of the building, with stage wings of only about eight feet on either side. A purple velvet curtain hid all but the front six feet of the stage from view.

Alex studied the program. It listed the summer's schedule, which included a mixture of drama, comedy, and musicals. Most were plays that had achieved fame on Broadway including *Heaven Can Wait, Once Upon A Mattress, Kiss Me Kate, Anastasia, Smoke On The Mountain, Foxfire*, and *Funny Valentine*. Two were original plays written by members of the Okoboji Lakeside Theater cast, including tonight's play, *Sisterly Love*. What luck.

The program listed the cast from tonight's play and provided a short biographical sketch of each.

Simone Delaney was the manager of the theater. She had also written tonight's play, directed it, and had the female lead. Alex scoffed. "Simone Delaney," he thought to himself, "what an obvious attempt to create a stage name – real people don't have names like that. Sure, Alex Gideon was a stage name, too, but it was a good name – a believable name. And, the writer, director, and lead actress – what an ego trip she must be on." Alex wondered if she'd play the accordion during intermission.

Alex read on about Simone Delaney. Perhaps he had been a little hasty in his harsh criticism, for it was Simone Delaney, Ph.D. She was the chair of the Drama Department at the University of Arizona in Tucson. She first came to the Okoboji Lakeside Theater as a junior in college and fell in love with The Theater and with Okoboji. She had returned every summer since then and four years ago had assumed the role of theater manager. She had written a play that performed to sold out crowds at the theater each of the last three summers.

The article said Simone believed that the theater served a dual purpose – to entertain the audience and to nurture the creative talents of the cast and crew. Thus, she directed and starred in only one play per season. Each member of the theater troupe, except for the professional actors who were hired to play the lead in one or more plays, performed a different role in each play, ranging from playing bit parts, to playing the lead, to directing, to serving on the crew.

Alex studied Simone's photo. She had reddish brown hair, dark eyes, high cheekbones, and a slender face. It was a face with character that seemed strong and vulnerable, serious and mischievous, all at the same time. But then, she was an actor so how the hell would he know what that look on her face meant.

Filbert Kaufmann played the male lead. "Filbert has to be his real name," Alex thought to himself. "Nobody in their right mind would pick a name like that for themselves on purpose."

Filbert had graduated from Duke University with a double major in theater and music. This was his fifth summer at the Okoboji Lakeside Theater and he would perform in four of the ten plays this season. Filbert was a full-time performing actor. He had performed in theaters off-Broadway in New York, and had extended engagements in the Catskills, Chicago, New Orleans, and London. He had traveled with a cast of *Oklahoma* for over a year, playing in more than thirty cities. He also had television credits, having appeared on *All My Children* six times and on *As The World Turns* twice.

Alex studied Filbert's picture. He looked like a Filbert. Period.

Ted Payne played a supporting role. He was a dock builder and lived in Arnolds Park. This was his fourth summer at the theater. He had been an offensive lineman on the University of South Dakota football team and also played the tuba.

Sally Monroe was a senior at the University of Iowa, majoring in theater. She played a supporting role in this play, but had played the lead in *Kiss Me Kate*, which was presented earlier in the summer. After graduating from college, she planned to move to Hollywood to pursue a movie career. Alex winced. He wished he could talk to her and pound some sense into her head, but, of course, he couldn't risk it.

62

Eric Gibson was a graduate student in theater at Northwestern University in Chicago and was playing a supporting role in this play. He had received his bachelor's degree three years ago and had performed in more than two dozen plays off-off-off Broadway and in small venues around the country since then. He had the distinction, it said, of performing in one of the world's shortest running plays, *Whodonedat?*, which folded at intermission on its first night when the entire audience left and failed to return.

The piano player, which is always an important role in most of these plays, was a woman named Mel. She was a music teacher in the Okoboji school district.

There were short bios of the remaining cast and crew also, mostly college students getting their first taste of the theater, and a sprinking of locals who were enjoying their fifteen minutes.

"I've seen this play twice already," Martha said, "and I'm going again tomorrow night. You're welcome to come with me if you want."

"Thanks, but once is usually my limit," Alex said.

"If you change your mind, let me know," she said.

Alex now had two friends in Okoboji – Deano and Martha – and he could probably stretch that a bit and include Herman, Cindy Fred, and Bev in that category, too. Including Lyin' Louie and Whitey from The Iowa Navy in his new circle of friends might be stretching it a bit too much.

Mel launched into a rousing version of "Oh! Susanna," on the old upright perched on the corner of the stage. She continued with a rollicking medley of other Stephen Foster songs including "Camptown Races," "Way Down Upon The Swanee River," "Jeanie With The Light Brown Hair," and "My Old Kentucky Home." The lights were dimmed, the curtain was raised, and the show was on.

63

The play was set in the 1850's south, prior to the Civil War. Savanna, played by Simone, and her father, Matt, played by Ted, were sitting on the veranda of the antebellum mansion, enjoying a glass of sweet tea. They were anxiously awaiting the arrival of Savanna's sister, Marion, who had been away to boarding school in Boston. Marion was played by Sally.

The sound of horses announced that Marion and the hired hand, William, who had picked her up from the train had arrived. William was played by Eric Gibson.

Marion had been away to school for nine months and had grown into a young lady of charm, grace, and sophistication – at least that's how she perceived herself compared to her older sister, Savanna, who had been toiling on the plantation, taking care of their aging father. Savanna, the level-headed, hard-working dutiful daughter, tried her best to overlook Marion's condescending attitude and aversion to physical labor, attributing it to youthful immaturity.

When Savanna's fiancé, Nathan, played by Filbert, arrived on the scene, Marion flirted with him shamelessly, demonstrating time and again how she was so much more worldly and sophisticated than Savanna. Nathan, the arrogant and self-centered neighboring plantation owner, basked in the attention.

William, the hired hand, had grown up on a small cotton farm just a couple of miles from Savanna's plantation and the two had been friends since childhood. William's parents were poor sharecroppers and when it was time for William to go out on his own, he felt fortunate to land a job on the plantation. William and Savanna remained friends, although Nathan loathed the sharecropper's son and forbid Savanna to even talk to William in his presence.

In this time of turmoil, Savanna turned to William for support and comfort. The first act ended with Savanna pouring her heart out to William, telling him how she felt so awkward and plain compared to Marion and how she felt the love of her life, Nathan, may be falling for Marion. At the same time, on the other side of the stage, Nathan and Marion were seen embracing and kissing.

The curtain was dropped, Mel tore into the Stephen Foster medley, the house lights were turned up, and it was intermission.

Alex checked his watch. An hour had flown by. He turned to speak to Martha. She was wiping tears from her eyes. "I just feel so sorry for Savanna," she said. "But silly me, it's just a play, isn't it."

And then Martha smiled. She was back on top. "Well, what do you think of our little small-town theater so far?" she asked.

"To be honest, I expected a one-horse operation with a feeble play written by some hometown hack and a bunch of lame actors," Alex said, "but nothing could be further from the truth. I'm very impressed – ah, based on my limited knowledge of plays and acting, that is."

"What do you think of Simmy?" Martha asked.

"Simone? Alex asked.

"We all call her Simmy."

"Is she married?" Alex asked.

"I guess that answers my question," Martha said, without answering Alex's.

"And that guy, Filbert," Alex said, "he's playing the part of Nathan beautifully."

"He's an asshole," Martha said, "and he's not acting."

The Stephen Foster medley rang from Mel's piano, the house lights were dimmed, the curtain was raised, and Act Two was underway.

Nathan assured Savanna that he truly loved her and that he was merely trying to build a bond with his future sister-in-law, Marion. In the meantime, Nathan and Marion continued with their clandestine love affair and Marion continued with her

65

obnoxious behavior toward Savanna.

Nathan pressed Savanna to marry him immediately rather than to wait until Thanksgiving as they had planned. When he was alone with Marion, he begged her, too, to run off with him and to get married.

William found a few boll weevils attacking cotton balls on a field bordering Nathan's plantation. He checked Nathan's plantation and found the entire crop was infested with boll weevils, beyond the point of being able to save the crop. Nathan had apparently spent too much time romancing Savanna and Marion to pay attention to his crop and he was about to be ruined.

Savanna and Marion's father, Matt, was in failing health and was unable to care for his fields. William reported to Matt that he had discovered the boll weevils and had gotten rid of them, saving the crop and saving the plantation from financial ruin.

After saving the cotton crop, William set out to save Savanna and Marion from Nathan. First he took Savanna to secretly eavesdrop on Nathan and Marion. She overheard Nathan pledge his love to her and tell her that Savanna meant nothing to him and that he wanted to marry her immediately.

Next, he took Marion to secretly eavesdrop on Nathan and Savanna. Nathan used the same identical words to pledge his love to Savanna as he told her that Marion meant nothing to him and that he wanted to marry Savanna immediately.

Marion and William jumped from their hiding place as the two sisters confronted Nathan. The smooth talker tried to worm his way out of the situation, but he was cornered. William produced a cotton ball crawling with boll weevils that he had taken from Nathan's plantation and accused him of desperately trying to marry either of the sisters, it didn't matter which one, to save his plantation.

Nathan exited the stage in disgrace. Marion realized what a

fool she had been and apologized to Savanna, who graciously forgave her. William seized the moment to confess to Savanna that he had always loved her and wanted to marry her if she would have him. She, too, realized that she loved William and jumped into his arms as Mel flew into the medley with gusto and the curtain was dropped to a thunderous standing ovation.

Alex found himself on his feet, clapping wildly and whistling. That had been one hell of a performance.

The curtain rose, and the entire cast took a bow. The applause grew louder. Alex couldn't take his eyes off of Simone. Two hours ago he had regarded her as some country bumpkin and now he was in awe. She had written a play that had drama, mystery, wit, humor, tenderness, and a theme of redemption. And, she could act. She could really act.

The cast exited, all except for Simone, who stood alone at center stage.

"Thank you so much," she said. The applause continued, wildly.

Simone waved her hands for the crowd to stop applauding. Clearly she enjoyed it, but she wanted it to stop so she could move on. Finally, the applause subsided enough for her to speak.

"Thank you so kindly for your support tonight and for your support of the Okoboji Lakeside Theater through the entire season and throughout all of the years that the theater has been in existence," she said. "But now, I have something of grave importance that I want to talk to you about tonight."

The auditorium fell deathly silent. Simone was dead serious and the audience gave her respect.

"As many of you know, the amusement park, Roof Garden Ballroom, Maritime Museum, this theater, and the grounds, known locally as *The Park*, occupy about twenty acres of land, with over eight hundred feet of frontage on West Lake Okoboji. This is very valuable property, with lakeshore property selling for over $12,000 a running foot these days. Three and a half weeks ago, the owner of this property sold it to a developer from Des Moines who intends to tear down all of the existing structures, or move them, and build high-rise condominiums on these grounds."

A collective moan came from the audience. Alex glanced at Martha – she was again wiping tears from her eyes.

"The sales price was ten million dollars, Simone continued, "and it did not include the amusement park rides, which are to be moved elsewhere by the current owner.

"Residents of the Okoboji area were shocked, as were people from all over Iowa and many states around – and from around the country. Former residents and tourists, now living all over America, have fond memories of summer days at the amusement park, of hot summer nights at the Roof Garden Ballroom, and, I hope, of memorable times at this very theater as well.

"The Board of Directors of the Maritime Museum approached the developer and asked him to name a price for which he would sell the property back. He said he would sell it back for eleven million dollars, if the Museum could come up with the money in one month. Steve Kennedy, founder of the Maritime Museum, along with several others, immediately set about spearheading a fundraising effort. Hundreds of people have joined the effort by volunteering their time and thousands of people, from school children to corporate CEO's, have donated money. The original owner of the property has pledged to donate all of the amusement park rides and buildings, valued at around three and a half million dollars, if the fundraising project is successful.

"The support has been overwhelming, but still, we are over three million dollars short of our goal. Our deadline is five p.m. this coming Monday – that's just a little less than four days away. We will not give up. We cannot give up. We must save The

Park – not just for you and me, but for all of those who have fond memories of good times in Okoboji and for all of the future generations who deserve the opportunity to build their own memories right here in The Park, in Okoboji."

They were on their feet again, and Alex was with them. Simone was passionate, truly passionate. He had known plenty of starlets who were passionate, but their passion was accompanied by heavy breathing and panting. Simone's passion came from her heart and her soul. She wasn't acting, this was real.

Simone waved her arms back and forth to get the crowd to stop applauding and to get them to sit down and listen.

"It's true," Simone continued, "we could build a new amusement park, a new ballroom, a new museum, and a new theater somewhere else in Okoboji, but this is home. This is where it belongs."

They were applauding again, loudly, and again Simone got them to settle down.

"We're going to pass a hat for donations. Are there angels among you? Please give all that you can. Give until it hurts – give until it feels good. And, thank you very, very much. And, don't leave, I have one more announcement."

Filbert, Eric, and Ted, still in costume, each took a section of the auditorium and passed the hats they had worn in the play. When the hat got to Alex and Martha, the hat was almost overflowing already. Alex glanced at the hat and saw a few ones and fives, but mostly they were twenties, fifties, and even a few hundreds.

Alex reached for his money clip, loosened the hinge, and slipped the entire bankroll into his hand. Usually, he tried to keep at least $500 in the money clip and the rest of his cash in the wad in his pants pocket. Alex always kept the big bills on the inside with a few ones on the outside so no one would know how much money he was carrying. Alex nonchalantly slipped

69

the bills into the hat as he handed it to Martha.

Martha set the hat in her lap. She took her left hand and pulled the diamond ring from the index finger of her right hand – the biggest ring with the biggest diamonds. She dropped the ring in the hat, shook it a little so it would settle to the bottom, and passed the hat on.

Martha leaned over to Alex and whispered, "That'll fix the son-of-a-bitch, and tomorrow I'm going to go buy a new one."

Back in L.A. they called that Kiss-My-Ass-Rich, and they probably called it that out here too.

The hats were passed and delivered to the front of the theater. Two armed policemen appeared from the wings, dumped the contents into a bank bag, locked it, gave the key to Simone, and left with the bag. Alex, for one, appreciated their penchant for security.

"Thank you all very much for your generosity," Simone said. "It is very, very much appreciated. Also, 'Save The Park' T-shirts are on sale in the foyer for fifteen dollars. The shirts have all been donated by C & C Screenprinting, so it is pure profit."

Alex had seen dozens of people wearing those "Save The Park" shirts and had seen signs all over Okoboji with the same slogan. Now, it all finally made sense.

"This will only take a moment, but I want to make one more announcement – two, actually," Simone continued.

Simone looked into the wings, pointed to someone, and motioned for them to join her on stage. Eric, who had played William in the play, obeyed and joined Simone front and center.

"Eric has been with us for the past two months and has done a wonderful job," Simone said. "He received word this afternoon that his grandmother, who had been ill for some time, passed away at age ninety-one. Eric will be leaving in the morning to be with his family in Illinois and will miss the final three

70

appearances of this particular play. Will you all please join me in thanking Eric for sharing his talents with us and in wishing him God's speed."

Simone turned to Eric and led the applause and then walked over to him and gave him a hug. Eric left the stage as he waved goodbye.

"And, that brings me to the final announcement of the evening – we need a new Eric," she said, "or, I should say, a new William, for the next three nights. Even though William is on stage quite a bit, he actually has only eighteen lines to say – I counted them just today. It's night work and the pay isn't good, but if you have an interest in trying out for the part we'll be conducting auditions as soon as the theater is cleared out – in about fifteen minutes."

There was another round of applause, not as fervent this time, as people rose to exit the theater.

Martha poked Alex in the ribs, "Go for it," she said.

"Well, I don't know…" Alex began.

"What are you, a chickenshit?" Martha asked.

They both laughed.

"Okay, I will. I'll give it a try," Alex promised.

Martha and Alex hugged and said their good-byes, each saying they hoped to meet again. Somehow, Alex knew that they would.

There was only one other man who hung around for the audition, a guy named Peterson, several years older than Alex, who was a business teacher at the local community college.

Filbert and Ted approached them and introduced themselves. With a name like Filbert, one would assume he'd want to be addressed as Phil or Bert – but not Filbert – he made it clear that his name was FILBERT. Ted, the former college lineman, was bigger up close than he had looked on stage – maybe six four or six five and three hundred pounds – a real buffet buster.

Even his ears were fat. He wanted to be called Big Teddy. That was fine with Alex – hell, he would have called him Mr. Big Teddy or Sir Big Teddy if he wanted.

Apparently Filbert and Big Teddy came out to warm them up with a little small talk before their audition. "Do you play golf?" Alex did; Peterson did, kinda. "Do you like boating," Alex did; Peterson did, kinda. "Did you play any organized basketball," Alex did, kinda – high school intramurals; Peterson did, high school varsity. "Do you do any running to keep in shape?" Alex lied and said he didn't; Peterson did, kinda.

Simone appeared with three scripts and gave Filbert and Big Teddy a dourful look. Apparently she wanted to conduct the audition herself without the help of these two.

Simone had changed from her costume into jeans and a T-shirt with the "Save The Park" motto on the front. Alex didn't want to appear too obvious but he couldn't resist the temptation to look her over while she had turned away from him and Peterson to shoo Filbert and Big Teddy off to a corner. She was slender and trim with all the right curves in all the right places. If there was one thing Alex knew about in this world, it was beautiful women, and Simone fit right in with the best of them.

"I'm Simone," she said, apparently not considering Peterson and himself to be worthy of calling her Simmy.

Simone asked her own questions, which seemed to make a little more sense than Filbert's and Big Teddy's. "Did you see the play tonight – are you familiar with the part of William?" Alex had and was; Peterson had and was. "Could you rehearse for three hours tomorrow morning?" Alex could; Peterson could. "Have you ever done any acting?" Alex lied, saying he had not. Peterson had been in a high school play years ago, as a barking dog. "As you saw, William strums a few chords on a guitar; do you play?" Alex said, truthfully, that he had once owned a ukulele; Peterson said he didn't know – he'd never tried.

Next, Simone handed each of them a script and asked them to study the scene where William was comforting Savanna at the end of the first act.

Simone first read the scene with Peterson. He wasn't much of an actor. He would be well advised to keep his teaching certificate current.

Next, she read with Alex. He wanted to strike a delicate balance between being obviously better than Peterson, but not so good that he drew suspicion to himself. Even though it was only an audition, Simone gave her part her all. Her magnificent performance inspired Alex and he had to fight to stifle the urge to give a command performance right on the spot.

"Simmy, can Filbert and I talk to you for a minute?" Big Teddy asked.

Simone glared at the two of them for a moment and then frowned and said, "Sure, backstage."

It was a small stage and the acoustics were great, so Alex and Peterson could hear the entire conversation word for word.

"We think Peterson would be best for the part," Big Teddy said.

"He can't act," Simone said.

"Neither can the other guy, Al," Filbert said.

"Martha was right," Alex thought to himself. Filbert was an asshole.

"I think he has potential," Simone said.

"Potential for what?" Filbert sneered.

Simone ignored the inference.

"But Peterson has acting experience," Big Teddy pleaded.

"He was a barking dog," Simone said sarcastically.

"But...," Filbert started.

"I know what you two are up to," She said with a sharp edge to her voice.

"What?" "What?" they said in unison.

73

"I heard the two of you out there asking questions." Simone's voice was now dripping with sarcasm, "Do you play golf? Do you boat?" Do you play *basket-ball?*"

"This is the best chance we've ever had to win the championship," Big Teddy said. "With a little luck, and Peterson, we can beat Scratches tomorrow."

"That is assuming," Simone said, "that Peterson is a better basketball player than he is an actor."

Alex glanced at Peterson. He was taking his bashing like a man. But, he was sweating bullets – he must have wanted the part real bad.

"What you need is Eric Gibson," Simone said, "but his grandmother had the audacity to die right in the middle of your basketball tournament – maybe at age ninety-one she's entitled."

"You're right – Eric carried us this far, but we're so close – so close to finally beating those guys. We're tired of those beer guzzling jugheads making fun of us because we're actors and not jocks," Filbert said. "Give us Peterson, please."

Alex took another look at Peterson – he was sweating mortar shells.

"Listen," Simone said compassionately, "I don't know if Peterson can play basketball or not – but I do know he can't act. And even if he can play basketball, it's going to be pretty tough to beat Scratches' team without Eric."

"Please."

"Guys, I'm trying to run a theater here," she said, "and I've got to do what I think is best for the play, for the rest of the cast, and for the theater."

"Please."

"I'm the director of this play," she said firmly, "and I'll cast the part – it's Al's if he wants it."

Alex hoped that Peterson didn't take it too hard – it appeared that he wanted the part so badly. Alex looked at Peterson out of the corner of his eye. He was smiling like he had just won the lottery. It looked like the weight of the world had been lifted from his shoulders. Peterson jumped up, grabbed Alex's hand, pumped it several times, said "Congratulations, you'll do great," and charged out of the theater before Simone had a chance to change her mind.

"And besides," Simone said, taking a parting shot as she walked away from Filbert and Big Teddy, "Eric's costume will fit Al and it won't fit Peterson."

Alex gulped. He, Alex Gideon, one of the most famous movie stars in the world, had come within one or two suit sizes of getting beat out for a part by a business teacher. That hurt.

"Where's Peterson," Simone said as she appeared on stage.

"I think he changed his mind," Alex said.

"You heard?" Simone asked.

"Ya," Alex answered, "we both heard."

Simone winced. "Did Peterson take it ha…"

"He was relieved. I think he regretted throwing his hat in the ring," Alex said.

"I'd hate to hurt his feelings," Simone said.

"I think you did him a big favor," Alex said.

"And what about you? Why did you try out for the part?"

"By chance I ended up sitting next to this gray-haired lady, Martha. She put me up to it," Alex answered.

"Twelfth row, aisle seats?"

"How did you know?" Alex asked.

"She's one of the grand ladies of this theater, and one of its biggest benefactors," Simone said. "She was an actress, and a good one, they tell me – played the lead opposite George C. Scott when he performed here one summer – back some years ago.

"Why, that old broad," Alex thought to himself with a smile.

"Can you rehearse tomorrow morning, say nine a.m.?"

Simone asked. "We'll be done by noon."

"Sure," Alex answered.

"Here's the script," she said. "I hope you'll have a chance to study it before our rehearsal."

"I will," Alex promised.

"Good," she said as she turned and walked toward the wing. "See you right here at nine – and you can call me Simmy, if you like."

"Simmy," Alex said to himself as he walked toward the rear of the theater. "Simmy."

Big Teddy was waiting for Alex in the foyer. Alex didn't know if Big Teddy was going to break his legs so Peterson would get the part, and a spot on the theater basketball team, but he was soon to find out.

"Al," he said, "congratulations on winning the audition – you'll do just fine. If I can help in any way, let me know."

Alex was relieved. He had suspected that Filbert and Big Teddy would hold a grudge, so he was pleased to see that they didn't – at least not Big Teddy.

"I don't know if anybody told you, but the Summer Games are in progress here in Okoboji this week and this weekend," Big Teddy said. "The theater has a basketball team and, after winning three games this week, we're in the championship game tomorrow afternoon. We play Scratches bar, which has won the tournament for the last seven years. Scratches is a sports bar and they load up their team with former basketball and football players from Iowa State, Iowa, Nebraska, and even Minnesota. It's the first year our theater team has even made it past the first round so we're excited to be in the championship game. Scratches is awesome and they'll probably kick our ass. But anyway, if you'd like to play, we would be happy to have you."

"What time is the game?" Alex asked.

"One o'clock – at the Spirit Lake High School gym. Do you

76

know where it is?"

"I'll find it," Alex answered. "See you there."

One of the great regrets of Alex's life was that The Kaiser had moved his family from base to base so often that Alex was never able to play on an official high school basketball team. He would have relished the competition. He would have welcomed the challenge of seeing how he stacked up against other players from other teams. He would have had the answer to the question that had haunted him ever since he graduated from high school – was he good enough to have played college ball? Could he have made it to the pros? How would he have stacked up against the best?

One of the fruits of stardom is that you get to meet other stars, from all fields of endeavor. Alex had met famous musicians, singers, golfers, football players, Olympic heroes, business tycoons, boxers, and authors. But, the stars that he really liked to hang out with were the professional basketball players. His friends and acquaintances included Michael Jordan, Larry Bird, Magic Johnson, and most of the current players on the Lakers team. The player that he spent more time on the court with than anyone else was former Laker great, Magic Johnson. During the season, Magic was up to his ears in basketball, conducting clinics, scouting players, and doing television commentary, so he and Alex rarely played. In the summer, though, Alex and Magic shot hoops, played horse, and played one-on-one two or three times a week on the tennis court behind Alex's house.

Now, Alex wasn't about to try to convince anyone that he was in Magic's league, because he wasn't. And he never knew if Magic tried his best against him. But, he always felt that there must be one player in the NBA, somewhere, that he could out-play - that there would have been a spot for him.

Alex looked forward to the game against Scratches. It would be an opportunity to test his mettle, to see how he stacked up, to get a little closer to answering that nagging question - would he have been good enough?

☙

The Four Seasons' parking lot had become overrun since Alex had left for the theater. Kitty corner across the street, The Ritz parking lot was swelled to overflowing also.

Alex walked into the Dry Dock in search of his newfound friend, Deano. He had a couple of urgent questions on his mind.

The bar was L-shaped, with glass windows overlooking the waters of West Lake Okoboji. There were about ten barstools, all of which were occupied, and people stood two or three deep all along the bar. Every table was full and the place was alive with noisy conversation and laughter. Alex could hear Deano, but he couldn't see him.

Finally, he located Deano at the far end of the bar. Deano saw him coming and broke into that grin of his.

"Al," he yelled, "Al, over here."

Alex made his way through the crowd and found a spot next to Deano. Deano put his arm around Alex and introduced him to the woman that he had his other arm draped around.

"Al, Jodell. Jodell, Al." You can't get an introduction shorter and more direct than that.

This was, no doubt, Deano's lady friend – the one he went to the Black Hills with and the one he had gone to the theater with just last night. She looked like she belonged with Deano.

"What're ya drinkin'?" Deano asked.

Alex's choice of alcoholic beverage had been a source of much good-natured ribbing among his well-heeled and world-ly acquaintances in Los Angeles. While they poured down Glenlevit scotch, Gray Goose vodka, or Chateau Margaux, 1986, of course, at $550 a bottle, Alex preferred a good cold

78

bottle of Bud Light, as in Budweiser.

"I'll have a Bud Light," Alex answered.

The bartender delivered the bottle of Bud Light and Deano nodded to him and said, "Put it on my tab – wages."

Deano continued, "Al, this is Brian, he tends bar at a couple of places around town and helps us out on Thursday nights. This is Al, he'll be around for ten days or so, take good care of him."

Brian was wearing a baseball cap with the Iowa Hawkeye logo on the front.

"Hawkeyes had a good year – eleven and two," Alex said, referring to last year's football team as he pointed to the tiger hawk on Brian's cap.

Brian beamed. Alex had found his hot button and had made a friend for life. "They were picked to finish ninth in the Big Ten by every sports writer in the country. Before the season started, though, I predicted they'd go nine and three and was roundly laughed out of every bar in Okoboji. I'll never let any of them forget it. To be honest, it surprised the hell out of me, too."

"Well," Deano said, "do I owe you for the price of a theater ticket?"

Before Alex could answer, Deano turned to Jodell and said, "I told Al I'd pay for his ticket if he didn't like the play."

"So, how did you like it?" Jodell asked.

"I was, I was very impressed," Alex said. "I never expected anything that good out here."

"We didn't all just fall off the turnip wagon yesterday, you know," Deano said.

"I didn't mean it that way," Alex explained. "I mean I wouldn't expect to see an original play that good anywhere."

"I figured you'd like it," Deano said.

"By the way, do you know Simone Delaney?" Alex asked.

"Doc?" Deano asked. "Everybody knows Doc. She's a Phud, you know – that's short for Ph.D."

79

"Deano calls her 'Doc,'" Jodell said, "but the rest of us call her Simmy."

"Is she married?" Alex asked.

"Why do you ask?" Jodell asked.

That was twice now that Alex had asked someone if Simone was married and twice that they had answered his question with another question. Perhaps they were trying to protect her from guys like Alex.

"She's married." Deano said.

Alex's heart sunk. "To who?" he asked.

"She's married to the theater." Deano answered.

"All that girl does is work, work, work," Jodell said. "We've all tried to talk her into getting a life outside of the theater, but that is her life."

"How about Filbert?" Alex asked.

"He's an asshole," Deano said, "but he can act."

"I mean, is there something going on between Simone and Filbert?"

"Jeez," Jodell said, "give the girl a little credit. If there's anything going on between those two it's only in Filbert's mind, but you've got to give him credit, he keeps right on trying."

"You're sure asking a lot of questions," Deano said. "You wouldn't be the first tourist who came to Okoboji and took a run at Doc, but it's not going to happen, believe me. If you're looking for some action, check out the big blonde at the end of the bar – she's been giving you the eye ever since you walked in."

Alex turned to look in her direction and that was all the encouragement that she needed. In a flash she was standing chest-to-chest with Alex, spilling her drink on his shoes. "Let's go dance," she said.

"There isn't any music," Alex said.

"We'll make our own music," she answered.

Gawd. Alex had heard those lines before, from the

Hollywood bimbos like those that he had come here to Okoboji to escape. Alex glanced at Deano. He was loving this, grinning like a lunatic.

Alex had a lot of experience in situations like this. "Excuse me," he said to the blonde, as he turned his back to her and joined in conversation with Deano and Jodell.

"What a prick," the blonde said as she staggered away.

She didn't know it, and maybe she never would, but she had just insulted the hottest sex symbol in America.

"I'm going to be in Simone's play the next three nights – as a supporting actor. One of the guys' grandmother passed away and he had to go home for the funeral – I'm taking his place."

"That would be Eric," Jodell said. "His grandmother's been ill for some time."

"Does everybody know everybody and know everything about everybody in this town?" Alex asked.

"Pretty much," she said. "Pretty much."

"This is my son, Mike. He's the Mayor of Arnolds Park," Deano said proudly, "and this is his wife, Jill."

They both said a quick "hello" and hustled back to serving the overflow crowd.

By this time Deano had two more Bud Lights lined up on the bar in front of Alex. Alex had learned long ago that two beers were his limit on a night before he had acting to do. He had found that out the hard way on his second Bunny Boy movie, having consumed ten or twelve beers on a wild night with Shana LaDue on a beach in Gulf Shores, Alabama. He had made it through the next day's shoot, but it was a brutal struggle. He had promised himself he'd never do that again, not even for a wild night with Shana LaDue.

81

Alex stood on his deck, enjoying the peacefulness as he watched the red and green boat lights float over the lake. He had been in Okoboji for less than twelve hours, but the hours had been very eventful. It reminded him of the old joke that comedians often tell about spending a day in a boring town, "I spent a month there, one day."

Alex felt the same way - he felt like he had spent a month in Okoboji this day, but it had been a good month. He reflected on all of the events of the day starting with the plane ride from Phoenix to the truck ride from Sioux Falls, to Lyin' Louie, to Whitey and the Iowa Navy, to Deano, to the bonehead talking to himself in the restaurant, to the theater, to Martha, to Simone... Simone …. He rushed back into his motel room, settled into the recliner and grabbed the script. He had work to do. After all, he was an actor – an actor with a real part to play.

7

Alex had never been one for eating a big breakfast, but he wanted a little something before he met with Simone for rehearsal. He had noticed a coffee house on the far end of Broadway Street in Arnolds Park, past the bars and restaurants, named Arnolds Perk. He thought the name was clever, so he pulled the Orange Blossom Special right up in front.

Arnolds Perk had the appearance and flavor of a real coffee house – not one of those chain outfits that had sprung up in the malls in recent years, that you just knew had been designed in some board room.

Nothing matched. The chairs, the couches, the tables – they all looked like they had been gathered by the participants in a scavenger hunt. This was the way a coffee house was supposed to be. Informal, relaxed, easy, cool. Alex felt at home the minute he stepped across the threshold.

Alex ordered a scotcheroo and a cup of coffee, black. That, too, his preference for regular ground black coffee, had caused his hotsy-totsy friends to poke fun at him, in a good-natured way. They, to be sure, drank latte, mocha, cappuccino, spiced cocoa, and other concoctions that Alex couldn't even pronounce.

Alex felt the urge to log onto one of the computers in Arnolds Perk to check his e-mail messages back home. But he knew what he would find – a dozen messages from Charlie reminding him that he was escorting Heather Devreaux to last night's Save The Universe banquet – and then a couple dozen messages from Charlie giving him hell for not showing up.

He hadn't given it any thought, but at about the time he was sitting in the Okoboji Lakeside Theater with Martha, he was supposed to be sitting with Heather Devreaux at the Beverly Hilton. Given those two choices, he'd take Martha any day.

The image of scenes that probably played out in Los Angeles last night danced in Alex's mind and made him smile. There was Heather Devreaux, wearing a skin-tight red sequined dress, sitting on a velvet chair, chewing bubble gum, blowing bubbles, and checking her watch, wondering what was keeping "The Bunny Boy." There was Charlie at the entrance of the Beverly Hilton, wearing his tuxedo and black patent leather shoes, checking his watch every thirty seconds, pacing back and forth, wondering if Alex had finally gone through with his threat this time, and wishing he'd gone into another line of work, like being a mortician. It may have been cruel, but it made Alex smile, and he didn't give a damn.

Alex checked his watch – fifteen minutes to nine. If Simone was as much a taskmaster as Jodell had described her as being, she was probably punctual also, and probably had no time for those who weren't. He ordered two cups of coffee to go, black.

The Orange Blossom Special, of course, had no drink holders, so Alex set the two cups of coffee on the front seat. It would be a miracle if he made it to the theater without their spilling.

Miracles happen, sometimes. The coffee didn't spill. His timing was perfect. Simone arrived at the same time and pulled her car, a black Mercedes SLK two-seat roadster with retractable top, right up next to the Orange Blossom Special. He had a car almost identical to hers, back in Beverly Hills, but that was nothing that he could tell her, at least not now.

Simone looked the Orange Blossom Special over from top to bottom, front to back. A smile, bordering on a giggle, played on her lips. "Nice car," she said.

That removed all doubt. This was the fourth or fifth time someone had said, "nice car" about the Orange Blossom Special. This town was full of comedians. Well, maybe one day he would take miss smarty pants Simone Delaney for a ride in his Aston Martin - that would wipe that smile off her face.

"I call it the Orange Blossom…"

"Special," Simone said, finishing his sentence.

"How'd you know?" he asked.

"Just a wild guess," she said.

"Coffee?" Alex asked, holding out the paper cup.

"Black?" she asked, as she took the cup.

"Of course," Alex said.

Simone was dressed in a tight pink "Save The Park" T-shirt and white shorts. For a woman who had been depicted as a workaholic, she seemed to be dressed rather sensuously. Had she dressed like that for Alex? Was she teasing him? Was she making a play for him? He could only hope. Or, was it just summertime in Okoboji?

"After you," Alex said, as he pulled open the front door to the theater. Sure, it was the gentlemanly thing to do – to let the lady go first - but in reality, he wanted to get a good look.

Most of the guys that Alex knew back in Los Angeles, especially the professional athletes, were "boobs men." Alex didn't give a lick about that. For Alex, sex appeal started with a woman's legs and went from there. And, Simone Delaney had Betty Grable legs.

Simone left Alex standing on the stage and excused herself, saying she would be back in a moment.

Alex used the spare time to rehearse his strategy. Sure, he could give a command performance, right out of the box, that would knock Simone into the third row. But, he didn't want to give a flawless performance right away - not when he had been allotted three hours of rehearsal time alone, one-on-one, with Simone Delaney.

No, he would bumble and stumble a bit at the start. Then, he would allow her to direct and guide him as he made slow and steady progress. And finally, toward the end of the three-hour rehearsal, he would nail the part and Simone could take credit for molding this hopeless, babbling idiot into an *actor*. He would be her protégé. She would be his mentor. It was the perfect script.

Simone returned wearing a loose-fitting jogging suit. That answered the question about whether she had purposefully dressed provocatively for him – hell no, he had simply showed up ten minutes early and had caught her in the parking lot before she changed into her work clothes. Damn.

Simone got right down to work, this would be a work session – the pleasantries were over.

"You've never acted before?" she asked.

"No," Alex lied. But then, most of the movie critics in the world would agree with that statement – No, Alex Gideon had never acted.

"Well, forget about everything you've ever heard about acting and ever thought about acting, and may have ever known about acting and we'll start from the beginning," Simone said.

Again, the critics would have said that this would be an easy task for the Bunny Boy, since he knew absolutely nothing about acting.

"First of all," Simone began, "the play is performed in front of a live audience, which can cause an actor a certain amount of tension and anxiety. Try to ignore the audience. Focus totally on the scene that you are involved in. Realize that from the audience's point of view, they are observing a private conversation that you are a part of. When you speak, you are not speaking to the audience - you are talking to the other characters in the scene. The audience is like a window peeper – they're observing your private activities and conversations, but you don't know they're there. Ignore them."

That was easy for her to say. She had been acting in front of live audiences for years. All of Alex's acting had been done in front of a camera. He hadn't given it any thought until now, but there would be real, live people sitting out there watching every move, listening to every word. And, he would have to get it right the first time – there were no retakes. Often, in shooting a movie, they would shoot a scene over and over and over again until they finally got it right – maybe twenty or thirty times. Ignore the audience, she had said. Pretend that they're not there. Easy for her to say.

"If at any time before or during the performance you feel tension, take a deep breath and exhale slowly. Do it several times until you feel calm."

Apparently, Simone had never heard about Inderal. Almost every actor and actress that Alex knew suffered from stage fright. Some of the biggest stars in the world were so afraid of getting up in front of a live audience that they had to be begged, coaxed, bribed, threatened, and sometimes beaten, before they would take the stage. But, if they took an Inderal tablet ninety minutes before their appearance, it would relax them, remove the tension, allow them to take the stage like a whirlwind, and deliver a critically-acclaimed performance. Inderal was that powerful. And, it was a legal prescription obtained from a doctor, was inexpensive, and was non-habit forming. Actually, it was a pill routinely prescribed by doctors for people with heart conditions. For an actor, it simply slows down and controls the racing heart that causes stage fright and allows the actor to function normally. In fact, a clinical study reported in the *Journal of*

Modern Medical Discoveries said that a speech or presentation made while using Inderal was twenty percent more effective than one delivered without it. How they figured that out, nobody seemed to know, but every actor and actress Alex knew had heard of the study and carried a bottle of Inderal with them at all times. Everybody but Alex. How did he know he was going to end up in a play? In a play in front of live people?

"I heard somewhere that there's a prescription medicine that actors take that eliminates stage fright," Alex said.

"It's called Inderal," Simone said. "The generic brand is called Propanolol. It's effective, it's harmless – and I don't have any."

Oh, oh. Alex would be flying without a net, in front of a live audience. Take a deep breath, she had said. He would try to remember that.

"When it comes to acting your part as William, don't act," she said. "You must become William, you must be William."

That, Alex had heard a hundred times before from the three different directors and six different assistant directors that he had worked with on his movies. He could handle it. From this moment on, whenever he stepped on this stage, he was William.

Simone looked at him, observing his metamorphosis from Alex to William and got that smile, bordering on a giggle on her face.

"I can see that you're becoming William already," she said.

From what Alex could tell, she was serious. But then, she was one heck of an actress, so how could he tell if she was serious?

"Did you get a chance to study your lines?" Simone asked.

"Yes," Alex replied, "I studied them last night and again this morning. I'm ready to give it a try."

Alex was known as a quick study in the movie industry. He could memorize all of his lines for an entire movie in just two or three days. But then, when the majority of your lines consisted of "Hey, Baby," "Whatcha doin' tonight, Babe?" and crap like that, who couldn't?

"Let me set up your first scene," Simone said. "You are off stage. You have just brought Marion home to the plantation from the train. There is the sound of horses' hooves drawing closer and a horse whinnies. The horses come to a stop. Marion speaks, off stage, 'Nice seeing you again, William, stop by and see me sometime.'"

Simone's voice dripped with smooth southern honey. Alex could listen to her talk in that southern drawl all day long.

Simone gestured for Alex to say his lines. His mind went blank. He blurted out "I'd like to see you sometime, too."

He wasn't putting on – he was a bona fide babbling idiot.

Simone smiled. "I believe the line is, 'It was a pleasure, Miss Marion. Say hello to your daddy - and to Savanna, too.'"

"Let me try it again," Alex said.

Simone led him into his lines by repeating Marion's part, "Nice seeing you again, William, stop by and see me sometime."

"It was a pleasure, Miss Marion. Say hello to your daddy – and to Savanna, too."

"That was good, William, real good," Simone said to Alex with a little smile. "Let's go over it again and this time give it a little more southern drawl and talk a little bit slower."

They rehearsed the scene five more times before they moved onto the next scene. William appeared in a total of nine scenes, but he spoke in only six of them. Alex was thankful for that.

Alex had looked forward to the final scene. That's where the boy gets the girl – where he, William, gets Savanna, played by Simone.

"Savanna, I might be out of line here, but I just have to say what I've got to say – and you might hate me forever - but I love you. I've always loved you, and I will always love you."

"Oh William, I've been such a fool, wasting my time on that terrible man when you were right here all the time. I love you, too."

And with that Simone took two quick steps toward Alex and jumped into his arms.

Alex had held a lot of women in his arms in his day – sometimes for roles he was playing and sometimes for real, but he could not recall ever holding more woman than he was right now.

"We do a theatrical kiss here," Simone said. "We don't actually kiss, but we make it appear to the audience that we do. Turn slowly until my back is to the audience."

Alex followed her directions.

"Now, put your left hand on the back of my head. Let your hand flow with the movement of my head while I move it back and forth to make it appear that I am passionately kissing you. Hold your mouth, closed, about an inch from mine and move your head back and forth also, slowly. We need to do this for only two or three seconds while the curtain drops."

"Wouldn't it be simpler to just go ahead and kiss?" Alex asked. "You know, for the sake of reality in the play."

"Nice try," Simone said, "but we'll do it my way. I am the director, you know."

They rehearsed the scene twice more and then went back and rehearsed each scene one more time in rapid succession.

Alex had been through auditions with hundreds of hopefuls after Shanna LaDue bailed out on him and had played parts opposite dozens of actresses in his movies. It was hard to explain – impossible to explain without experiencing it firsthand – but the thing that an actor always looked for with another actor was that chemistry, that interaction that produced that synergistic effect of 1 + 1 = 3. Alex felt that magic with Simone. He wondered if she felt it, too – he wondered how she could miss it.

"Now, the guitar," Simone said as she picked up the Martin acoustic that was resting against the wall. "You don't play, right?"

"I owned a ukulele once," Alex said.

"Could you play it?" she asked.

"No," he answered.

"Nobody could," Simone said, "except for Arthur Godfrey and Tiny Tim, and neither of them were very good at it."

"I heard that said somewhere before," Alex said, thinking back to his youth when he had bought the damned thing and had owned it for less than one day.

Simone showed Alex how to hold the guitar. Then she took his fingers in her hands and placed them, one by one, on the proper strings for the first chord he was to play. Alex hoped she didn't see the calluses on the tips of his fingers from years of playing.

He strummed the chord. It almost made the hair stand up on the back of his neck. Simone again placed his fingers on the right strings and Alex tried it again. It sounded better, but he didn't have it yet.

After about five delightful minutes of playing footsy with Simone's fingers, Alex finally had the two chords down.

"One more thing before we're done," Simone said, pointing to William's costume draped over a chair. "The men's dressing room is back there."

It was a community dressing room – the kind that the extras shared in the movies that Alex had made. He, of course, had a private dressing room, with his name embossed on a silver star on the door.

Alex slipped into the costume and appraised himself in the mirror. He made a pretty good-looking southern plantation field worker, or whatever they were called.

Alex entered the stage, stopped about ten feet from Simone, and struck an aristocratic pose.

Simone looked him over carefully. "William," she said approvingly. "It's William."

Alex checked his watch for the first time in several hours. It was twelve thirty.

"Are you playing in the basketball game?" Simone asked.

"Yes, at one – at the Spirit Lake High School Gym."

"You can still make it," she said. "It's only about fifteen minutes."

"Well, I'm the new guy on the team. I probably won't get to play 'till later in the game, anyway. I heard them last night, you know - Filbert and Big Teddy – they wanted Peterson."

"It was my call," she said. "I made the right choice."

"Thanks," Alex said. "That means a lot to me." And, it did.

"Are you coming to the game?" he asked.

"I'm going to the Maritime Museum to see if I can help out with the Save The Park fundraiser. If I can slip away, I'll try to catch part of the game," she said.

Alex pointed the Orange Blossom Special north on Highway 71, toward Spirit Lake. The game would be starting about the time he got there but that didn't matter – Simone wouldn't be there until later on.

He had spent over three and a half hours with Simone and it had seemed like five minutes. He had expected that he would need only about fifteen minutes of rehearsal time to have his part down, but he had been wrong. There was a lot more to this acting than he had anticipated. Charlie was right – there was a difference between being a movie star and being an actor. In three and a half hours Alex had learned more about acting from Simone than he had learned in the past seven years making eight movies. He was eager to learn more. He would need to move cautiously, though, slowly releasing only a small amount of that famous Alex Gideon charm at a time. Unleashing it all at once would be too much for any woman to handle, even Simone Delaney. Ha.

8

It was five minutes to one when Alex walked into the gymnasium. The teams were just finishing their warm-ups. "Come along," Big Teddy said as the theater team headed for the locker room. Filbert looked at Alex and glared - if the team lost the game he already knew whose fault it would be – Alex's.

There were seven players on the team, including Alex. Big Teddy was by far the biggest, but a couple of the others, who had apparently been stage hands on *Sisterly Love*, looked like they might have been athletes at some point in their lives. Alex had never heard of an athlete named Filbert and he suspected that when this day was over he still wouldn't have.

Big Teddy would start at center, Mike and Bill would play forwards and Ken and the ever-so-dangerous Filbert would start at guards.

Big Teddy gave the pre-game pep talk. "We've got a chance against these guys, even without Eric. Did you watch them during warm-ups? Those guys are hung over. They had a big party last night. A couple of them are still drunk. And, they're overconfident. If we can hang in there with them until the last ten minutes, we might be able to wear 'em down. Let's go out and show 'em what we're made of."

And with that, the Okoboji Lakeside Theater basketball

team charged onto the floor to do battle with Scratches Sports Bar for the Okoboji Summer Games championship.

Alex got dressed for the game. He was alone in the locker room and looked around for a place to stash his wad of cash. They had taken a bag to the gym for the players' valuables, but Alex wasn't about to let anyone see his bankroll. Finally, he decided to stash it in the toe of one of the shoes he had just taken off. This was Iowa – nobody was going to steal his shoes. He took his money clip with him to the gym to be deposited in the valuables bag.

Alex got his first glimpse of Scratches' team. They may have been hung over, drunk, and out of shape, but they were big, strong, and athletic – they looked like over-the-hill jocks are supposed to look. They all wore red T-shirts with SCRATCH-ES and the bar's motto, "Scratch Where It Itches," emblazoned in gold letters.

There were maybe fifty fans behind Scratches' bench. They looked like the cocktail crowd – bartenders, cocktail waitresses, drinkers. They were a rowdy bunch. Most of them looked like they had been at the party last night and they looked like they were getting primed for another one tonight.

There were a couple of dozen fans behind the theater team's bench. Sally, who would play Marion opposite Alex in the play tonight was there, as were several others who had small parts in *Sisterly Love*. The rest were probably stagehands and part of the crew.

Scratches got the tip and scored in three seconds. The theater team turned the ball over the first two times they got their hands on it and Scratches scored both times. Big Teddy was a stallion, snaring rebounds, blocking shots, and holding his own in the middle against the studs from Scratches. Alex could see that Mike, Bill, and Ken had played ball before and they each had their moments, stealing a ball here, blocking a shot there, and scoring now and then. The weak link was Filbert. He looked like an actor playing the role of a basketball player. He was a double threat, capable of fouling up equally well on either end of the court.

Mike got poked in the eye and asked Alex if he wanted to replace him for a few minutes. Alex suggested that the other substitute, Jerry, go in, since he had been with the team through their three preceding tournament victories and he deserved the minutes. After Jerry got on the floor, Alex could see why Mike had asked him to go in – Jerry glided from one end of the court to the other like a gazelle and was always going in the opposite direction of the flow of the game. Alex was content to sit on the bench, for now – observing, thinking, planning. Besides, Simone had not yet arrived.

Scratches was ahead at halftime 56-32. If they hadn't been goofing around, they could have been ahead by twenty more. The theater team walked to the locker room and simply sprawled out on the floor. No strategy talk, no rousing pep talks, just silence, except for the heavy breathing and wheezing.

The second half began with a continuation of Scratches' onslaught. The score ballooned to 75-39. But, Alex could see that Big Teddy's prediction was coming true. The Scratches players were shot. They weren't only breathing hard, they were gasping for breath. They no longer sprinted from one end of the court to the other, they shuffled. They didn't run on defense, they stood.

The theater team wasn't much better off, but at least they weren't throwing up as some of the Scratches players were. Perhaps they could reach down and find renewed energy if they needed to.

Alex heard a commotion in the stands behind the bench. He glanced out of the corner of his eye – Simone had arrived. Just then, Filbert picked up his fourth foul and finally took himself out, wanting to save himself for a rally at the end of the game, no doubt. Alex checked the clock – there was thirteen minutes remaining in the game.

It was Alex time.

Alex was the only player on the court with fresh legs and good lungs. The first time down the court, he caught a pass from Bill and launched it from two feet beyond the three-point arc – swish. Alex had noticed that Scratches' players were sloppy with their in-bound passes and he sneaked up and swiped the ball. Alex took two dribbles, sprang into the air and slammed home a mighty dunk.

"Holy shit," one of the Scratches players groaned.

"Where the hell have you been?" Big Teddy asked.

On the other end of the court, Alex stole the ball and drove for the basket, being chased by a pack of lead footed, wheezing Scratches players. Alex was ten feet in front of the nearest pursuer when he pulled up behind the three point line and launched another one – swish. Scratches players were slow learners and Alex again stole the in-bounds pass and slammed it through. In less than twenty seconds, Alex had scored ten points and had Scratches back on their heels.

Scratches called time out. They needed a rest and they needed a strategy.

Alex trotted toward the theater team's bench. He could see the theater team's fans going crazy. They were jumping, yelling, screaming. Simone joined in on the merriment, but was more reserved, refined, and restrained than the rest. Alex felt like a high school kid trying to impress the cheerleading captain. He wasn't sure if it was working.

Big Teddy was going nuts in the huddle. Filbert, trying to re-establish himself as the team leader, was babbling something that made no sense at all. Bill, Mike, and Ken were fired up.

Scratches' defensive strategy was, predictably, to double team

Alex and to play a zone with the remaining three players. It didn't work. Alex was too fresh, too quick, and too good.

Scratches switched defenses – this time they had three guys guard Alex, leaving only two players to guard the other four players on the theater team. If there was one thing that Alex could do better than shoot a basketball, it was pass one. His razor sharp passes sliced Scratches' defense to pieces as Big Teddy, Mike, Bill, and Ken scored one easy lay-up after another. Big Teddy caught his second wind and charged from one end of the floor to the other like a gladiator, waving a clenched fist in the air. There would be no stopping the mighty theater team. Not this day.

The final score was 94-86. The theater team was the Summer Games Basketball Tournament champion. There were high fives all around. Everybody was laughing and smiling. Even Filbert had a smile plastered on his face, but Alex could see that beneath the smile Filbert was seething. He wasn't as good an actor as everybody thought.

Before Alex had arrived, Filbert had been the big man on campus, the actor who had performed off-Broadway, in London, and on television. Now, this Al from Rapid City, South Dakota, had appeared on the scene and was an instant hero, just because he made a couple of baskets in a game against a bunch of out-of-shape, hungover, has-beens. Maybe this guy, Al, was a hero here in front of sixty or seventy fans in this gymnasium, but tonight Filbert would be the hero where it really mattered, on the stage in front of a packed house.

The theater team's small contingency of fans stormed the floor and surrounded the team. Alex was pleased to see that Simone was among them, laughing and screaming like the rest. There was a true camaraderie with this group – a kinship. This was a true team victory and the entire theater troupe was on the team.

"Can I have your attention, please," a voice said over the loud-speaker, "for the presentation of the trophy. Attention please."

The place quieted down. The voice continued, "Golly, gee, that was an exciting game."

Alex's head snapped in the direction of the speaker, although he didn't need to look.

Herman was grinning from ear to ear and his eyes sparkled with excitement. He held a magnificent two-foot high trophy in his hand – these guys took the Summer Games seriously. "On behalf of the University of Okoboji, I present this Okoboji Summer Games championship trophy to the Okoboji Lakeside Theater basketball team."

The theater team's fans hooted and hollered and even the Scratches' fans and team offered respectful applause. Filbert charged to the center of the floor, followed by Big Teddy and the rest of the team. Alex stood on the sideline – this was their team, their trophy.

Herman spotted Alex standing on the sideline and reached him in a dozen big steps. "Gosh," he said, "that was a wonderful performance. Golly, gee, it's great having you here in Okoboji."

"It's good to be here," Alex said. "It really is."

Herman headed for the exit, stopping to greet the Scratches players, who were heading in Alex's direction en masse. Alex didn't know if he should run and hide or stand and fight. He didn't have to make that decision.

"Great job," the first player said, and the others joined in, "Fantastic game," "Love that jumper," "Fun playing against you," – the compliments went on.

One guy, Jake, looked Alex straight in the eye and said, "You beat us today when we were hung over, out of shape, tired, and wore out – but if we had been in our prime, sober, and in shape – you'd have whipped our butts anyway." It was a high compliment.

Three or four of the players invited Alex down to Scratches bar for a few drinks, on the house. He promised he would, sometime.

The theater team retreated to the locker room to change clothes. Alex could tell at a glance that someone had been through his clothes. He had left nothing in his pockets – no ID, no money, nothing. His shoes were still there, but he was suspicious. He slipped off his basketball shoes and slipped his foot into the shoe where he had hidden the wad of cash. His foot slipped all the way in, comfortably. He had been robbed – here in Iowa.

Alex showered and got dressed. He was perturbed. Oh, losing ten or twelve grand didn't bother him so much – he'd lost that amount on a single hand of blackjack at the Bellagio in Vegas. What upset him was that someone had gone through his clothes looking for something, and it probably wasn't money. After all, the team had placed their valuables in a bag and had taken it to the gymnasium and set it on the bench in full view.

Alex vowed to keep his guard up and to not make any mistakes. He had things going for himself in Okoboji, good things, and he wasn't about to mess it up.

Alex checked the cash in his money clip - $480. That would go quite a ways in Okoboji, but it wouldn't last another eight days – not with some of the plans he had. He didn't want to do it, but maybe he'd have to break down and call Charlie to have him send some money. Sure, Charlie would scream and holler and probably even cry, but Alex was entitled to a vacation now and then and Charlie would just have to get used to it.

9

Alex was at the theater at quarter to six as Simone had instructed him. She wanted him to quickly run through his lines with each of the actors that he would be doing a scene with.

His first scene was with Sally, who played the part of Marion, the spoiled younger sister. Sally may have been slightly over-weight, but she was still a very attractive and desirable young woman. Sally was quiet and shy, but when she assumed the role of Marion she became a vixen. They had several scenes togeth-er and the rehearsal went well.

Alex rehearsed each scene with the actors involved in them. Two of the scenes involved Filbert playing the role of arrogant Nathan. It was apparent to Alex that Filbert didn't like him. Much to Alex's surprise, though, even the rehearsal scenes with Filbert went well and Filbert didn't try to throw him any curve balls. Apparently Filbert's love of the theater and his pride of presenting a good performance outweighed his dislike for Alex.

Alex's favorite scene was the final one where the boy gets the girl and Simone jumps into his arms. Alex would have liked to rehearse that scene several times, but Simone announced "it's a wrap," after just one go-through.

Simone gathered the cast and crew behind the curtain for a couple of announcements. "Remember the Summer Games parade is tomorrow morning at ten. Meet here at nine to change into your costumes. Mike will have the float here and we'll board it at nine fifteen and go to the parade starting point. The parade should be over by eleven. Don't forget the Save The Park rally at four tomorrow afternoon. End of announcements."

Alex could hear the audience talking and laughing. It was ten minutes to showtime. He slowly pulled back the corner of the curtain and peeked out. The place was packed. There was hardly an empty seat in the house and people were still coming in. Last night, while sitting in the audience, Alex had estimated that the theater held maybe six or seven hundred. Tonight, looking at it from a different vantage point, he was sure it held two or three thousand. Alex checked the twelfth row on the aisle — two empty seats.

Alex's mouth was dry, his stomach felt queasy, his heart was racing, his palms were sweaty, and his knees felt like they could buckle at any moment. A classic case of stage fright. "Breathe deeply," he said to himself. "Breathe deeply."

Alex felt a hand lightly on his arm. "You'll do fine," she said. Alex turned and looked into the eyes of a beautiful southern belle. It was Savanna. He would not let her down.

The entire cast and crew gathered in a circle on the stage behind the curtain. They all joined hands and lowered their heads in silence for a moment. Alex didn't know if they were all sick like him, if they were clearing their minds and mentally assuming the personas of their characters, or if they were praying. Alex chose to pray. He discovered that the difference between praying in church and praying backstage before you're about to face a live audience is that when you pray backstage, you really, really mean it.

"Let's make some magic," Simone said softly. The group disbanded. Everyone headed for the wings except for Simone and Big Teddy, who took their places on the veranda, and Mel, who

102

headed for the piano. Alex and Sally held hands just off stage.

The strains of "Oh! Susanna" filled the theater, followed by the other songs in the medley. The curtain rose – this was it.

"They should be here any moment now," Savanna said.

"I'm sure looking forward to seeing her. I'll bet she's all growed up," Matt said.

The sound effects guy pushed the button on the tape player and the sound of approaching horses rang out. The horses came to a stop and whinnied.

"Nice seeing you again, William, stop by and see me sometime," Marion said.

"It was a pleasure, Miss Marion. Say hello to your daddy – and to Savanna, too," William said.

Alex had delivered his first two lines – like a virtuoso. Only sixteen lines to go.

About five minutes later, or so it seemed, Alex heard himself speaking again.

"Savanna, I might be out of line here, but I just have to say what I've got to say – and you might hate me forever – but I love you. I've always loved you, and I will always love you."

"Oh William, I've been such a fool, wasting my time on that terrible man when you were right here all the time. I love you, too," Savanna said.

And with that, Savanna took two steps and jumped into William's arms. Savanna and William kissed, theatrical style, the curtain was dropped, and the crowd went wild.

Alex held Simone in his arms for a moment before putting her down. "You did great," she said, and gave Alex a soft kiss on the cheek before turning to walk away.

Alex had been kissed passionately and mauled by some of the most beautiful starlets in Hollywood, both on and off camera, and it had left him cold, sometimes. That little peck on the cheek by Simone, however, had his blood boiling.

103

The cast lined up at center stage for a curtain call. The audience was on their feet. The applause was deafening. Alex was experiencing first-hand the warmth, interaction, and magnetism of live theater. The most positive response he'd ever had to any of his movies was a lukewarm sitting ovation from the audience and a two-star review from a critic, but here they were on their feet, damned near ready to charge the stage.

Alex's eyes searched for the twelfth row, aisle seats. There was Martha! She was on her feet. Alex couldn't tell if she was laughing or crying, but she was brushing away a tear. Next to her was a dapper white-haired gentleman dressed in a blue and white striped sport coat and white pants. He looked into Martha's eyes, she looked into his, and they swooned. Either the wayward husband had come home or Martha had worked fast.

Simone finally got the audience to settle down and to take their seats. "I have several announcements," she said. "Tonight making his first appearance ever on the stage, and doing a wonderful job – Al, playing the part of William."

Simone motioned for Alex to step forward to be acknowledged. The crowd was on their feet again. This time the applause was for Alex, and Alex alone. He bowed slightly and stepped back in line with the rest of the cast. This live theater was great. In the movie business, the best you could hope for was a sitting ovation from the moviegoers as they held their bag of popcorn in one hand and clapped with the other. This was a moment Alex would always remember.

"We are also proud to recognize tonight the Summer Games Basketball Tournament Champions – the Okoboji Lakeside Theater team," Simone said as Mike, Bill, Ken, and Jerry entered carrying the trophy. Filbert, Big Teddy, and Alex stepped forward to join them to polite applause.

The cast and crew exited the stage, except for Simone who launched into her spiel for the Save-The-Park fundraiser.

Big Teddy, Filbert, and Alex were called forth to pass their hats for the collection. When Alex got to the twelfth row, aisle seats, Martha stood and gave him a big hug.

"This is my husband, John," she said.

John rose and offered a warm handshake. "Martha has told me wonderful things about you, it's a pleasure. Enjoyed your performance tonight," he said.

John dug his wallet out of his back pocket and sorted through a wad of bills. Martha leaned over and whispered to Alex, "He fired his secretary. Isn't life grand!"

Martha raised her right hand slightly and motioned to it with her eyes. Alex glanced down – there on her index finger was the huge diamond ring that she had dropped in the hat last night. "I bought it back for ten thousand," she said with a smile. "It was a bargain – he doesn't know a damn thing about it."

John continued to dig through his wallet, trying to find a suitable bill. Martha reached over, grabbed the whole works and threw it in the hat. John looked at her, nodded his head in agreement, and sat down.

The chant started in the women's dressing room and was soon picked up by the men, "Maestro," "Maestro," "Maestro," "Maestro."

"Come along," Big Teddy said, "we're all going to Ruebin's to see the Maestro. It's a Friday night tradition here at the theater."

"Ruebin's? Maestro?" Alex asked.

"It's a bar where this guy Tim Horsman plays – everybody calls him Maestro," Big Teddy said.

Alex recalled having seen Ruebins in that two or three block stretch that was lined with bars and restaurants on Broadway Street. "Does everybody go?" Alex asked.

"Ya," Big Teddy answered

"Everybody?" Alex asked.

"Absolutely everybody."

Then that would include Simone. "Maestro," Alex shouted, joining in on the chant, "Maestro."

10

When Alex had driven the Orange Blossom Special past Ruebins on his way to the theater at about five thirty, you could have driven a beer truck down Broadway Street sideways and not hit anything or anybody. Now, some three and a half-hours later, the street was a madhouse and the lunatics were running wild. Tim Schumacher's Hooterville All Stars was playing to a standing-room-only crowd at Whiskey Dick's. There was a line of maybe fifty people waiting their turn to get into Captain's Getaway to see the Fishheads, a popular band from Omaha. A guitar player and singer, Gary, was knocking 'em dead in Smokin' Jakes. A band named Free Beer was performing at Kalsows and live music came from about every open door and window all along Broadway Street. Hundreds of partiers drifted from one bar to another and hung out in small groups on the sidewalk, enjoying the eighty-degree summer evening.

The owner of Ruebins, Jim Hentges, was standing on the sidewalk in front of the bar, checking ID's and controlling the influx of patrons. "Your table is ready," he said to Big Teddy, who led the charge into the bar.

Ruebins was a long narrow bar with the stage located directly inside the door to the left. The bar was ahead and to the right and was maybe thirty feet long. Tables and chairs occupied the front two-thirds of the bar. The back third was a game room with two pool tables, a snooker table, darts, foosball, and a variety of other games. The walls were decorated with an assortment of posters of movie stars and musicians. Alex didn't even search the walls for a poster of the Bunny Boy – this wasn't the kind of place that would have a Bunny Boy poster, unless they used it for warming up for their dart games. Besides, it was too dark for anybody to get a good look at a poster or of Alex to try to make a comparison.

Memorabilia of all sorts hung from the higher reaches of the walls and from the ceiling. There was a giant moose head mounted on the wall above the bar with the slogan, "A saloon without a moose is just a bar."

An old bicycle, a beat-up suitcase, a pair of ice skates, some water skis, a couple of football helmets, numerous beer signs, a boat oar, some mangled golf clubs, a couple of tennis racquets, some battered highway signs, and the like served as décor.

The size and décor of Ruebins reminded Alex of the time his sixth grade class in Rapid City had taken a field trip to Deadwood, about forty-five miles away. First they visited a museum filled with artifacts, circa 1876, when the gold rush was on in the Black Hills. There were miner's picks, shovels, and pans, clothes, furniture, lamps, and horse tack from the era – none of which was very interesting to a group of sixth graders.

Mount Mariah cemetery, where Wild Bill Hickok, Calamity Jane, and Potato Creek Johnny are buried high on a hill overlooking the town of Deadwood, was more interesting than the museum, mostly because some of the stuff written on the tombstones was pretty crazy. Stuff like, "Oh why, Sweet Jesus, have you taken the youngest and best of us before his time, why?" Or, "Here's lies a dirty polecat who died suddenly, with his boots on." Or, "Now do you believe I'm sick?"

The most interesting stop on the class trip, though, was

Saloon No. 10. This was, the tour guide had said, one of the most famous saloons in all the world. That's because this is where Wild Bill Hickok was shot to death while playing poker. He was holding a hand of aces and eights, which became known forevermore as the "Deadman's Hand." They even had the chair Wild Bill was sitting on when he got shot displayed above the door with a spotlight shining on it. Stuff like that will really get the attention of a bunch of sixth graders.

Saloon No. 10 had thousands of antiques from the old days hanging on the walls and hanging from the ceiling. There was maybe a hundred stuffed animals including wild turkeys, deer, moose, elk, fox, raccoon, and buffalo. Thousands of guns, animal traps, old roulette wheels, wagon wheels, horse tack, and similar items from the 1800's covered every square inch. The tour guide had said that Saloon No. 10 was the only bar in the world with a museum. Or maybe it was the other way around. Anyway, it had been over fifteen years ago and Alex remembered it vividly.

Ruebins was definitely the Saloon No. 10 of Okoboji. He wondered if fifteen years from now he would remember this night in Ruebins.

Big Teddy led the way to a reserved table right up front, at the edge of the dance floor. This was just like in Hollywood, actors had pull and got the best tables.

Big Teddy motioned for Alex to sit next to him. Sally sat next to Alex on the other side – Simone was across the table. Filbert grabbed a chair next to Simone, almost knocking one of the stagehands to the floor in the process.

The bartender saw them enter and approached the table. He spoke to Big Teddy as if he were in awe of some miracle. "I heard," he said. "Congratulations."

"Have you seen the guys from Scratches?" Big Teddy asked.

"Jake and the guys were in for a couple of shots right after the game," he answered.

"Were they pissed off?" Big Teddy asked.

"No, not at all," he said. "They were raving about your new player."

Big Teddy pointed to Alex. "That would be Al, right here," he said. "This is Mark Happe."

"Call me Hap," he said with a smile. "I heard you had a great game."

When he was in high school, Alex had daydreamed about being the game's hero and being interviewed on television after the game. He had rehearsed in his mind saying things like "It was a great team victory," or "I was just glad to be part of the team." The kind of stuff that every player said after every game where he was the big star and thought he was supposed to sound like a modest team player, even though he was bursting inside to yell, "I am the greatest."

Now, he was finally having that post-game interview, sort of, here with Hap at Ruebins. "It was a lot of fun," Alex said simply. "I enjoyed playing with the guys."

"I'll send Lois over to take your order," Hap said as he headed back to the bar.

"Lois works for a company that distributes books and DVD's and she's in charge of racking half a dozen Wal-Marts, or something like that," Big Teddy said to Alex. "With the money that she earned in tips at Ruebins working weekends the past couple of years she's managed to buy two or three rental houses. A lot of places bartenders and waitresses are looked down upon as second-class citizens, but not here in Okoboji. They are well respected – they make the economy go. Without the bartenders and waitresses, and us dock builders, too, Okoboji would come to a sudden stop."

Lois was there in an instant. Back in Beverly Hills, Alex would have gladly handed her a hundred for the round and told her to keep the change. Tonight, though, he would not. First of all, after being robbed, he wasn't in a position to do it. Second, he wanted to continue with his low profile image of being just an average guy – a tourist from Rapid City.

Lois delivered the drinks and Alex took a sip of his Bud Light. It was tooth-cracking cold, just the way he liked it.

The round came to $65. "Let's all throw a $20 in the pot and we'll drink off of that," Big Teddy suggested.

Before anyone could get their money out, Filbert handed Lois a $100 and said, "Keep the change."

Filbert glanced at Alex and their eyes locked. "That son-of-a-bitch," Alex said to himself as he stared at Filbert.

Filbert had a little sneer on his face as if to say, "And what are you gonna do about it?"

Filbert was smart. He knew that because Alex hadn't said a word about being robbed and that since the police weren't questioning everyone who had been in the gym, Alex had not reported the theft. And, he would not report the theft. Most people don't walk around with twelve G's in their pocket unless they've got something to hide. And when they've got something to hide, they don't go to the police.

"Jeez, Filbert," Big Teddy said, "what did you do – win the lottery?"

"Something like that," Filbert said with a smile. And then he made a quick glance at Alex, looked away, and sneered.

There would be no point in confronting Filbert, since the bills were unmarked and untraceable. Who's to say that a famous actor like Filbert Kauffman couldn't have a wad of $100's in his pocket. A semi-famous actor like Filbert Kauffman.

Alex doubted that anyone had noticed the little silent exchange between Filbert and himself. No one but perhaps Simone - he wasn't sure.

Alex was happy to throw a $20 in the pot like everyone else. That's all he wanted to be, right now, like everyone else, part of the group. Especially when the group included Simone Delaney.

The troupe was a lively bunch and the conversation was spirited and animated. Filbert was trying his damndest to monopolize Simone's attention, but it was evident that she wanted to interact with everyone.

"Simone," Alex said, "that's French, isn't it?" trying to divert her attention away from Filbert.

A collective groan went up from the table, followed by a host of rapid comments, "Oh, no!" "You just had to ask, didn't you!" "Not again," "I'm leaving," "Here we go," and "Let's get it over with."

Simone was smiling and laughing, as were the rest of them. It was some kind of an inside joke that Alex had unwittingly stumbled into.

"Well," Simone began, trying to act serious, "My great, great, great, great grandfather, Ferdinand Grillier, was a full-blooded Frenchman. He fought in Napoleon's army when they invaded Russia. He was a cavalier, which means he rode a horse instead of being a foot soldier. Napoleon's army was beaten badly by the Russian army, and when they retreated it was every man for themselves, trying to get out of Russia and make it back to France. My great, great, great great grandfather, Ferdinand Grillier, was captured by the Russian soldiers and they took his horse. They were going to kill him, but then they decided to let him go because…"

Simone paused for a moment and the whole table groaned again. "Why did they let him go?" a couple of them asked as if on cue.

"They let him go," Simone said, "because he was such - a handsome man." Simone was smiling again - that half smile, half giggle.

They were groaning again.

Simone waved her hands up and down to quiet them down so

she could finish the story.

"My great, great, great great grandfather, Ferdinand Grillier, walked and crawled out of Russia, trying to make it back home to France. He collapsed, however, exhausted, when he got to Germany and was befriended by this German farm family, who nursed him back to health. He fell in love with the farmer's daughter, Amalia, and they were married and lived happily ever after."

The troupe gave Simone polite, although mocked, applause for her performance.

Simone looked straight at Alex. "So to answer your question, yes, Simone is a French name. I am one-thirty-second Frenchwoman. Thanks for asking." She was doing that half laugh, half giggle again.

"And," Big Teddy said to Alex, "don't ever ask if she's French again."

"French?" Simone shouted, snapping to attention. "Did I ever tell you about my great, great, great grandfather, Ferdinand Gril…"

The groans and shouts drowned her out. Now they were throwing straws and napkins at Simone. She was laughing again. They were all laughing.

"Like I said," Big Teddy said to Alex, "don't say it again – that word. That word that sets her off."

Mel, the piano player, and her husband, Terry, joined the group. He owned a restaurant in Estherville and had just gotten off work and was thirsty. He ordered a round for the whole table and paid for it with a $100. This town was floating in $100's.

The chant started with somebody down at the end of the table and soon the entire troupe was doing it, "Maestro," "Maestro," "Maestro," "Maestro," "Maestro."

He had a striking resemblance to Paul McCartney of The Beatles. "How was the show tonight?" he asked no one in particular as he approached the table.

"Great." "Fine." "Wonderful." "Packed house." "Knocked 'em dead." "Broke a couple of legs."

Maestro shook hands with several of the guys at the table including Big Teddy and Filbert and gave Simone and Sally a hug. Every town has its heroes and its celebrities, and this was one of the biggest in Okoboji.

"Well, I've got to get a drink and then get back to work," Maestro said.

No sooner had he headed for the bar when Lyle, the Harley rider, walked in the door. He looked taller, broader, and bigger to Alex than when he had met him yesterday – kinda met him.

Lyle walked straight to the troupe's table. Filbert said "Hello," and stuck out his hand. Lyle totally ignored him as he went straight to Simone and gave her a big hug.

Lyle looked the table over, waving to some, nodding to others, shaking hands with some. It was obvious that Lyle was a revered member of the Okoboji community. He shook hands with Big Teddy – and then he noticed Alex. He looked at Alex for a moment with those steely eyes. Then he smiled and said "Al, good seeing you again," as he stuck out his hand for a shake.

That was it. Alex was now an official Okobojian. Lyle had anointed him, more or less. Alex could sense that his stature had just increased among the troupe. All of the troupe, that is, but Filbert, who was stoic.

Alex had been a little skeptical about all of the enthusiasm the troupe had displayed over going to see a one-man band. He had seen dozens of one-man bands at cocktail parties in Beverly Hills and most of them were about as exciting as a sleeping pill. Maestro took the stage. He hoisted a shot of tequila and made a silent toast to Big Teddy, who also had gotten his hands on a shot, somehow, and slammed it back. It was show time.

Maestro's hands flew across the keyboard as he opened the set with a hot version of Jimmy Buffet's "Margaritaville." The piano sang, it wailed, it barked, it honked. Jerry Lee Lewis would have been proud. He might have been jealous. If Alex had closed his eyes, he would have sworn he was listening to a three-piece band, maybe four piece. This wasn't your father's one-man band.

Filbert jumped up, grabbed Simone by the arm, and pulled her out of her chair. Big Teddy grabbed Sally, and the entire troupe hit the dance floor - all but Alex who didn't have a partner. He didn't mind. His partner was dancing with Filbert and there was no one else he cared to dance with.

Alex watched Simone and Filbert dance. He had always admired dancers who created their own unique style, moves, and steps. Simone's dancing was classy, it was stylish, and it was sexy. Filbert's dancing, on the other hand, resembled those guys in the wineries who stomp grapes with their bare feet.

Filbert was smiling at Simone, he was grinning, he was winking. He touched her hand, he felt her arm, he grazed her butt – anything to cop a feel, all in the name of dancing. He was giving it his best shot. Alex watched Simone. She was looking at Maestro, she was looking at the other dancers, she was looking at the clock, she was looking at the wall, she was looking at the floor – anything and everything but Filbert. As an actor, Alex was keenly aware of the loud and unmistakable messages spoken by body language. Perhaps Simone wasn't even aware of what her body was saying to Filbert, but from where Alex was sitting he could see that it was shouting, "Filbert, you're a jerk."

"There's music now," the voice said. Alex turned to face the blonde bombshell that had tried to hustle him at the Dry Dock last night. She grabbed him by the ears and dragged him to the dance floor. She, too, had her own unique dance style. It amounted to trying to bounce Alex off the wall by hitting him in the chest with her boobs. Alex could see that Maestro was watching the show and enjoying it – how anybody could sing with a grin like that on his face was just amazing. It was the longest version of "Margaritaville" that Alex had ever heard. Finally, it ended and Alex and the bombshell walked off the floor.

"Do you know my friend sitting over there?" Alex asked as he pointed to Filbert.

"No," she replied.

"That's the famous actor, Filbert Kauffman. Why, he's been on *All My Children* six times and ..."

"Oh, my God," she screamed, "a real live movie star here in Okoboji – I love *All My Children* - I watch it all the time," and she was off after Filbert like a hound chasing a rabbit. She walked up to him, stuck those boobs in his face, said, "Let's dance," and dragged him out onto the dance floor. He didn't resist.

Simone was smiling. "I saw what you did," she said.

Alex smiled, too. "I did you a favor," he said.

"That's true," she said. "But how about you, don't you like blondes?"

"I don't like them that blonde," Alex replied.

Maestro was playing Van Morrison's "Brown-Eyed Girl" with a vengeance.

"He's playing your song," Alex said.

"They're not brown," she said, "but that's close enough."

Alex had dance moves that would make his moves on the basketball court look like grade school stuff. He was, after all, the star of that fabulous movie, *Dancing Bunny*. But, he had showed off enough for one day, on the basketball court and by giving a flawless performance in the theater, if he had to say so himself. Alex would show her a few dance moves, but not everything – had to be careful, you know, not to unleash too much of that Alex Gideon charm at one time.

It was the shortest version of "Brown-Eyed Girl" that Alex

116

had ever heard. They had just set foot on the dance floor and now they were walking off.

"The blonde worked Filbert over pretty good," Alex said with a smile.

"I didn't notice," she said.

Of course she didn't. How could she when she had spent every moment on the dance floor looking at Alex.

Alex glanced to his left – the blonde had Filbert pinned against the wall. Ah, the perks of stardom.

The theater troupe's table was like a train station, with a constant flow of people coming and going, stopping to say hello or to chat for a minute or two.

A couple stopped by to talk with Mel and Terry. "Scratches is packed," he said. "The Mudruckers are playing and there's a hundred people waiting in line."

"Did you get in?" Mel asked.

"We just walked up to the head of the line like we owned the place, I flashed a $20 at the doorman and, Bingo-Bango, we were in."

"Was the band good?" Terry asked.

"Long story short, we're here," he said.

The parade of visitors continued and Big Teddy made sure that Alex met every one of them. There was Andy, Ramona, Dean, Judy, Linda, Gary, Doris, Delbert, Paloni, Jerry, Esther, Diamond Dave, Boots, Mike, Jach, Rick, … they just kept on coming.

"One of the neat things about Okoboji," Big Teddy said, "is that everybody is accepted – it doesn't matter if you're a millionaire or a hundredaire, unemployed or a CEO – we're all just here for a good time. Why right now in Ruebins there's at least twenty-five millionaires and maybe twenty-five guys who are flat broke – I'll bet you can't tell one from the other."

Alex surveyed the crowd. There were tall people, short people, skinny people, fat people, and everything in between – a cross-section of humanity. They were dressed up and they were dressed down. But, there were no telltale signs of great wealth or great poverty. He couldn't tell. It looked like everybody felt fortunate to be spending a Friday night in Okoboji, having a blast right here in Ruebins.

Alex did a double take. What the hell was he doing here in Okoboji? In Ruebins? Alex looked again. He was sure it was him – B.J. Thomas. With a tall brunette beauty.

Alex had met B.J. at the premiere of *Dancing Bunny*. B.J. sang the theme song, "Boogaloo Bunny," for the movie. It was a real coup to get B.J. to sing the theme song since B.J. had sung some of the biggest selling movie theme songs ever, including "Raindrops Keep Falling On My Head" from *Butch Cassidy and The Sundance Kid,* starring Paul Newman and Robert Redford. Even though *Dancing Bunny* was crap, it had been a huge box office success and it propelled "Boogaloo Bunny" to five weeks at number one on the charts.

And now, could it be that both of the stars of that movie, B.J. Thomas and Alex Gideon, had coincidentally ended up here, a thousand miles from anywhere, drinking Bud Lights on a Friday night in Ruebins? Couldn't be.

"Who's that guy over there?" Alex asked Big Teddy, pointing to B.J.

"The guy who looks like a middle-aged Patrick Swayzee?"

"Or a young B.J. Thomas," Alex said.

"That's Bob, with his girlfriend, Barb. He runs a body shop in Milford."

End of story. Alex told himself to relax. He was a thousand miles from anyone who knew him or had ever seen him in person. He was paranoid. He was self-conscious. He was overreacting. He was being an alarmist. It was time to forget about Alex Gideon – he was Al from Rapid City.

Maestro continued belting them out. His repertoire consisted of hard driving classic rock 'n roll from the sixties, seventies, and eighties – well, maybe a few from the eighties. There was Del Shannon's "Runaway," Buddy Holly's "Maybe Baby," Looking Glass's "Brandy," Delbert McClinton's "Shotgun Rider," Van Morrison's "Wild Nights," The Ides of March's "Vehicle," Creedence Clearwater's "Lodi," Elvis's "Burning Love," and The Beatles' "I Want to Hold Your Hand." Alex knew them all. Even though the songs may not have been from his generation, they were the songs his mother had loved and he learned them from her. Many of them were songs he played on the guitar for his own amusement. It would be a blast to grab a guitar and join Maestro on stage but, of course, that was out of the question. Low profile, you know.

Maestro stopped in the middle of "Walkin' in Memphis" and shouted a warning, "Tomcat in the house, Tomcat in the house."

He strolled in with a swagger that was somewhere between a good James Dean and a bad John Wayne. He was of medium height, maybe five foot nine, and slender. He wore a T-shirt that said "TOMKAT," in big letters on the front. He stopped at the edge of the dance floor, took a deep breath and let out an ear-piercing scream, "Heeeeeee, Heeeeeeeeeeee," to let everyone know that the Tomkat had, in fact, arrived.

He sauntered over to the troupe's table and hugged a few of the women, including Simone, and shook hands with a few of the guys.

Tomkat saw Alex and he froze. He just stared. He swaggered around the table, slipped up behind Alex and whispered in his ear, "I know who you are, Heeeee, Heeeee." And then he strolled off toward the bar.

It had finally happened, and it wasn't paranoia this time – Alex had been busted. By a Tomkat, nonetheless. He was standing there at the end of the bar, drinking a beer and just staring

119

at Alex. He mouthed the words, "I know who you are, Heeeee, Heeeee."

A guy named George Stewart, who looked more like Ernest Hemingway than Hemingway himself and Scotty Moore, a native American with a long pony tail joined the table. George was a local philosopher and writer. Scotty was a local hero for having retired somewhere around age forty. This was a resort community and those who didn't work were far more admired than those who worked their butts off.

He was staring again and mouthing the words, "I know who you are, Heeeee, Heeeeee. I know who you are, Heeeee, Heeeeee."

It was time for a showdown. Alex got up and walked to the bar. He held up two fingers and in a flash Hap set two cold beers in front of them. Alex put his arm around Tomkat's shoulder and squeezed, "Okay, Turkey," he said, "who am I?"

"Jeez," Tomkat said, pulling loose from Alex's grasp, "you don't have to get sore."

"Well, who do you think I am?"

Tomkat looked at him in disbelief, "Why, why, you're the King – you're Elvis," he said.

Alex heaved a sigh of relief. He patted Tomkat on the shoulder. "Can we just keep this our little secret?" he whispered.

"You can count on me, King, I won't tell a soul. But, can I get your autograph?" Tomkat asked.

Alex grabbed a napkin and pulled a pen from his shirt pocket. He scribbled something that had an "E" and a "P" in it and handed it to Tomkat. He beamed. "Mum's the word, King. Your secret's safe with me."

And, Alex knew that it was. He had dodged the bullet again. "Relax," he told himself. "Take a deep breath."

"One more song, and then I'll take a little break," Maestro said. It had been a long and rousing set. Alex had enjoyed it and had danced with Simone three times, but he looked forward to a little peace and quiet so he could talk to her. He was making nice progress. Slow and steady, but nice – he could feel it.

The door to Ruebins flew open and in walked an absolutely beautiful young woman, all alone and looking out of place. Anyone wearing a trench coat in Okoboji in the summertime would look out of place. Maestro had just started playing Billy Joel's "Only the Good Die Young" when she walked out onto the empty dance floor, stood in front of him for a moment, and whipped open the coat. Even sitting behind her you didn't have to guess. Maestro's face said it all – that and the sour notes his fingers had suddenly produced. She stood there for a full three or four seconds and then closed the coat and exited as fast as she had entered. Maestro tried to regroup, but it was a struggle. Finally, he got back on track – "Only the Good Die Young" seemed to have a little more zing and zest this time around.

"That's Candy," Big Teddy whispered to Alex with great reverence. "She dances at Boji Nites – it's a strip joint two doors down. Me and Filbert and the guys will probably go over there later – come along."

"No thanks," Alex said. He had his reasons, and most of them were sitting across the table from him. He recalled what Paul Newman had told him once in explaining why he never had an affair in all the years he had been married to Joanne Woodward – "Why go out for hamburger when you've got steak at home."

"She's a legend," Big Teddy continued. "See those two guys over there – the two with the white headbands and big smiles."

"Yes, I see them," Alex replied, spotting two guys that might have been in their early twenties, who appeared to be in a daze.

Big Teddy was like a little kid telling his buddies that he had spied on his sister's pajama party. "There's chairs all around the stage where the girls dance," Big Teddy began. "Candy does a somersault off the stage and lands with her head in a guy's lap,

121

face down. Somehow, without using her hands, she gets ahold of the guy's underwear with her teeth and she chews through them just below the elastic band. Then, she snaps her head back and, quick as a flash, rips the elastic band clean off. That's what those two goofy guys have wrapped around their heads – their underwear elastic. It's the damndest thing I've ever seen."

"Sounds like quite a show," Alex said.

"Oohhh, Gawd," Big Teddy moaned.

Two new guys, Norm and Sparky, joined the table. Norm was a tall, lanky guy who could easily have been the prototype for the Marlboro Man. Sparky was a little shorter with a moptop hairdo, perfect Alex Gideon pearly whites, and glasses that kept slipping down on his nose. Of course, they both headed straight for Simone for a hug. The thought occurred to Alex that he was about the only guy in the place that hadn't hugged her. Maybe that was a good sign, in some weird kind of way.

Filbert's big blonde took a liking to Norm and followed him to the bar. Just when Alex was about to start making some serious moves on Simone, like "Can I give you a ride home?" or something like that, Filbert was back in the picture.

It was a glass-shattering scream and it was coming from Sally, sitting right next to Alex. He checked his hands – they were both on top of the table – it wasn't him.

The bar fell silent. Had someone been murdered? Had someone had their first taste of whiskey? Had someone told the big blonde that there wasn't a Santa Claus?

"Turn it up, turn it up," Sally yelled to Hap behind the bar as she pointed at the television set mounted on the wall a few feet from the troupe's table. Alex looked up and it suddenly felt like someone had hit him in the face with a shovel. There on the TV was a full screen picture of him, with the caption – "Alex Gideon – Missing."

Alex froze. He could feel a hundred eyes looking straight at him - maybe two or three hundred. Staring, piercing, probing. He couldn't move. He could hardly breathe. He was too young to have a heart attack, but then again, maybe not. He glanced across the table. He dared to venture a peek around the room. They were all looking in his direction, hundreds of eyes – but they were looking at Sally sitting next to him. He had been spared again but, perhaps, only momentarily.

By now, Hap had found the remote and turned up the volume. It was CBS newscaster Peter Jenkins. "We interrupt this program to bring you this late-breaking news from Beverly Hills, California. Actor Alex Gideon, also known as the Bunny Boy, has apparently disappeared. Foul play is suspected. When Mr. Gideon failed to show up at the Save The Universe banquet last night, his manager and his date for the event, Heather Devreaux, became suspicious and called authorities. That's all we know right now. We will bring you updates as we learn more about this late-breaking story. Once again, actor Alex Gideon is missing and foul play is suspected. Good evening."

Sally was weeping uncontrollably. Simone rushed to her side to console her.

"He's the most wonderful man in the world," Sally sobbed. "He's kind, he's talented, he's…"

"He's a joke," Filbert said with a snarl. "He couldn't act his way out of North Dakota."

"He's a fabulous actor," Sally sobbed.

"This is Peter Jenkins with more developments in the disappearance of actor Alex Gideon," the voice on the TV said as the picture of Alex again filled the screen.

Sally held her breath. All eyes were on the TV. Alex held his breath, too, wondering what bombshell was about to be dropped next. At least Jenkins had referred to him as an "actor" this time instead of as the "Bunny Boy" as he had on the previous news flash – that was an improvement.

Peter Jenkins continued. "An anonymous source has confirmed that there was a break-in at Mr. Gideon's thirty-six room Beverly Hills mansion sometime Wednesday or Thursday of this week. A quantity of blood identified as being that of Mr. Gideon was found in at least two rooms of the mansion. Apparently Mr. Gideon put up a ferocious fight before being abducted. Authorities refused to reveal if a ransom note was found at the scene. Again, Alex Gideon, known as the Bunny Boy for his role in some eight Bunny movies, featuring skimpily clad starlets romping in a variety of settings, has apparently been abducted from his Beverly Hills mansion. Foul play has been confirmed."

"That jerk," Alex said to himself, "he didn't have to call me the Bunny Boy. And, it has *thirty-eight* rooms."

Alex looked at his finger. The cut suffered when he put up that ferocious fight with a piece of broken glass was completely healed. What a bunch of idiots.

Sally was wailing again, crying uncontrollably. "I pray to God that he's all right," she sobbed. "I can't bear the thought of living without having Alex Gideon in my life."

"Oh my Gawd," Filbert sneered. "He's just a phony movie star. He can't act, and besides, I understand he doesn't even like women – he's a fag."

Alex restrained himself. He had to remain calm. He could not defend Alex Gideon – not now. But his time would come, and when it did, POW! For Filbert Kauffman did not realize it, but he had just slandered the star of that fabulous movie, *Boxing Bunny.*

Mild-mannered, quiet, shy, reserved Sally jumped to her feet and screamed at Filbert, "You son-of-a-bitch, Filbert Kauffman – he's more man than you'll ever be, and he can act circles around you, too." And having said that, she lunged across the table for Filbert's throat.

Simone grabbed Sally from one side and Alex got her from the other before she could reach Filbert. It was very painful for Alex to hold her back when she was about to do such good works. Alex had liked this sweet, quiet, shy girl, Sally. But now that he saw another side of her, he adored her.

Filbert was smiling. Alex didn't know which he enjoyed the most, bashing Alex Gideon or tantalizing a true Bunny Boy fan, but he was having a ball.

"You're just upset, dear," Simone said. "He'll be okay, he really will. He's just missing – maybe he ran off with one of his other girlfriends for the weekend."

"But, I'm so afraid for him," Sally said.

"I'm sure he's fine. He's in no danger. He's off somewhere having fun with friends. He'll show up, laughing at the world in a few days. Trust me. He's okay,"

Alex spoke the words with such sincerity and conviction that Sally stopped crying on the spot. She wiped her eyes. She regained control.

"But what about the blood that they found?" she asked.

"Oh, he probably cut his finger on a broken glass or something. You know how those reporters jump to conclusions and make things up just to have a sensational story to make themselves look important," Alex said.

"Do you really think so?" Sally asked hopefully.

"I know so," Alex said firmly. "Trust me."

There it was – as close as you could get to an out and out full confession that he, Al from Rapid City, South Dakota, was, in fact, Alex Gideon, the Bunny Boy. But nobody listened. Nobody paid attention. Nobody caught it.

Sally looked at Alex with thankful eyes and gave him a big kiss right on the lips. If she had known that she was kissing her idol, Alex Gideon, she probably would have been the one to have the heart attack.

"You have made me feel so much better," Sally said. "I can't explain it, but I just believe what you say is true – that my Bunny Boy is safe and sound."

Alex had threatened to kill people for calling him the Bunny Boy, but Sally was exempt. She could call him that – that name if she wanted.

"Now that everyone has calmed down a bit, I think some apologies are in order," Simone said. She was looking straight at Filbert.

Filbert looked down at the floor, he looked up at the ceiling, he looked around the room, he looked at Simone and frowned. She stared back at him. Finally, he said it, "Sally, I'm sorry."

"And, I'm sorry that I called you a bad name and tried to choke you," Sally said, "but you did say some terrible things about Alex Gideon."

"Like I said, I'm sorry," Filbert stated. "I don't deny that I feel that way about him, but I'm sorry I upset you."

Filbert got up from his chair, walked around the table and he and Sally hugged each other.

The table was under control. The mutiny that had threatened to tear the theater troupe apart had been averted.

"Now that we're friends again, can we talk?" Filbert asked.

"Go ahead," Sally said.

"Doctor Delaney," he said to Simone, "you're a student of acting and actors – have you ever seen a Bunny Boy movie?"

"Yes I have, several," she said.

Alex was shocked. Everybody at the table was shocked. What was she doing watching trash like that?

"Well, do you think he can act?" He had set Simone up for the obvious answer to prove his point.

Simone thought for a moment, "I think he has potential," she said.

"Potential for what?" Filbert blurted out.

126

Alex had heard this exchange before, between these two, word for word. It was when Simone had selected Alex over Peterson for the part of William in the play.

"How about you, Al," Filbert said, "do you think Alex Gideon is a fag?" He was sneering again.

Alex's first impulse was to jump up and finish the job that Sally had started – to choke the living hell out of this arrogant, condescending, mean-spirited, son-of-a-bitch named Filbert Kauffman. But, Alex restrained himself – it was one of his better acting jobs, ever. "I think he likes women," Alex said nonchalantly. "I would guess that he likes women a lot."

"For God's sake, Filbert, everybody on earth knows he made it with Shauna LaDue and he's probably making it with Heather Devreaux, too," Big Teddy said. "He likes women, you can take that to the bank."

Alex said a silent prayer, thanking The Lord for Big Teddy and Sally, who had unknowingly come to his defense so ably.

"You're just jealous because he has millions of fans that love him with all their heart," Sally said.

A voice from the end of the table chimed in, "I understand that yesterday someone bought every Alex Gideon poster and photo that they had in the Funhouse Gallery – about a thousand dollars worth."

"That proves what I've always said about Okoboji," Big Teddy said, "somebody's granddaddy has too damned much money."

It was Peter Jenkins again. "We have additional developments in the disappearance of actor Alex Gideon. And now live from Beverly Hills, here is Mr. Gideon's manager and long-time friend, Charlie Waller."

Big as life, there he was – Charlie. He was wearing a light blue shirt, dark blue suit, and blue and red striped tie. Alex would bet a hundred that it took Charlie two hours to pick out the outfit for this show and that he was wearing his black patent leather shoes, too.

127

Charlie looked sad. He looked worried. He looked despondent. He looked like hell.

Charlie began slowly, sadly, "I would like to thank the millions of Alex Gideon fans worldwide who, undoubtedly, at this moment are expressing care, concern, and love during this very, very difficult time. We do not know what has happened to Alex. He disappeared suddenly and without a trace. We are sad to say that it appears that foul play is involved. Alex Gideon is a kind, warm, wonderful, and talented person. If anyone knows anything about the disappearance of Alex Gideon or knows anything about his whereabouts, I beg of you, please come forward. And, if anyone is holding him against his will, please..." Charlie's voice cracked and he paused for a moment to compose himself, "...please do not harm him and please - let him go. He is like a son to me." And with that Charlie broke down into a sobbing mess.

Alex was touched. He almost cried himself. This was a different side of Charlie than he had ever seen before. Alex had always viewed Charlie as being interested in three things and three things only – money, money, money. That every move Charlie planned and every decision he made, was designed to enhance the image of Alex Gideon for one purpose and one purpose only – and that was to put more money in Charlie Waller's pocket. That Charlie viewed Alex as a puppet that he could manipulate for his own ends. But, in those thirty seconds that Charlie was on television, Alex could see that he was completely wrong. Underneath that slippery exterior was a warm and caring human being. Alex was ashamed of himself for having harbored such suspicions of Charlie's motives for all these years. And, he realized that it had been selfish of him to disappear without telling Charlie and to cause his good friend and mentor, who thought of him as a son, such worry, grief, and heartache.

The gig was up. Alex would phone Charlie yet this night – it was not yet midnight in California. He would not tell Charlie where he was, for he had a life to live, too, here in Okoboji for another week or so. But, he would place the call and let Charlie know that he was safe and then he would let Charlie deal with the mess back there in California. Poor Charlie. Alex's heart ached for him. Yes, Alex was very ashamed of himself.

The camera held on Charlie for a moment after he had finished talking, wanting to wring every ounce of emotion out of this scene that they could. And then, just a split second before the camera cut away, Alex saw it. Charlie was transformed in a flash from a sobbing, grieving heap into his normal cold, calculating self. Alex doubted that anyone else had noticed, since it was only visible for a split second and no one else would have known what to look for.

"Why that dirty, rotten, low-down, scheming scoundrel," Alex said to himself. Everybody in the whole world, including the media, the police, and Charlie as well, thinks that he has been kidnapped, – but Charlie has one goal in mind – to milk it for all the publicity he can get. Why this could sell a couple million extra movie tickets and who knows how many posters, photos, and action figures. And, Alex's picture might be on the cover of a thousand magazines…

No, he would not call Charlie Waller this night. He would let Charlie Waller wallow in the mess that was brewing in California. He had things to attend to here in Okoboji.

"What a shyster," Big Teddy said.

"You got that right," Alex said.

"I think it's all a publicity stunt," Filbert said. "Your Bunny Boy is sitting on some island in the Caribbean right now with a rainbow – a blonde, a brunette, and a redhead. Wise up."

"His manager might be a shit," Sally said, "but Alex Gideon would never be a part of anything like that. He's missing, and his manager is trying to take advantage of the situation – but he's missing. What do you think, Al?"

"I think you're right – absolutely right," Alex said. This girl had undying faith in Alex Gideon, the likes of which he had never seen. So, she wanted to go to Hollywood to become a movie star, did she? Well, she didn't know it, but that was going to happen – he, Alex Gideon, would see to it.

Heading straight for the table, were the erstwhile actor, Peterson, and Bev from the Funhouse Gallery – the same Bev who had sold him all of those Alex Gideon posters and photos that had been discussed at the table just moments ago. Alex's ship had survived one torpedo after another this night, but he had the feeling that it was about to be broadsided. Peterson headed straight for him.

"I heard you did a great job in the play tonight," Peterson said. "Good going, I'm happy for you."

"I'm sorry about last night," Simone said.

"Oh no - I should thank you," he said shaking her hand. "I've had this crazy idea for years that I wanted to become an actor and when it came down to it, I was terrified. You did me a big favor. And now that I've got that out of my head, I'm going to write a book."

Simone looked relieved. "Thank you," she said, "and good luck with the book. I'd love to read it when you get it finished."

Alex turned to Bev, "Hello," he said, bracing himself for the inevitable reference to all of his Alex Gideon purchases, particularly since they probably tripled in value in the past hour.

"Hello," she said, "nice seeing you."

And that was it. No "Nice seeing you, *again.*" No mention of the posters. No mention of the Bunny Boy. No mention of the Funhouse Gallery. Confidentiality. They believed in confidentiality.

The two of them headed off to join B.J. Thomas and his girlfriend. He had been spared again. He was living a charmed life here in Okoboji.

Peter Jenkins was back. "We continue with our coverage of the Alex Gideon disappearance. Live from Los Angeles, here is Mr. Gideon's date for the banquet that he failed to attend, Heather Devreaux."

The camera showed her from the waist up – always best to display a person's best attributes. She looked into the camera for a moment, supposedly composing herself before beginning.

"Ooohhhh, my Gawwwddd," Big Teddy moaned. "He's dead. He's gotta be dead. What else could keep him from a date with *that*."

"Whew," Filbert whistled.

Alex had to admit, she was fabulously beautiful. The most beautiful woman in the world, some say. But, just wait boys - wait until she opens her mouth.

Heather, the genius, began to speak, "Alex Gideon and I are very close. We have been seeing each other for some time. I miss him terribly. I fear for his safety. If you have Alex, please let him come home. Let him come home to me." And then she whimpered a couple of times and jiggled the best part of her anatomy at the camera.

Big Teddy and Filbert, as well as half the guys in the place, were moaning. Their wives and girlfriends wouldn't sleep tonight.

Alex could see that she, too, was wringing every ounce of publicity out of this that she could. It was apparent that someone had written her script and had rehearsed her until she was able to deliver it so she didn't sound like the idiot that she was. "We are very close..." Where in the hell did that come from? He had escorted her to one event and had sent her home with the limo driver, alone, while he took a cab home. That was it. And that whimpering at the end – you call that acting?

131

Simone had remained noncommittal throughout this exchange involving the missing Alex Gideon. Perhaps she was occupied comforting Sally. Perhaps she found it all silly. Perhaps she was observing human nature unravel. Perhaps she knew.

It seemed like an hour since Maestro had played a note, but it had been only twenty minutes. He was back on the stage now, ready to go. Hap, thank God, had turned the sound down on the television sets, and Maestro launched into "Proud Mary." Alex was never so glad to hear a song in his life.

Simone and Sally rose from the table. "I'm going to give Sally a ride home," Simone said. "See you all at nine at the theater for the parade."

And, she was gone. All of Alex's groundwork was down the drain. Damn that Alex Gideon. If only he hadn't disappeared…

11

Alex jumped out of bed at seven o'clock, showered, and got dressed. Back home in Beverly Hills, he would normally get up at the crack of nine, eat a leisurely breakfast of cereal and fresh fruit, work out for an hour or so, and lounge around until noon before he got rolling. But, this was Okoboji and he had things to do.

It was a beautiful morning for a parade. The sun was shining, there wasn't a cloud in the sky, and it was about seventy-five degrees.

Alex bought a copy of the Des Moines Register from a vending machine outside the motel office – he made the front page, picture and all. Alex quickly read the story. There were some more quotes from Charlie about how he was so worried and how he was grieving. There was some babbling from Heather, but besides that, basically there was nothing new. That was good news. It appeared that Alex would have one more full day here in Okoboji without any serious Bunny Boy complications.

Alex walked into the Dry Dock for some breakfast. The place was packed. At the bar were several of the guys Alex had met the night before in Ruebins, drinking Bloody Mary breakfast specials. "Come join us," George, the guy who looked like Hemingway said. "You know everybody, don't you – Scotty, Norm, Sparky, Diamond Dave. It's Summer Games, let's party."

Alex declined, preferring a breakfast that he could chew.

Mayor Mike was helping out in the kitchen, frying eggs and buttering toast. His wife, Jill, was waiting tables as were a couple of others, Deb and Cindy. The bartender, Wanda, was mixing Bloody Marys as fast as she could but still couldn't keep up with the demand. Alex checked his watch – had he overslept by five or six hours? No, it was eight o'clock – in the morning. You had to be tough to live in Okoboji.

Alex was eager to see Simone and was concerned about Sally, so he arrived at the theater early - at about eight thirty.

Simone was already there, sweeping the floor of the stage. That would be the day when someone like Shana LaDue or Heather Devreaux, or even Charlie, would sweep a stage floor.

"Don't you have stagehands who do that?" Alex asked.

"I like to do it," she replied. "Keeps me grounded."

"Mind if I help?" Alex asked.

"Suit yourself, there's another broom over there," she said as she motioned to the wing. "How was Candy?"

"I didn't go – I went straight back to my room about five minutes after Sally and you left," Alex said.

"Why didn't you go?" Simone asked. "All of the guys in the troupe go to Boji Nites on Friday night – it's a tradition."

"Do you want the truth?" Alex asked.

"I think I can handle it," Simone said with a smile.

"Well, I was really hoping to spend some time with you – talking, like we are now. When you went home, I went home, too," Alex said. "Would you like to go out to dinner some evening?"

"I don't go out much," she said. "I've got a theater to run and I'm going to be pretty tied up with the Save The Park fundraiser for a while. I don't think so – not now."

She was pleasant. She was kind. But she was also distant, preoccupied.

134

"Is something wrong?" he asked.

"I'm just so worried about the fundraiser. That's all I have on my mind right now. We've only got three days to go – less than three days - and we still need to raise over two million dollars. I don't know if we can do it, but we're gonna keep trying."

Alex seized the opening. "How can I help?"

"Well, we're looking for volunteers. Can you handle a telephone?"

"I once did telemarketing, and I won three sales awards my first month," Alex said, not telling her that two of them were simply for showing up for work on time.

"You're hired," Simone said.

"How's Sally?" Alex asked.

"She dearly loves that man, Alex Gideon, and she's terribly worried about him. But, she's young and resilient – she'll be okay."

"And, what do you think of him?" Alex asked

"He's okay," She said.

That wasn't much of an answer, but it appeared to be all that Alex was going to get. At least she didn't hate him, probably.

It was nearly nine and the troupe started to trickle in. Sally looked like hell. She looked like she had been crying again.

"Are you okay?" Alex asked.

"I'm so worried," she said. "I watched the eight o'clock news on CNN this morning and they still don't know anything. And that Heather Devreaux makes me sick – she's just using this for publicity – she doesn't really care about him. Not like I do."

Alex gave Sally a hug. "He'll be okay. Remember, I promised. Trust me. I can just sense that he's with a dear friend at this very moment, as we speak."

"When you assure me that he's okay," Sally said, "I just feel such a connection to him – it's kinda weird – I can't explain it. But, I feel better already."

135

Sally headed to the women's dressing room to put on her costume for the parade. That was more than a bounce in her step - she was walking on air. Alex could do that to women. He wished it would work with Simone.

She had watched the whole thing between Sally and Alex from the corner of the stage. "Thank you. Thank you very much," Simone said, as she turned and headed for the dressing room.

The theater float was a hayrack that had been borrowed from a local farmer. A hand-lettered sign hung down about three feet on each side with the lettering, "Okoboji Lakeside Theater." Drawings of masks depicting the theater symbols for comedy and tragedy adorned the sign. A big sign saying "Save The Park – And The Theater," hung from the back of the hayrack.

Everybody, except Big Teddy, was onboard. Mike, who had played on the theater basketball team, was elected to drive the tractor that would pull the float. He started up the John Deere, put it in gear, and they headed for the parade route.

It was a splendid group, all dressed up in their costumes from *Sisterly Love* and the previous play, *Once Upon A Mattress*. The conversation was lively, recounting the previous night's escapades and planning for the day's Summer Games activities. Everybody seemed to be involved in something.

Mike and Bill were going to ride in the bicycle race that started at The Ritz bar at noon and went all the way around West Lake. Simone would take a short break from her fundraising duties to enter the paddlewheel race with Sally. Filbert and Big Teddy were going to be in the canoe race. Others were going to enter the water ski competition, Jet Ski races, or sail boat races. A couple of the women were going to participate in the ecology dive, where scuba divers scour the lake bottom for junk, and maybe treasures. Everybody was going to watch the battle between the Iowa Navy and the Nebraska Navy.

136

Jerry, the guy who raced up and down the basketball court like a gazelle, was already in the midst of running a marathon. The race had started at six-thirty this morning in a small town named Marathon and would end in Arnolds Park. It wasn't an official marathon distance – the town of Marathon was some twenty five or thirty miles south of Okoboji – nobody knew for sure and nobody gave a damn. The race had been dubbed "The Marathon From Marathon," and over five hundred runners had started the race. It was expected that over two hundred might actually finish, sooner or later.

The final mile of The Marathon From Marathon was along the Summer Games parade route. The six-thirty starting time was selected so that the front runners should be able to finish the race between ten o'clock and eleven o'clock while the parade was in progress. The runners who finish the marathon during that hour's time frame will run the parade route to the cheers of thousands of onlookers. Those who finish after that will limp into town virtually unnoticed. It was a good reason to get the lead out – or to cheat.

A mobile unit from KUOO Radio in Spirit Lake was following the race and reported in every fifteen minutes. At last report, Jerry, the gazelle, was holding his own, in twentieth place. Even though the radio station's call letters, KUOO, were taken from the University Of Okoboji, it was a serious, bona fide radio station, unlike The University itself.

There were already a dozen floats in the Okoboji Middle School parking lot at the corner of Highway 71 and Broadway Street, where the parade entries were to assemble. Other parade units were coming from all directions. Mayor Mike and First Lady Jill were in charge of lining up the parade units. In a small town, you wear a lot of different hats.

The Okoboji High School and Middle School bands were standing in formation on Broadway Street, which had been

137

blocked off for the parade. The Okoboji music program was one of the top music programs in the state and the bands were always one of the highlights of the Summer Games parades.

Each year, the parade committee invites one guest band to march in the parade and to play the "Star Spangled Banner" at lakeside before the official start of the day's games. This year, the guest band was from Mergen, Minnesota, about a hundred miles north of Okoboji. Rumor had it that the Mergen band director had visited Okoboji as a teenager and had lost his virginity in a boat out on West Lake. He has been wild about the place ever since. He had petitioned the parade committee each of the last four years, wanting to be the guest band, and they had finally given in.

The parade committee had found that selecting a guest band, sight unseen, was like playing Russian roulette. Sometimes you got a direct hit – sometimes you got a complete miss. With the Summer Games parade crowd, though, the worse the guest marching band plays, the better they seem to like them, so it really didn't matter.

Big Teddy finally showed up in a Volkswagen Rabbit with the bell of a tuba sticking out of the sunroof. After much effort, Big Teddy finally extricated himself and the tuba from the Volkswagen and climbed aboard the float. Alex had heard a one-man piano band last night and it appeared that he was about to hear a one-man tuba band today.

Lyle pulled up on his chopper, followed by a dozen guys on Harleys and Indian motorcycles. Farther down the line were a half dozen riders on Victory motorcycles from the local Polaris plant. Bikers have a great deal of loyalty and pride in the brand that they ride and in Los Angeles, a mixture of Harleys, Indians, and Victories on the same street would lead to some serious trash talking or even a good old-fashioned rumble. Here in Okoboji, at least on Summer Games parade day, everybody was here to party, not to fight, and they joined forces to ride together in the parade.

Several groups were going to march in the parade and they were milling around the parking lot or Broadway Street. Hap, Jim, Lois, Autumn, Jenny, Jeremy, and the rest of them from Ruebins, totaling about ten people, were going to march and they were sitting on aluminum lawn chairs in the middle of the street.

Over three dozen floats and about eight or ten convertibles that would haul various dignitaries and beauty queens were in place for the start of the parade.

Mayor Mike lined up the first parade units on Broadway Street. After that, he and Jill would signal other units when they were to pull out of the parking lot and join the parade.

The first unit was the fire truck, then came two police cars. After that would be the parade marshal riding on a beautiful palomino horse followed by the Mergen High School marching band.

The parade marshal, sitting on his palomino, was talking to a couple of pretty girls from the Mergen band, killing a little time before the parade began. A raw-boned farm boy named Kopischke, reached over with his slide trombone and scratched the palomino's belly, slowly moving the slide back and forth. The horse whinnied and it sighed and it whinnied some more. It was in ecstasy. Kopischke gawked around, looking at the girls in the Okoboji band and nonchalantly checking out the sites of the city, while he continued to massage the palomino's belly with his slide trombone.

Finally, the fire truck blew its whistle and the parade was under way. The two police cars fell in behind the fire truck and the parade marshal followed on his palomino – his palomino that had become aroused by Kopischke's slide trombone. We're talking about a horse here – use your imagination.

The parade goers applauded politely when the fire truck and police cars passed, but when the parade marshal came into view on his horse, they went wild. They laughed, they screamed, they howled, they cried, they took pictures, and they took more pictures. He had been asked to be parade marshal twice before but he had turned it down. If he had known that the parade marshal got this kind of reception, he'd have done it long ago. He waved at the crowd, wildly, enjoying immensely his newfound popularity.

Mothers covered their daughter's eyes and a couple of spinsters recoiled in self-righteous indignation, and then grabbed their binoculars to make sure they were seeing what they thought they were seeing.

Two of the strippers from Boji Nites had an orgasm and three virgins fainted before the parade marshal discovered what was going on and fixed the palomino's condition with a baseball bat.

The Mergen High School band was made up of a bunch of players and marchers. Unfortunately, those who could play couldn't march and those who could march couldn't play. To make matters worse, those who couldn't play faked it, blowing as loud as they could and moving their fingers on their instrument keys as fast as they could, including a trumpet player named Hammermeister, who hit a couple of notes that they don't even have on the charts yet. To the casual observer, then, it would appear that these were the real band members, capable of marching and playing like mad at the same time. In comparison, those who could actually play looked like a bunch of stumble-bums compared to the fakers because they couldn't march in line or in step and they moved their fingers so slowly on their instruments. Throw this all together and it sounded like one of those kitchen bands that show up on television every once in a while where everyone plays music on some type of kitchen utensil, pot, pan, or rolling pin. It was a mess, but the crowd loved them.

140

The theater float pulled out of the parking lot and joined the parade as Big Teddy launched into a rousing version of "Oh! Susanna" on the tuba. You haven't lived until you've heard "Oh! Susanna" played on the tuba, and you're not sure if you want to continue living.

Riders on most of the floats threw candy and strings of beads to the parade goers. The theater troupe threw plastic masks depicting either comedy or tragedy. They were a big hit.

The Ruebins' crew was two places ahead of the theater float so everyone on the float had a good view of them as they marched along the parade route. Before the parade, the Ruebins crew had been sitting on aluminum lawn chairs in the middle of Broadway Street. When it was their turn to join the parade, they folded them up and took them along. Good to be prepared, you know, if the parade stalls and you've got to wait a bit. When they got in front of Ruebins, where a big crowd was gathered, they all stopped, unfolded their lawn chairs, sat down, and leaned back like they were about to take a little snooze. Was it a boycott? Was it a protest? Did they need a drink? You could see that everyone along the parade route, including those on the theater float, was puzzled.

Suddenly, in unison, they all jumped up, folded up their chairs, and smacked the frame of the chairs down on the street, three times. They picked up the chairs, threw them in the air about five feet, caught them, smacked the street twice, sat down, jumped up, switched chairs, sat down, jumped up, marched in a circle, threw the chairs about ten feet in the air, caught them, smacked the street twice, marched back and forth in two rows, sat down, jumped up, marched in a circle, and finally took off down the parade route. It was a hell of a show – the likes of which most people hadn't seen since Ed Sullivan went off the air.

When the theater float was about halfway through the parade

route a mighty roar could be heard coming from the viewers along both sides of the route behind them. It was building quickly, getting closer. Everyone on the float turned to look — the first of the Marathon From Marathon runners had arrived to thunderous applause. There were two runners, side by side, giving it all they had. They had run twenty-five or thirty miles of lonely blacktop roads this morning with nothing but a few cattle, hogs, and chickens for an audience. Now, there were thousands of spectators and they were putting on a show. The applause was building louder and louder as the runners approached the float, and then they were past and the applause moved on ahead of the float and on down the parade route, eeeeeeeeeoooooooooooooo.

The applause was beginning to build again from behind the float — it was Jerry, the Gazelle, in a dead heat with another runner. Maybe he couldn't play basketball, but he was one hell of a runner. The troupe went wild. One of their own was on stage and he was about to steal the show. The Gazelle fed off of their excitement and reached deep down within himself and kicked in his afterburner, eeeeeeeeeoooooooooooo. He was past them, gaining on the leaders.

More runners entered the parade route and picked up their pace, being fueled by the tremendous applause all along the gauntlet.

The parade route extended down Broadway Street and past the yellow building housing the Maritime Museum and University of Okoboji Foundation offices. From there, it turned right at the roller coaster, went two blocks to the state pier and ended. The parade entries then turned right and continued onto the large grass area where they disbanded.

The rowdy hour-long parade ride was no time for Alex to try to talk to Simone, so he observed and he reflected. He had seen her strong, intelligent, and brilliant as an actor and theater manager. He had seen her concerned, involved, and passionate in the Save The Park effort. He had seen her loyal and comforting to her friends. He had seen her having fun and being silly out on the town. He had seen her as a peacemaker. He had seen her rolling up her sleeves and doing menial work that no Hollywood star, or even starlet, would consider. And he had seen within her a deep sadness when she realized that the fundraising effort might fall short and that the theater might be lost. She was real. She was genuine. She was magnificent. Now, what was Alex Gideon going to do about it? What could he do about it?

The final parade unit rolled into the grassy area and the parade viewers followed it in, as if it were the Pied Piper.

A small stage had been erected next to the theater, along the lakeshore. The thousands of people who had lined the parade route had gathered for a few words of wisdom from Mayor Mike and for the official beginning of the day's Summer Games events.

Mayor Mike thanked everyone for coming and read a list of the events that were to take place during the day and evening. He introduced the winner of the Marathon From Marathon – it was some guy from the Iowa State University track team who had won four events at the Drake Relays the previous spring. Then he introduced the runner-up – it was the Gazelle. They both received a thunderous ovation.

Mayor Mike introduced the guest band from Mergen, Minnesota, and announced that they would play the "Star Spangled Banner" before The Games would officially begin for the day.

The band director had positioned the band facing the stage, which meant they were facing the lake, which meant they were also facing the beach. And therein, as it turned out, was the problem.

The director raised his arms, took a deep breath, and kicked off the band by making those little triangles in the air like music directors make. The band got off to a good start, with most of them starting at about the same time. They were moving along well and the director was giving it all he had when three shapely young women in bikinis showed up on the beach for a little sunbathing.

The first ones to notice the sunbathers were the trombone section, consisting of Kopischke and three other farm boys. They had enough trouble trying to play and march at the same time, so trying to play and watch some half-naked women at the same time was strictly out. They opted for the women. The trumpet section, including Hammermeister, was the next to fall. Then the tuba players dropped out. And from there, the whole band collapsed - right there, during the "Star Spangled Banner." The only one still going was the bass drum - Boom, Boom, Boom, Boom.

The band director was furiously making those triangles in the air with his right hand while he motioned c'mon, c'mon, with his left hand. Occasionally, somebody, like a clarinet player, would try to jump in, but invariably the damned thing would just squeak and they'd jump back out again. Still, the director led his band forward, Boom, Boom, Boom, Boom to the bitter end of the National Anthem. It was a memorable performance.

The band instructor was totally exhausted. No doubt, this was God's way of extracting penance from him for screwing that Iowa girl out on the lake those many years ago.

It was a hard act to follow. All Mayor Mike could say was, "Well."

The start of most solemn events justifies calling out the local VFW to shoot off a twenty-one gun salute. Not so for the Okoboji Summer Games. Three guys wearing Hawaiian shirts, shorts, and sandals were poised behind three strange looking contraptions identified as *potato launchers*. Each launcher, made from plastic PVC pipe, was about four feet long and resembled a bazooka. Each guy crammed a potato down the barrel of the launcher. Then, they unscrewed the cover from the bottom of the launcher and sprayed hair spray into the compartment. They screwed the cover back on, pointed the potato launcher in the air, and held a match below the compartment containing the hair spray. POOF! POOF! POOF! Each of the potato launchers fired a potato a couple of hundred feet into the air and several hundred yards out onto the lake.

The crowd erupted in thunderous applause and Mayor Mike yelled, "Let the games begin!" And, the Okoboji Summer Games were officially underway.

The last time Alex had been in a parade was a year ago the previous New Year's Day when he had been the Grand Marshal of the Tournament of Roses Parade in Pasadena and had been squired along the parade route in a Rolls Royce convertible. Now, a year and a half later, he was here in Okoboji and had ridden in a crazy one-mile parade standing up on a hayrack surrounded by twenty other people. If only his mother could see him now!

12

Simone led Alex through a side door of the Maritime Museum. It resembled a politician's boiler room operation during election year with tables and phones everywhere and charts on the wall keeping track of progress. Dozens of people answered ringing phones at a furious pace. The donations were still coming in.

Simone introduced Alex to several people that he would need to know in order to work the phones and take donations. The Liberty Bank from Arnolds Park, which Alex recalled seeing across the street from the Middle School parking lot, was the official depository for the donations. Employees had worked as volunteers on their days off since the crisis began nearly a month ago. Today, Marjo, Sara, Steve, Karen, and Lisa were all there. Any credit card donations or electronic transfers were to be routed to them.

The tote board on the wall showed that they had donations of $8,447,150. Alex did some mental math – they needed eleven million – that left them over two and a half million short of the goal. It took three and a half weeks to collect around nine million – how would they ever be able to collect two and a half mil in less than three days? No wonder Simone was worried.

Some of the volunteers were making outbound calls, trying to solicit donations from the wealthy. They weren't having much luck reaching anyone, though - this was a Saturday in the summer and it was time to play.

Since Alex didn't know anyone that he could call for donations, he was assigned to fielding incoming calls from people making pledges. In an hour Alex received six calls with donations of $20, $50, $100, $25, $15, and $50. Again Alex did a little math, at this rate of collecting, say $225 an hour from each phone, and with ten phone lines going full time, it would take over a thousand hours to collect the money to meet the goal. They had only about fifty-three hours until the five p.m. deadline Monday.

Alex felt sick. He felt sick for all of these volunteers who had worked so hard. He felt sick for all of those who had been to the amusement park, the Roof Garden Ballroom, the Maritime Museum, and the Okoboji Lakeside Theater years ago and who could never return to revisit those memories. He felt sick for those who would never have a chance to build wonderful memories here. And, mostly, he felt sick for Simone. The theater was her life – it was her dream – it was her.

"How are the solicitations going?" Alex asked one of the men making out-bound calls during a lull.

"We have pretty well tapped out all of the potential big givers that we have been able to come up with – and there have been some huge donations. I can't mention any names, but we've had three donations of a half million dollars each and several donations in the one-, two-, three- and four hundred thousand dollar range. There has been a fabulous outpouring of support for the Save The Park project and people have given very, very generously. And we've gone back to those big donors and hit them up two and three times. Besides the big givers there have been literally thousands of people who have given what they can – maybe $5, $10, $50 or $100. It's just that we needed too much money and we had too little time. But we have not given up and we will not give up."

At about one-thirty the phones went dead. Nobody called.

"We're done for the day," Simone said. "Everybody's at the Summer Games. No need to sit around here."

The museum was only a block from the theater where their cars were parked. Alex had not fared well when he had asked Simone out for dinner, but he was not one to give up easily.

"A paddlewheel's one of those little boats that two people sit in and peddle something like a bicycle, right?" he asked.

"Right," Simone said, "and as you peddle it turns the paddle-wheel on the back, which makes it go."

"Where does your race start?" he asked.

"At Fillenwarth's Beach Resort, just on the other side of The Central Emporium. We race to the Arnolds Park Beach – right next to the Dry Dock – just past Water's Edge Condos."

Alex knew it well. That's where he had been bombed by Whitey and the Iowa Navy.

"Can I drop you off at Fillenwarth's?" Alex asked.

Simone paused for a moment, in thought.

"Parking might be tight by Fillenwarth's," Alex continued.

"Well, okay," she said.

And so, he was off on a date with Simone Delaney, kinda. The traffic was bumper to bumper and there was no parking space anywhere within a half-mile of Fillenwarth's.

"A great place to watch the end of the races is from the lawn in front of Water's Edge Condos – it's right by the finish line." Simone said as she got out of the car. "And, by the way, you aren't going to find a parking spot anywhere around here or around the Four Seasons Resort – I'd park back by the theater, if I were you."

"Why you, why you, she-devil," Alex said. "You conned me into giving you a ride up here."

"You volunteered," Simone said with that half-laugh, half-giggle. "See you after my race."

149

"She likes me," Alex said to himself. "Why else would she pull a dirty stunt like that on me."

Alex drove back to the theater in more bumper to bumper traffic and parked next to Simone's Mercedes. He was beginning to see that the trucker had been right about the traffic in Okoboji. He checked his watch. He had over a mile walk ahead of him, but he'd easily make it before the paddlewheel racers made it to the finish line.

Simone had been right – you couldn't have squeezed a bicycle into any of the parking lots around the Four Seasons or The Ritz, let alone a tank like the Orange Blossom Special. They were parked willy-nilly in all directions and two-thirds of the cars were boxed in by someone who had parked behind them. Most likely, during the Summer Games, no one cared.

The Water's Edge Condo lawn next to the Dry Dock was packed. Alex squeezed in behind a couple of guys with the elastic bands from their underwear tied around their heads. The lawn was sloped toward the lake and Alex was able to get a good view of the finish line. Off in the distance, he could see the paddlewheelers. They were moving very slowly in his direction. There were several thousand people standing along the lakeshore and hundreds of boats were anchored in the bay, filled with people watching the action from that vantage point.

"William, William," someone was calling from the deck on the second floor of the condo. "William, William." They kept it up, "William, William."

Alex turned around to see who the screaming idiots were and to get a look at this deaf guy, William. They pointed in his direction – it looked like they were pointing at him.

Alex looked around. No one else was looking in their direction. Alex pointed to himself, "Me?" he asked.

"William," they yelled again and motioned for him to join them on the deck.

Alex climbed the spiral staircase up to the deck.

"I'm Jeff and this is Dougherty – and you're William," he said. It appeared that they might have been imbibing a wee bit, but then, most of Okoboji seemed to have been imbibing a wee bit today. After all, it was the Summer Games.

"Saw you in the play last night," Dougherty said. "Fabulous job, William."

"We got beer, whiskey, gin, scotch, vodka, wine – what'll it be?" Jeff asked.

"I'll pass," Alex said, "I've got to work tonight – the theater, you know."

Jeff and Dougherty stared at him like he was some kind of a freak. Finally, Dougherty said, "That makes sense," and he flashed a big Irish smile. "But, after the show tonight," he said, "I'm going to buy you a cocktail, William."

"Fair enough," Alex said.

The deck of the condo provided a fabulous view of the lake and of the race. There were about ten paddlewheelers and the leader was nearing the finish line. The rest were bunched about twenty yards behind them. Alex spotted Simone and Sally buried in the pack.

"Ever try to paddle one of those things, William?" Jeff asked.

"No, I haven't," Alex answered.

"Don't," he said. "It's like walking in quicksand."

The first paddlewheeler crossed the finish line uncontested. The battle would be for second place, and third, and fourth, and fifth.

The paddlewheelers neared the finish line in a bunch. They were laughing and screaming and exchanging good-natured barbs and banging into each other.

The crowd was into it now and everybody was screaming for somebody. Alex never knew that paddlewheeling was taken so seriously in some parts.

151

Simone and Sally finished somewhere in the middle of the pack. They beached their paddlewheeler and flopped down on the sand, as did the rest of them, exhausted.

Finally, Simone and Sally headed toward the Water's Edge lawn. Jeff spotted them and began yelling, "Simmy, Simmy."

Simone spotted them and she and Sally climbed the spiral staircase to the deck.

"Look who we've got here," Jeff said. "It's William."

"Darned if it isn't," Simone said. "I need to sit down. Have you ever peddled one of those things – don't."

The canoe race had started at the state pier and they were now gliding across the lake, a hundred yards from the finish line. Big Teddy and Filbert were in the lead by a good ten yards and were increasing the lead. By the time they got within twenty yards of the finish line, they had it won. Big Teddy stood up and pumped his fist into the air like a gladiator, as he had done on the basketball court. This time, however, he was in a canoe, which is about as easy to stand up in as a hammock. In a split second the canoe flipped over and Big Teddy and Filbert were in the water. They were thrashing around, trying to hang onto the canoe and trying to keep their heads above water.

"Help, I can't swim," Filbert yelled. "Help, help, help."

Filbert disappeared below the surface and Big Teddy grabbed him and pulled him back up. Filbert was coughing and sputtering and trying to hold onto Big Teddy. Big Teddy lost his grip and Filbert disappeared again, only to be fished out by Big Teddy. This happened five or six times before Big Teddy finally hauled Filbert to shore, coughing, wheezing, and sputtering.

The crowd found the whole thing to be hilarious. Falling-down-on-the-ground hilarious. But nobody found it to be as funny as Alex. Had he been down there, he could have saved Filbert in a flash, because he was, after all, the star of that fabulous movie, *Boating Bunny*. But then, he wasn't down there, was he.

They say people go to auto races because they want to see the cars crash. Obviously people go to a canoe race for about the same reason - to see a canoe capsize so they can watch the Filberts of the world almost drown. And today they saw a spectacular crash.

"Oh, no, no, no," Sally screamed from inside the condo. They all rushed in to see what was wrong. She was watching TV and there on the screen was Heather Devreaux.

"...and I just love him with all my heart," she said, and then she finished the interview with a whimper.

Sally was seething.

"What happened now?" Simone asked, putting her arm around Sally.

"She said that Alex Gideon and she were secretly engaged but she felt that she had to tell the full story now because his fans deserved to know. She just made that up to get publicity - I know she did. If she really cared about him she'd be out looking for him."

Alex had expected more babbling from Heather and Charlie, but things were starting to get out of control.

"Next thing she's gonna come up with is that she's pregnant," Jeff said, howling at his own wit.

Sally shot him a look that could kill.

Dougherty stepped in to help his buddy save face and to comfort Sally, "Sometimes naughty girls like that Heather Devreaux take advantage of nice guys like that Alex Gideon."

"True story," Jeff agreed.

It didn't help. Sally was still upset.

"What do you think?" Simone asked Alex.

Alex looked Sally straight in the eyes. "There is no way that he is engaged to her. She may be pretty, but she is an air-headed idiot. He wouldn't go for a woman like that. He would like someone who is more, more grounded. He would never, ever fall

153

in love with someone like Heather Devreaux."

He was talking to Sally and he was looking in her eyes, but he was pleading his case to Simone. He hadn't figured out if Simone knew he was Alex Gideon, but it was inevitable that she would find out soon. If Heather and Charlie kept it up, he'd be forced to tell her and then he'd have to go public before this thing really got out of hand.

"And do you think he might have gotten her pregnant?" Sally asked.

"That was these two guys who said that," Alex exclaimed, pointing to Jeff and Dougherty. "She never said that, now did she?"

"No she didn't," Sally said, "but I was just wondering if you thought maybe ..."

"Not many people know this, but it's true," Alex said. "Alex Gideon and Heather Devreaux have been together exactly one time, when that idiot manager of his arranged for him to escort her to the Academy Awards for publicity. After the Awards show, Alex Gideon sent her home alone in the limo and he took a taxi home. And, that's the one and only time he has ever been with her." He was definitely stating his case to Simone.

"Gosh, how do you know all that?" Dougherty asked.

"I read it," he said, "and it wasn't in the National Enquirer."

"You believe that, don't you?" Alex said looking directly at Simone.

She smiled and shrugged, "If you say so."

"See," Alex said to Sally, "even Simone believes it. Don't let that airheaded bimbo get to you."

"You made me feel better again," Sally said with a smile. "Thanks. I'll be okay now."

Alex didn't give a damn about what Heather or Charlie said or did — he could straighten that out in ten minutes at a news conference when he got back to L.A. What did concern him, though, was his fans. All over the world there were millions of Sally's who adored him and loved him with all their hearts. He was able to comfort Sally, one-on-one, but even that had been difficult. He could not wait too long before he put an end to this for the sake of his grieving fans.

The discussion of Alex Gideon and Heather Devreaux was interrupted by loud shouting and clapping outside the condo.

"It's the battle of the navies," Jeff shouted as he headed for the deck followed by the rest of them.

About fifty yards from shore, off to the left was the Nebraska Navy's ship - a pontoon painted red and white. Off to the right was the Iowa Navy's ship - a pontoon painted black and gold. Each pontoon flew its state's flag and the U.S. flag and carried several large crates on its deck. In addition to the helmsman, there were six crewmembers on each ship. They were nattily dressed in their all-whites, from the top of their caps to their shoes.

The ships were on parade, slowly traveling in an oval as the crew waved to the onlookers on the shore and saluted those in boats out on the water. In return, the crowd cheered or jeered, depending upon which pontoon passed by.

Alex spotted Whitey, who he met when the Iowa Navy bombed him when he first arrived in Arnolds Park. He was having a large time, waving and saluting with both hands.

The Iowa Navy and the Nebraska Navy were now engaging in foreplay, making passes at each other and shouting and waving their fists at one another. The crowd was cheering and jeering like crazy.

"How do they decide who wins the battle?" Alex asked.

"See those large crates on the pontoons – those are filled with water-filled balloons." Dougherty said. "Each navy has a balloon launcher and the object is to bomb the other navy's pontoon. The first one to make ten direct hits wins the war. The referee

155

is in that small motor boat out there – he decides when a direct hit has been made and he also keeps score."

The referee raised a starter's pistol and pulled the trigger. The battle between the Iowa Navy and the Nebraska Navy was underway. One crewmember held each side of the balloon launcher, another pulled it back in shooting position, another removed the balloons from the crates, another loaded the shells, and another – that would be the Rear Admiral - gave the command to fire.

The balloons were flying fast and furiously and neither Navy had any better accuracy than the day Alex had been bombed. The balloons landed in the water, they landed in the boats out on the lake, they landed on the beach, and they landed among the crowd of onlookers. Finally, the Nebraska Navy scored a hit, to the uproarious approval of their supporters and to the boos of the Iowa Navy supporters. Then, the Iowa Navy charged the Nebraska ship and scored three direct hits in quick succession. The Nebraska Navy retaliated by charging and scoring two hits, while being hit once in return. At least one or two crewmembers were hit with every shot that landed and most of them were soaking wet.

By this time at least three dozen misguided water filled balloons had bombed the crowd of onlookers and half the crowd was also soaked.

After a fierce half-hour battle, the referee declared that the Iowa Navy had scored its tenth hit and was therefore the winner of the battle, for the second year in a row. To salute the crowd for their support, the two navies launched their remaining shells into the crowd and at the boats on the water. Now everyone was soaked. Alex was glad he was up on high ground, although three of the shots had hit the Water's Edge Condo a little down from where he was standing.

As a celebrity, Alex had the opportunity to witness in person major sporting events of all kinds including the Super Bowl, NCAA basketball Final Four, College football championship game, Wimbledon, and championship boxing matches. Never in his wildest dreams did he ever imagine that in a single day he would witness a paddlewheel race and a sea battle between the Iowa Navy and the Nebraska Navy. When he returned to L.A., he would have some stories to tell Brad, Ben, Denzel, Mariah, Orlando and the rest of them that they simply were not going to believe.

"Come here, quick," Sally yelled from inside the condo. "They're going to have an update on Alex Gideon."

It was Peter Jenkins again. Didn't that guy ever sleep?

"We have an update in the Alex Gideon disappearance," he said. "This afternoon, with permission of Mr. Gideon's manager, Charlie Waller, Beverly Hills police entered Mr. Gideon's home for further investigation, during which this film footage was shot. The film has been edited to bring you the highlights of that investigation."

The screen showed a dozen or more people milling around Alex's den. In the middle of the group, making sure he was always on camera, was Charlie. Somebody picked up Alex's guitar and strummed it a couple of times and somebody else plopped down on his couch.

"This is fascinating," Sally said, "getting a glimpse of his house and the way he lives. No one from the media has ever been allowed to take pictures inside his home. Look – there's a dartboard on the wall – and there's his desk. They say he spends almost all of his time right there, in the den. It's where he rehearses for his movies."

It was a weird feeling for Alex, sitting there in Okoboji, watching the inside of his home on television – and watching a dozen people wandering around. Alex's den was sacred ground and his guitar was the Holy Grail. What in the hell was Charlie

157

thinking, anyway.

Alex was soon to find out as the footage continued. The camera showed Charlie walk over to the picture on the wall and pull on it, revealing the wall safe. That was it – when Alex got back to L.A. he would fire one Charlie Waller. He had gone too far this time.

Now the film footage showed some guy wearing a metal mask with a small window in the front. That made perfect sense, because he was now firing up an acetylene blowtorch. And now, he was using that blowtorch to cut open Alex's wall safe. No, Alex would not fire Charlie Waller. He would kill him.

Alex tried to maintain a casual, expressionless exterior while his interior was boiling. Out of the corner of his eye, Alex thought that he caught Simone glancing back and forth between the television set and him. He wasn't sure, but if she was watching his reaction to the newscast, there would be none.

Peter Jenkins was on the screen again. "According to Mr. Gideon's manager, Charlie Waller, Mr. Gideon keeps large sums of cash in the safe in his den, perhaps as much as one hundred thousand dollars. As you can see, the safe is being cut open to see if the contents have been removed."

The screen switched back to the guy with the blowtorch as he finished cutting through the door of the safe and it fell onto the floor. A crack Beverly Hills detective looked inside, turned to the camera, posed, and spoke, sounding damned near like Geraldo Rivera. "It's empty," he said.

The camera cut to Charlie, who had apparently collapsed upon discovering that the safe was empty. By this time, most people following the newscasts about Alex's disappearance had probably figured out that Charlie was a shyster. Most likely, they would accuse him of faking a collapse just to add drama to the situation, realizing that in the movies people collapse when they find a grave is empty – not when they find a safe is empty. Alex, however, knew that this was pure, honest, unadulterated, uncensored emotion on Charlie's part – he wasn't faking a thing.

No, Alex would not kill Charlie Waller. He would torture him. He would use Chinese water torture. He would drive toothpicks under his fingernails. He would take money from Charlie's billfold and burn it in front of him. He would...

"And, that's our update in the continuing saga of the disappearance of Alex Gideon," Peter Jenkins said as the station returned to regular programming.

"If they took the money, why would they take him, too?" Dougherty asked.

"Maybe they didn't want to leave any witnesses," Jeff said.

Alex shot a quick glance at Sally, expecting her to start wailing at the mere thought that her Alex Gideon might have been done away with. But, she was learning to ignore any theories from those two guys and she appeared to be getting stronger. She was fine.

"We'd better get going if we're going to make it to the rally," Simone said, interrupting the discussion.

Alex was thankful that the Alex Gideon discussion was over, at least for now. He longed to be alone with Simone, to talk to her, to look at her, to touch her, but there were always so damned many people around. He would have to find a way to change that.

The original Roof Garden Ballroom had occupied the entire second floor of a two-story wood frame building perhaps thirty yards from the shore of West Lake Okoboji. On warm summer evenings, large windows would be swung open, allowing the soft lake breezes to flow through the ballroom. The Roof Garden was legendary, known by concertgoers and dancers throughout the Midwest and by entertainers throughout the country. Many notable big bands played there in the 40's and 50's. In the early days of rock 'n roll in the late 50's and the 60's, nearly anybody who was anybody, played the Roof Garden to crowds of four or five thousand dancers. When the place was really rocking, the dance floor would move up and down five or six inches. Predictions that the ballroom would collapse under the weight of too many dancers never came true. Eventually, the ballroom was torn down, much to the disappointment of the thousands of people who had such fond memories of "The Roof."

Perhaps it was because of the demise of the original Roof Garden Ballroom that Okobojians were so fervent in their desire to save The Park. They had already seen one beloved landmark disappear and they mourned its loss. If they could fulfill their dream to save The Park, they would not mourn again.

The Save The Park rally was held in the new Roof Garden Ballroom. It was a building built on a cement slab next to the wooden roller coaster in the amusement park, across the street from the original Roof Garden. It served the purpose of providing a place where people could gather for concerts, to dance, or to hold meetings. To those who fondly remembered the original Roof Garden with its swaying floors and steep outside stairs, however, it lacked character and atmosphere. On this night, though, everyone was happy that the new Roof Garden was there to provide a meeting place for this important rally.

Perhaps two thousand people were packed into the Roof Garden for the Save The Park rally. These rallies had been held weekly since the crisis began. This would be the final one. The purpose of the rally was to inform everyone on the progress of the fundraiser, to generate support, and to create enthusiasm. The rallies were short and simple, lasting only a half-hour.

Everyone at the rally seemed to know Simone and felt obligated to stop by to say hello. Alex may be a worldwide movie idol, but here in Okoboji, Simone was a star in her own right.

Simone started introducing Alex as "my friend," which was a small step forward in their relationship, if, in fact, any relationship existed at all. As far as Alex was concerned, a relationship existed – a serious one. But, he was afraid that Simone simply looked upon him as another semi-interesting tourist who came into and went out of her life in a two-week Okoboji summer vacation.

"Did you get the check?" the man asked Simone, trying to stay out of Alex's earshot.

"Yes, and it even cleared the bank," Simone said with a smile.

"We're going to hold that lot for you – forever, if necessary," his companion said.

"Go ahead and sell it if you get the chance," Simone said. "I don't expect you to keep it for me."

"It's yours, whenever you want it, it's yours – and at the same price we paid you," the first one said.

Simone heaved a sigh of gratitude, "Thanks, guys, that's very nice of you – very sweet," she said.

"Who were those guys?" Alex asked as they disappeared into the crowd.

That's Blaine and Ken – they're developing the Emerald Meadows housing area on the Emerald Hills Golf Course.

"I couldn't help but overhear," Alex said.

"I was going to build my dream house, but decided I wanted a theater more – simple as that," she said.

What a contrast. Charlie, who dreamed of riches untold, had fainted when they found Alex's safe was empty. Simone sold the building site for her dream house so she could follow her dream of saving The Park. She would never fit into Hollywood. Never. That was why he was crazy about her.

Several Maritime Museum board members and Save The Park volunteers took the stage to begin the rally.

161

"In less than a month, we have raised more than eight and a half million dollars," the speaker said.

Applause, whistling, more applause.

"However," he continued, "we still have around two and a half million to go and only have forty-eight hours to do it. Are there angels among you? Can you give more to help save The Park? Do all that you can. We must not fail. Now, before we continue with the program, I would like to remind you that on Monday night at nine o'clock we are going to have a celebration right here in the Roof Garden. Hopefully, we will be celebrating that we have saved The Park. If our efforts fall short, though, come anyway and we will celebrate our tremendous joint effort in this project, and we will celebrate life, and we will celebrate each other."

Another speaker took the microphone. "We have a special guest who has something to say," he said.

A boy, maybe six years old, with braces on both of his legs hobbled across the stage toward the microphone. He carried a tin can with him. The crowd fell silent. The man who introduced the boy held the microphone for him to speak.

"I cannot run like some of the other children," he said. "And, I cannot play some of the games that they can play. But I can ride the rides in the amusement park and have as much fun as any of the other children. And, when I ride the rides, I feel that I am like all of the other children who can run and walk better than I can."

He held up the tin can he had carried across the stage. "I have saved my allowance for the last four weeks, and I sold lemonade from a stand in front of our house every day, and I sold my bicycle to get money to help save The Park. I have one hundred seventy-four dollars and thirty-five cents in this can. It is all of the money that I have in the world, but I am happy to give it to you to help save The Park." And with that, he handed the can to the

162

man with the microphone and limped off the stage.

Half the crowd was misty-eyed, including the guy on stage who had just received the donation in the tin can. And now everyone was applauding loudly as the little boy reached the edge of the stage and jumped into his mother's open arms.

Simone turned her head away from Alex, but he could still see tears streaming down her cheek. He gently put his arm around her shoulder and softly pulled her to his side as he patted her shoulder to comfort her. She looked up at Alex through glazed eyes and bit her lower lip. The moment their eyes met Alex was overwhelmed with a torrent of emotions. He had not cried since his mother died some ten years ago, but now tears welled up in his eyes and spilled over, running down his cheeks. Simone turned to him and they hugged. It was not a hug driven by passion, but rather it was one born of this heart-wrenching moment, fueled by despair, pride, and hope. Alex held Simone gently in his arms for perhaps ten or fifteen seconds before she slowly pulled away. She wiped the tears from her eyes and looked up at Alex and smiled weakly as he wiped away the tears from his cheeks. He smiled at Simone, put his arm around her shoulder, and gently pulled her near. She did not resist.

"I'm sorry," he said. "I haven't cried in years, but that little boy was a real show stopper."

"Yes, he was," she said, "and I appreciate a man who can show his emotions." And then she slipped her arm behind him and lightly patted him on the back twice before she pulled away and took a step forward to get a better view of the stage.

The tender moment was over, but it left Alex euphoric. He had held the woman of his dreams in his arms and they had shared real, genuine emotion. But then, when it felt to Alex like Simone was at the very brink of dropping her defenses, she had pulled away. He had sensed this in her before, but not as dramatically as this time. She did not give of herself easily as the starlets in Hollywood did.

The little guy was a show stopper, indeed, and he ignited a wave of donations the likes of which a Presidential candidate could only hope for. One after another, people approached the stage, check in hand to deposit in the collection box. The speaker's prayers had been answered – there was surely an angel among them, and he stood three and a half feet tall and was only six years old.

13

The theater was packed to the rafters. Alex pulled back the curtain and peeked out — row twelve, aisle seats — they were there and Alex was glad. John and Martha held hands and ogled each other. It's so wonderful to be in love — particularly when the one you are in love with loves you in return. At least, that's what Alex had always heard and it seemed to hold true with John and Martha.

This would be Alex's second performance in *Sisterly Love* and he felt like a real part of this theater troupe. His performance on the basketball court had opened the door for him, to be sure, but his stalwart performance in last night's play had blown the door off the hinges. He was eager for the play to begin. He was eager to get out there to show them what he could do. He was eager to be a part of this cast. But, to be honest, what he was really eager for was the final scene when Simone would jump into his arms and he would hold her for a few seconds while the crowd broke into wild, mad applause.

Simone gathered the cast together behind the curtain for their moment of silence. Last night, Alex had been so nervous he felt like he might jump right out of his skin. Tonight, he was a little tense, but a little tension was said to be good for an actor to help keep them sharp and focused.

The crew joined hands and stood silently in a circle with their heads bowed. Last night Alex had prayed, hard, for survival. Tonight he prayed, too, but what he prayed for would be much more difficult to obtain.

"Let's make some magic," Simone said, as the cast headed for the wings and Mel headed for the piano.

Mel launched into the Stephen Foster medley – it was show time.

A moment later, William was saying, "Savanna, I might be out of line here, but I just have to say what I've got to say – and you might hate me forever – but I love you. I've always loved you, and I will always love you." He said the words with great passion and conviction.

"Oh William, I've been such a fool, wasting my time on that terrible man when you were right here all the time. I love you, too," Savanna said. And then she took two steps and jumped into William's arms.

Alex wanted to kiss her right there, in front of the cast, the crew, the audience, and the whole world but he knew that a sophomoric stunt like that would wash away the fragile inroads that he had been able to build between himself and Simone. He opted for the theatrical kiss that the script called for and let it go at that.

Predictably, the audience was on its feet. They sounded even louder than the crowd last night, if that were possible.

It had been a stellar performance by the entire cast. Simone was magnificent as Savanna. Sally was superb as Marion. Big Teddy was solid and, if he had to say so himself, Alex had been outstanding as William. Filbert had struggled a bit from swallowing too much lake water and was a little green around the gills, but he had delivered a command performance, nevertheless. Filbert may have been a jerk, but when it came to the theater, Alex had to admit, he was a pro.

Simone delivered a powerful appeal for donations to the Save

166

The Park fundraiser and the hats overflowed with donations. It wasn't official, Simone had said, but preliminary calculations showed that over a half million dollars had been collected at the rally held at the Roof Garden earlier in the evening. Over nine million had now been collected and less than two million was needed to meet the goal. But, there was less than two days to go. "Are there angels among you?" she had asked, and they had responded with a resounding "Yes!" by opening up their pocket-books.

The chant started in the men's dressing room and soon spread to the women's as well, "Rock 'N Roll!" "Rock 'N Roll!" "Rock 'N Roll!"

"Come along," Big Teddy said. "We're all going to the Roof Garden for the Iowa Rock 'N Roll Hall of Fame concert."

"The what?" Alex asked.

"Every year the Iowa Rock 'N Roll Hall of Fame inducts bands, ballrooms, radio stations and others that have made a contribution to Iowa rock 'n roll music through the years - and tonight's the night. The induction ceremony is probably over, but six bands are going to play – we'll catch at least the last three or four, including Maestro's band, which is being inducted tonight. Come along," Big Teddy said, "it's a blast. Everybody's going."

"Everybody?" Alex asked.

Big Teddy studied Alex for a moment and then he smiled and said, "Ya, Simmy's going."

"I didn't know I was that obvious," Alex said.

"You are. But, hey, go for it," Big Teddy said. "Every year, about a half dozen tourists - and Filbert, too, try to get in her pants and it hasn't worked yet, but I can't blame you for trying."

"That's not my intentions," Alex said.

"Well, well, well," Big Teddy said with a smile, "you're in love. All those other guys – Filbert and the tourists – they've all been in lust, which is why it hasn't worked with Simmy. But, L-O-V-E," he said, spelling out the letters, "that might be a different matter."

"I never said I was in L-O-V-E," Alex said, mimicking Big Teddy as he spelled out the letters. "Don't jump to conclusions. It's just that she's a lot more fun to be around than guys like Filbert and you, that's all."

Big Teddy just rolled his eyes and sighed.

The entire theater troupe stormed the Roof Garden Ballroom. Somebody had a ticket for Alex, which was much appreciated since he was on a budget ever since being robbed of his wad of cash by Filbert.

There was a huge crowd for the concert and the theater troupe found an area towards the back where they could congregate. They were a lively group and Alex liked them, but he wished they would all go away so he could be alone with Simone. But, it appeared that was not going to happen.

The program said that six bands, all of which were from the 1960's or 1970's, were to be inducted into the Iowa Rock 'N Roll Hall of Fame tonight, including Maestro's band, The Traidmarx. Some of the bands hadn't played together for twenty-five or thirty years. When word came that they were going to be inducted into The Hall of Fame, they had hunted up their instruments and started practicing with a vengeance. Rehearsing was often difficult, or impossible, since many of the band members had scattered all over the country. In some cases, they had only one rehearsal as a full band, and that was the day of the concert. Since they were inducting earlier bands into The Hall of Fame first, while they were still alive, most of the band members were in their 50's or 60's. The Hall of Fame organizers had feared that one of these elder statesmen of rock 'n roll might have a heart attack on stage, but that had not happened, so far.

Each of the six bands were to play a half-hour set and the first three, The Velaires, The Seven Sons, and The Sensational Soul Company, had already finished when the theater troupe arrived. The Fabulous Morticians, who arrived at the Roof Garden in a hearse as they arrived for every gig in the 60's, was on stage.

Filbert looked like he might be a candidate for the Fabulous Morticians' hearse, but he was not about to miss out on a good party and he certainly wasn't going to go lay by his dish and let this new guy, Al, have Simone all to himself.

Filbert grabbed Simone by the arm and said, "Let's go dance."

"I don't like that song," she said as she pulled away from his grasp.

"Well, maybe the next one then," he said, and he just stood there, waiting.

Alex saw that Simone was going to be occupied by Filbert and the rest of the theater troupe for a while, so he wandered around the crowd. It only took him about five minutes to find what he was looking for.

"Remember me?" Alex asked.

"You're the friend of that movie star, Filbert," the wide-eyed big blonde answered.

"He really likes you," Alex said. "In fact, just a few minutes ago he was asking someone if you were here."

"R-e-a-l-l-y?" the blonde asked.

"Scout's honor. But, he's back there, you can go ask him yourse..." and, she was gone before Alex could finish the sentence.

Alex almost had to run to keep up with the big blonde, but he was not about to miss out on the show. And, if things worked as planned, someone would need to be there to take Filbert's place next to Simone, and that would be him.

The big blonde charged in between Filbert and Simone, stuck her chest out, swung her boobs back and forth a couple of times, reached up and grabbed him by the ears, and said, "Let's dance." Before Filbert could wipe that goofy grin off his face, she had him halfway to the dance floor.

As soon as the blonde hauled Filbert away, Alex stepped in beside Simone. She turned to him and gave him a smile that said, "I know what you did."

"Funny, how that blonde keeps popping up, isn't it," Simone said to Alex.

"I did you a favor," he said.

"That's true," she said. "Let's dance."

They walked hand in hand to the dance floor, which was at the front of the ballroom next to the stage. The Fabulous Morticians were on their last song and were giving it all they had on Tommy James's "Mony, Mony."

When some couples dance, they look like they're dancing to two different songs as one hops while the other bops and one swings as the other one sways. Alex and Simone, on the other hand, danced together in perfect rhythm and in sync like they had been practicing together for years. He studied her carefully, reading her body language like a master spy would read a message, trying to crack the secret code. Perhaps Simone would not admit it to herself, but her body was telling Alex loud and clear that she was smitten. Or, was he reading between the lines and filling in the blanks with wishful thinking? Perhaps he would need to do his homework and continue studying to find the answer.

Alex had also been watching Filbert and the big blonde dancing. Her body language was saying unmistakingly "I want you Mr. Movie Star, I want you in the worst way." And Filbert, being the humble star that he is, was not about to disappoint a true fan. Alex smiled to himself – spending a night with the big blonde would be a fate worse than death. Alex had vowed to get even with Filbert for stealing his money and especially for saying those rude, lewd, and crude things about that missing movie star, that real movie star, Alex Gideon. Sweet revenge, that's what they call it.

It took only five minutes for a stage change, as all of the bands used the same drum set and sound system. All they had to do was walk on stage, plug in their guitars, and they were ready to go.

The next band, Dee Jay and The Runaways, took the stage to a thunderous ovation. Back in the sixties they were a bunch of local kids in their teens and early twenties who had recorded the first national hit record ever recorded in the state of Iowa. The song, "Peter Rabbit," was recorded at Iowa Great Lakes Recording Studios just down the road in Milford. It became a regional hit on their IGL label and then was leased to Mercury records who distributed it nationwide. The band had toured America for a couple of years, and appeared on several national television shows, before they tired of the travel and came back home to assume more traditional lifestyles. Although Dee Jay and The Runaways had disbanded many years ago, most of the members continued to play in other bands on weekends, playing around a hundred gigs a year. The band sounded like a well-oiled machine. For their final song, they played their big hit, "Peter Rabbit," a novelty song of sorts with a hard-driving rock beat. Alex had never heard the song before but he liked it and it was a great song to dance to with Simone. It brought down the house.

Simone noticed the blonde mauling Filbert on the other side of the dance floor. "You should be ashamed of yourself," she said.

"He deserves it," Alex said. "Besides, I saved you from him."

"Maybe I didn't need saving," she replied.

"I know you can handle yourself, but I also know you were not enjoying his company," Alex said.

"So you think you know me better than I know myself, do you?" Simone teased.

Alex thought for a moment. "Yes," he said, "in some ways I think I do."

"Well, we'll just have to see, won't we," Simone said.

It was the type of light-hearted banter that Alex relished. Mental gymnastics. A matching of wits. Conversation. Simone was fun.

The final band of the night was The Traidmarx, which is the band that Maestro Tim Horsman had played in as a youth. After the Hall of Fame had passed over the band the past four years, patrons of Ruebins got up a petition nominating The Traidmarx. The petition, bearing over a thousand signatures, had been persuasive and now here they were, Iowa Rock 'N Roll Hall of Fame inductees. It was an eleven-piece band with drums, guitars, keyboards, and four horns, with Maestro Horsman on lead vocals. After the first half dozen notes from their first song, it was apparent why they had been chosen as the final band of the show – they about blew the walls out. Nobody would have wanted to follow them on stage. Besides that, they were great. They brought the house down with the Ides of March's "Vehicle," Chicago's "Make Me Smile," and The Flippers' "Harlem Shuffle."

Alex thought of his mother. How she would have enjoyed being here listening to this music that she loved. And, she was. When she died, Alex vowed that she would live through him and that he would carry her in his heart wherever he went. He raised his eyes upward and smiled.

For the grand finale, all of the Hall of Fame inductees got up on stage and played Bob Seeger's "Old Time Rock and Roll" over and over, with everyone taking a turn as the lead singer or instrumentalist.

It was a memorable evening. All of the bands played their

172

hearts out and, once again, nobody had a heart attack in the process.

"Some of the bands are going to have a jam session at Ruebins," Big Teddy said as he headed for the exit. "See you there."

Alex checked his watch. It was shortly before midnight - the shank of the evening. Going to Ruebins would be fun, but he had endured enough large groups of people for one night. Besides, he had other things on his mind.

"Want to go?" he asked Simone, just in case she intended to go.

"I've been around people enough for one day," she said, "but, go ahead, if you like."

"No, I'll walk you back to the theater," Alex said.

They walked slowly, hand in hand, down the street toward the lake. It was a magnificent evening – about eighty degrees and hardly a breeze at all. They sat on a bench on the state pier and admired the stars. It had been years since Alex had seen the galaxy in all of its glory, since in a city, the lights reflect off the sky and hide the stars.

"What are your plans for tomorrow?" Alex asked.

"Normally I would go to church on Sunday morning," Simone said, "but this is an unusually busy weekend and I'm going to skip it just this once. I've spent so much time on the fundraiser, and on Summer Games, that I've fallen behind in getting prepared for next week's play. Rehearsal starts on Monday."

"And then?" Alex asked.

"And then in the afternoon I'm going to work on the fundraiser at the Maritime Museum, and at night is the final presentation of *Sisterly Love*."

"I was hoping you might have time to go out to dinner sometime," Alex said.

173

"Well, I'm pretty tied up right now with the Save The Park project and rehearsals and the theater," Simone said. "Maybe later on."

"I may have to leave soon," Alex said.

"I know," she said. "Are you coming back?"

"I would like to come back," he said.

"When?"

"I don't know - it depends," he said.

"Well, maybe if you come back we can have dinner then," Simone said.

"Promise?" Alex asked.

"We'll see," She said.

Simone checked her watch. "It's been a lovely evening, but I really need to get some sleep."

"I'll walk you to your car," Alex said.

Alex felt like a schoolboy on his first date. Should he grab her and kiss her? Should he throw her over his shoulder and haul her off to the beach? Should he rip her clothes off? Should he grab her and throw her into the back seat of the car and jump in on top of her? Clearly, his mind had been warped by those Bunny Boy movies.

They reached Simone's car, which was parked next to the Orange Blossom Special.

"I could give you a ride home," Alex said, surprised to hear the words himself.

"I had a wonderful time, but I really need to go home and get some sleep," Simone said. And then, she leaned forward and kissed him gently on the lips. Before Alex could wrap his arms around her, she pulled back and got into her car.

"Are you going to help with the fundraiser tomorrow afternoon?" Simone asked.

"Yes, I'll see you there," Alex said.

He stood there for a moment, watching her taillights pull out of the parking lot. She had done it again. She had almost reached the point of surrendering to him, and then she had suddenly pulled away.

At first when he had met Simone he had kept most of that famous Alex Gideon charm bottled up, releasing only a small amount at a time so it would not overwhelm her. Now, however, he had been blasting her with both barrels and it didn't seem to phase her. He had come here to Okoboji to hide from Charlie and Heather Devreaux and the millions of fans who would faint at the mere touch of his hand. Now, when he had found the woman of his dreams, he did not have the power to coax anything more than a quick kiss on the lips from her. The tabloids would have fun with this story.

14

It was a clanging noise, coming from somewhere over there in the dark and it wouldn't stop. Alex crawled out of bed and groped for the light switch. Having found that, he could now see the phone sitting on the table. He checked his watch – it was eight thirty. He was reluctant to answer the phone. Hardly anyone knew he was here and he could think of no reason for any of them to be calling him at this time on a Sunday morning. But they were persistent and it appeared that they were not going to give up and go away. Probably Jeff and Dougherty calling for their new buddy, William.

"Hello," he said gingerly.

"Good morning," she said. It was the voice of an angel. "This is Simone."

"What's up?" he asked.

"I have a favor to ask of you – a big favor," she said.

"Anything," Alex said. "Just name it."

"Can you come down to the theater, right away?"

"Is something wrong? Are you okay?" he asked.

"I'm fine," Simone said. "I just need to ask a favor of you."

"I'll be there in forty-five minutes," Alex said.

He hung up the phone. That was strange, but it was wonderful. Simone needed someone to do her a favor and of all the people she knew in Okoboji she had called him, Alex Gideon.

Things were looking up, maybe.

Alex took a quick shower as the wheels turned in his mind. Maybe she wanted him to go pick up a donation from someone for the Save The Park fundraiser. Maybe something was wrong with her car. Maybe something needed to be fixed at the theater. Maybe something was wrong with his number one fan, Sally. There was no way to guess – he had to hurry and get to the theater to find out what Simone wanted him for – what she needed him for.

Alex took a minute of precious time to grab a newspaper from the vending machine and to glance through it for any stories on the disappearance of the Bunny Boy. He didn't have to look far – there on the front page of the Des Moines Register was his picture along with pictures of Charlie and Heather. The heading said "Ransom Demanded." The story went on to say that Mr. Gideon's manager, Charlie Waller, had received a ransom note the previous evening. Terms of the note were not discussed, but a "substantial amount of cash in unmarked bills" was demanded. Charlie was quoted extensively in the article, rehashing the same old crap about how Alex was like a son to him. Heather was widely quoted as well, babbling on about how close she and Alex were and how she missed him so much she couldn't sleep and that she was now under a doctor's care. The article ended with a quote from a Beverly Hills detective who said, "This ransom note is proof that Mr. Gideon is, in fact, the victim of foul play." Idiots. What a bunch of idiots.

Alex could hear Simone's voice coming from backstage as he entered the theater. She seemed to be talking to herself, pausing every now and then to gather her thoughts. When Alex got closer, he could tell that Simone was in the middle of a heated discussion with someone – a man - with a hoarse, raspy voice that was barely above a whisper.

"But, he can't act," the raspy voice said.

"I think he'll be able to handle it, just fine," Simone said.

"He'll never be able to learn the lines in time – it will be a flop," the raspy voice pleaded.

"Let me worry about that," Simone snapped.

"Okay, I wasn't going to tell you this, but he's a drug dealer – you don't want a drug dealer playing the lead in your play, do you?" the raspy voice said.

"He's no drug dealer – where did you get that crazy idea?" she asked.

"I can prove it," he said.

"Save your breath," Simone said.

Alex walked across the stage toward the voices, which were coming from Simone's office just past the women's dressing room. The door was open and Alex could see the back of the man that Simone was embroiled in discussion with. Simone saw Alex coming and glanced at him as he entered her office. The man with the raspy voice turned toward Alex – it was Filbert and he looked pale, worn, and beaten.

"I'm leaving," Filbert said to Simone in that hoarse, raspy voice, "but don't forget what I said." He shot Alex a vicious look as he stomped out of the office.

"Laryngitis?" Alex asked Simone.

"Too much lake water and too much big blonde," Simone said. "You're partly responsible for this, you know."

"I just sent the blonde his way and he took it from there. He could have walked away from her – I did, you might recall," Alex said.

"You're enjoying watching him suffer, aren't you?" Simone said.

"Well, I'll admit that Filbert isn't one of my favorite people. I think he's still mad because I got the part in the play instead of Peterson and he's jealous because I showed him up on the basketball court."

"Could be," Simone said, not venturing a guess of her own.

What Alex had really wanted to say is that Filbert views him as a rival for Simone's affections, but he had no evidence that Simone had any real affection for either one of them so he kept his mouth shut.

Alex looked around Simone's office. It was small, measuring maybe ten feet by twelve feet. Some of the producers Alex had worked with had bathrooms bigger than this in their offices. The walls were lined with framed photographs of people in costume. Undoubtedly, they were actors and actresses who had starred in plays here in the theater. There were posters, too, that had been used to publicize the plays. There was a row of shelves about eight feet high running the entire length of one wall that were stuffed with scripts and books on the theater and acting.

A photocopy machine sat on a small table two feet from Simone's desk and a computer sat on the desk. In the corner, mounted on the wall was a television set.

Alex was drawn to a framed photo a little larger than the rest. It was a handsome man and a beautiful woman staring into each other's eyes.

"George C. Scott," Simone said.

"And is that…"

"Martha," Simone said. "Wasn't she beautiful!"

"Yes," Alex said studying the photo. "Yes, she was beautiful, indeed – and she still is."

"That was taken in the 1950's – they were both in their mid twenties," Simone said. "They starred together and I have been told by people who saw them that they were magnificent."

"Were they lovers?" Alex asked.

"A lady doesn't tell," Simone answered.

"And a southern gentleman doesn't tell unless the lady does first – he was from Virginia, you know," Alex said.

"I know," Simone said. "Martha told me wonderful stories

about him."

"He passed away a few years ago," Alex said.

"Yes, in California. Martha grieved quietly for him," Simone said.

"Does her husband, John, know?" Alex asked.

"He knows they knew each other and that they starred in two plays together – I don't think he knows the rest," Simone said.

"Well, you had a favor to ask of me?" Alex asked, although he was sure he had already figured out what was coming.

"As you heard, Filbert has lost his voice and there's no doubt he won't get it back in time for tonight's performance. It's a lot to ask, but would you consider playing Filbert's role as Nathan tonight? You'd have a lot to learn in a short time – I know I'm really putting you on the spot," Simone said.

"Do you think I can do it?" Alex asked. He was fishing for compliments and praise. He knew darn well he could do it. He was, after all, a famous movie star.

"Yes, you can do it, but we'll have to get started quickly," she said.

"Who will play the part of William?" Alex asked.

"Eric is on his way back from Illinois – he'll be here late this afternoon. He'll play William, if you'll play Nathan. You know, Nathan is really a better character to play than William – the role has more depth," Simone said.

"I liked playing William because he ends up getting the girl," Alex said with a smile.

"It's only a play," Simone said. "Nathan's role is juicier. You'll have fun with it."

What Simone said was true. Actors loved playing the part of the mean, evil, villain and actresses loved playing the part of a woman who was a real bitch, mostly because it gave them a chance to play themselves in public and to get paid for it.

"I'll do it on one condition," Alex said with a little smile.

181

"That's blackmail," Simone answered.

"You know what the condition is, don't you?" he asked.

"I have an idea, but go ahead, let me hear it," Simone said.

"Dinner for two, tomorrow night," Alex said.

"You drive a hard bargain," she said.

"Then it's a deal?" Alex asked as he stuck his hand out for a handshake to seal it.

"Deal," Simone said as she raised her eyebrows and sighed as she shook Alex's hand.

"You've seen the play three times - once in the audience and twice as William, right?" Simone asked.

"Right," Alex answered.

"So, you understand the role pretty well. Even though Filbert can be a jerk, he's a good actor and he played the part well. You, of course, can bring your own interpretation to the role – don't try to be Filbert."

"Don't worry - I will not try to be Filbert. But, is there any way that Nathan can get the girl in the end?" Alex asked.

"William gets the girl – don't try to rewrite my play," Simone said. "Now, we'd better get started. William had eighteen lines in the play, Nathan has fifty-four. We have our work cut out for us."

Simone gave Alex a script for the play. Nathan's lines were highlighted with a marker.

"Why don't you go sit in a corner somewhere for a couple of hours and study your lines," Simone said. "Then this afternoon, you and I can rehearse. Almost all of Nathan's lines involve Savanna, so we won't need to rehearse with the rest of the cast."

That was music to Alex's ears. He would be alone with Simone for the entire afternoon. He would learn his lines well, but not too well. He would milk this rehearsal for all that he could.

Footsteps were rapidly approaching from the hallway outside

of Simone's office. Alex turned to see Sally coming at a near trot.

"Did you hear? Did you hear the news?" she asked, almost out of breath.

"What happened?" Simone asked.

Alex braced himself.

"Alex Gideon's slimy manager, that Charlie Waller, said he received a ransom note for a lot of money. They said on the news that it proves that he has met with foul play. But it also means that he's still alive, doesn't it? Kidnappers always keep their victim alive, don't they – so they have something to bargain with?" Sally was trying to convince herself as much as anyone.

"I think that's the way it works," Alex said. "Don't worry – his manager's got a lot of money and he'll pay the ransom and your Alex Gideon will be home safe in a day or two."

"Did you ever wonder," Simone began with a smile playing on her lips, "how such a wonderful guy like Alex Gideon ever got tied up with such a sleazy manager like that Charlie Waller?"

"I've been thinking that, too," Sally said wistfully.

"I understand that Charlie Waller discovered Alex Gideon when he was a nobody and when he was also green and dumb," Alex said. "He signed Gideon to a ten-year contract. I'd guess that Gideon realizes that his manager is a sleazeball but that he feels loyalty to him and that he'll honor his contract."

"That makes sense," Sally said. "Alex would be smart enough to realize his manager's a slimeball, but he'd be too loyal to fire him. Alex Gideon is simply too good of a person for his own good."

Alex couldn't agree more.

"Sally, Filbert has come down with laryngitis and Al has agreed to play the part of Nathan tonight," Simone said.

"I'll bet it was the big blonde that caused his laryngitis," Sally said.

"Well, whatever caused it, he's got it, and that's that. Eric is coming back to play William tonight," Simone said.

Sally looked at Alex. "I'll miss having you as William. You were a very good William. But, you'll be a good Nathan, too, and we'll get to play several scenes together. Now, I'd better get out of here and let you rehearse."

"Let us know if you hear anything more about Alex Gideon," Simone yelled after her.

"I will," Sally yelled back.

"She doesn't need encouragement," Alex said.

"Do you think they'll pay the ransom?" Simone asked.

"If it comes from Charlie Waller's pocket – no. If it comes from Alex Gideon's pocket – yes," Alex answered.

Simone was smiling. She had to know. But, Alex was not about to ask her, just in case she didn't.

Alex took the script and went to the back row of the theater. He had a lot to learn. The pressure was on. Playing the supporting role of William had been perfect. He had only eighteen lines to learn and he got the girl at the end of the play. Playing the lead as Nathan was an entirely different matter. He had three times as many lines to learn and the part called for much more emotion. As the Bunny Boy, he had played the part of a happy-go-lucky, upbeat, who-gives-a-shit voyeur who chased half naked women around in an hour and a half movie. As Nathan, he would need to transform himself into a mean, lowdown, doublecrossing, self-serving son-of-a-bitch. In real life, Alex's disposition was a lot closer to the Bunny Boy than it was to Nathan. He had a lot of work to do.

The afternoon rehearsal with Simone was wonderful – Alex had her all to himself. He had learned his lines, reasonably well, in only three hours of intensive study. That had pleased Simone. Now, they were working on his delivery. When Alex had rehearsed the part of William with Simone two days earlier, he had purposefully pretended to be a novice actor to extend his rehearsal time alone with Simone. Today, though, he wasn't pretending. The role was a stretch for him. Maybe if he pretended to be Filbert it would help.

Simone had been right. The part of Nathan, the evil, conniving, double-crossing fiancé was a meaty role that was great fun to play. But the best part was that he got to hug Savanna three times during the play. He'd trade the ending scene where she jumped into William's arms for the three hugs any day.

They had been rehearsing for three hours when Sally charged in, breathless. "Turn on the TV. There's going to be a big announcement. I just heard it on my car radio."

Simone and Alex followed Sally to the office. Sally already had the TV turned on and was nervously awaiting the news.

There he was again, Peter Jenkins. "We have shocking news in the Alex Gideon disappearance. Our news staff is finalizing the story as I speak. I will return with details after this commercial message."

"No, No," Sally screamed. "He can't be dead."

Alex put his arm around her. "He's not dead – just wait and see what they say."

Peter Jenkins returned. "We go live to Beverly Hills where an announcement will be made by the detective in charge of the investigation into the disappearance of actor Alex Gideon."

The same detective who had announced that Alex's safe was empty appeared on the screen. "The Beverly Hills Police Department, in cooperation with the LAPD and the FBI, has made a major breakthrough in the disappearance of Alex Gideon." He paused as he glanced at his notes.

This was perhaps the tenth time that Alex had braced himself for the news that would blow him out of the Okoboji waters. He was ready — let it come.

The detective continued, "Just moments ago Mr. Gideon's manager, Charles N. Waller, and Mary Ann Smith, better known as actress Heather Devreaux, were arrested on charges of conspiracy in the disappearance of Alex Gideon. An analysis of the ransom note that Mr. Waller provided to investigators yesterday was found to have been written by Mr. Waller himself. Additional investigation revealed that while Mr. Waller had signed a contract to be the exclusive agent of Alex Gideon, he was also secretly the agent for Ms. Devreaux. Investigators became suspicious of Ms. Devreaux, who claimed to be secretly engaged to Mr. Gideon, when it was learned that their only contact was when he escorted her one time - to the Academy Awards. Investigators also learned that on that night Mr. Gideon sent Ms. Devreaux home alone in the limo while he took a taxi to his own home. Ms. Devreaux's continual claims that she was in deep mourning to the extent that she needed to be under a doctor's care aroused the suspicion of the investigators. As Queen Gertrude said in Hamlet, 'The Lady doth protest too much, methinks.'"

"We will be back with Peter Jenkins in a moment, after these messages," a voice said as the station cut away for a commercial break.

"My, a cop who doth quote Shakespeare," Simone said with a laugh.

"That's Beverly Hills," Sally said.

Alex was stunned. Charlie was secretly Heather Devreaux's agent. So that's why Charlie insisted that he escort Heather Devreaux — it was to create publicity for *her*, not him. And then it hit Alex like a sledgehammer — by representing Heather Devreaux, Charlie had broken his exclusive contract with him. He was free. Free at last!

"Mary Ann Smith! She isn't a Frenchwoman, after all," Simone said as she laughed and slapped her knee.

"I just knew she was a phony. I knew she was only doing it as a publicity stunt. And, you were right," she continued, looking at Alex, "he sent her home alone from the Academy Awards."

"Like I told you," Alex said, looking at Sally but really speaking to Simone, "he wouldn't fall for an air-headed idiot like her. He would want a woman who was intelligent, and hard-working, and respectable, and talented, and grounded, and ..."

"Someone like Simmy, in other words," Sally said.

"Exactly," Alex said, "someone like Simone."

He glanced at Simone. She simply scoffed and looked away. Most likely she had heard it all before dozens of times from tourists in Okoboji and from professors on the make in Arizona.

Peter Jenkins was back. "Our affiliate in Los Angeles has provided us with exclusive film footage of the arrest today of Mr. Waller and Ms. Devreaux."

Charlie was the first one on the screen. He was wearing a black shirt, tan slacks, and tennis shoes – no power suit, no necktie, no black patent leather shoes, no gold chains, and no gold bracelets. The only bracelets he was wearing were handcuffs. He looked so weak, so frail. Alex almost felt sorry for him. Almost.

Next, they showed Heather Devreaux being led away in handcuffs. If they hadn't said it was Heather, Alex would not have recognized her. The long cotton-like blonde hair was gone and was replaced by a short, dishwater blonde disheveled mess. The eyelashes were gone, the long fingernails were gone. The boobs were still there, though. They may be store-boughts, but they were still there. They again cut away for a commercial break. If Charlie were there, he'd probably ask them for fifteen percent of the money the TV station collected from commercials – after all, he had created this program. But then, he was-

187

n't there, was he!

The silliness of the whole thing hit Alex all at once – millions of women around the world lusting for him while he was in Okoboji trying to romance a woman who didn't seem to want anything to do with him, Charlie writing a ransom note and getting caught at it, Charlie and Heather heading to jail in handcuffs, and Alex being free from Charlie at last.

He began to laugh. And he laughed, he howled, and he laughed some more – split-your-sides, in-stitches, tears-running-down-your-face laughter. He laughed so hard that his jaw hurt.

Finally, he stopped. Simone and Sally just sat there, staring at him.

"Are you okay?" Simone said. There was genuine concern in her voice.

"I'm fine," Alex said, laughing again. "I'm great. Everything's wonderful."

Peter Jenkins was back. "According to Beverly Hills detectives, the investigation continues. And there is one remaining question – just where is Alex Gideon?"

"Where do you think he is?" Sally asked Alex.

"Like I've said all along, I think he's off somewhere with friends. I think he's safe and happy, and no one has anything to worry about."

"Then you don't suspect foul play like they're always talking about on TV?" Sally asked hopefully.

"No, I don't. I think he's off on vacation in some remote part of the country, totally oblivious to this whole situation," Alex said.

"You're so wise," Sally said. "Sometimes I think you understand Alex Gideon better than he understands himself."

188

It was back – that rubbery knee, shortness of breath, cotton-mouth, heart pounding, dizzy sensation known as stage fright. Perhaps he had been too cavalier in his quest to be the shining knight, rescuing the damsel, Simone, from distress. Perhaps he had allowed his heart to do his thinking instead of his head. Perhaps he was in over his head this time – after all, he was a movie star, not an actor. Perhaps he would be lucky enough to have a heart attack before they opened the curtains. Perhaps he should run, now. Perhaps…

"You'll do just fine," she said, touching him lightly on the arm.

"Some guys will do anything to get a dinner date," Alex said weakly.

And then Simone gave him a quick kiss on the cheek. "For luck," she said.

They all joined hands behind the curtain and silently bowed their heads. Alex prayed harder than he could ever remember. No, he wasn't asking for a brilliant performance. No, he wasn't asking to be the shining star of this production. No, he wasn't even asking for the girl of his dreams. All he wanted was to survive.

"Let's make some magic," Simone said as everyone got into position.

Alex had always believed in miracles – tonight he would rely upon one.

Somewhere off in the distance someone was playing "Oh! Susanna" on the piano. Somebody opened the curtains and there were thousands of beady eyes staring at the stage. There were horses walking and whinnying, somewhere in the building. Familiar words were coming from over there – words that he should be speaking, but it was from someone else, "It was a pleasure, Miss Marion. Say hello to your daddy – and to Savanna, too."

Now he was standing there looking at a beautiful southern

189

belle. Words flowed from his mouth but they weren't coming from him, they were coming from someone else - from a smooth, charming gentleman with a slow southern drawl. "Miss Savanna, it is my pleasure, indeed, to call upon you this morning. And, Miss Marion, why, you're so all grown up I hardly recognized you. In just these few short months you have been away, you have been transformed from a girl into a lovely young woman."

"Oh, Nathan, you say the kindest things," she said in a southern drawl with a hint of eastern accent.

And now, they were all lined up in a row taking a bow as the audience was on their feet, applauding wildly.

Alex shook his head. This was the curtain call. This is what happened at the end of the play – after the play was over. The play had gone by in a flash. It was almost like he had undergone an out-of-body experience, where Nathan had inhabited his body and he had observed from above. And, from what he had observed, Nathan had not played a part in this play – he had, in fact, been there on that plantation in the 1850's, living it.

Alex felt a metamorphosis take place as he was now being transformed from a smooth, charming southern scoundrel named Nathan back into Alex Gideon.

Simone took Alex by the hand and stepped forward. The applause grew louder. Together, they bowed to the audience. They now were screaming, whistling, and yelling "Bravo," and "Encore."

Simone motioned for the crowd to quiet down. It took nearly a minute, but they finally stopped clapping and settled into their seats.

"Our guest professional actor, Filbert Kauffman, has so ably played the role of Nathan for all of the performances of *Sisterly Love* until tonight, when he was unable to perform because of laryngitis. At eight thirty this morning I placed a call to Al, asking

190

if he would play the role of Nathan tonight. In just one short day he not only learned the part of Nathan, but he became Nathan."

Simone stepped to the side several feet and swung her arm toward Alex, offering him to the audience. And then she curtsied to him, as a proper southern belle would.

The crowd was on their feet again, clapping, screaming, yelling, whistling, and stamping their feet. He bowed slightly, applauded the audience in return and spread his arms to them. He didn't know if this was proper theater etiquette, but it felt right. The crowd applauded, hooted, and hollered even louder.

This was a true, honest, unadulterated review, directly from the audience and not from some half-crazed critic who made a living by hacking up movies and actors and hiding behind some column in a newspaper. Maybe he *could* act, after all.

Alex couldn't help but think of Charlie. If he were here, Charlie would do two things. First, he would faint. Second, when he recovered, he'd want that fifteen percent. Alex was going to miss Charlie, but he had a feeling he'd get over it.

Alex was on a roll. The crowd was on its feet wildly applauding him. The cast was behind him applauding, and Simone was off to his left applauding him. He relished this moment. After all, this might be the one and only time he'd ever star in a live theater production. He turned to Simone and bowed. She curtsied. Then, in three quick steps he reached her. He swooped her up in his arms, and carried her off the stage as she flung her head back, laughing, kicking her legs, and waving to the crowd. It was a fitting grand finale to this fabulous play that had been performed in the Okoboji Lakeside Theater. The crowd went nuts - it was like throwing gasoline on a raging fire.

Alex carried Simone off the stage and into the wing. She was still laughing. It was an emotional release as much as anything. Twelve hours ago, it had appeared that the final performance of *Sisterly Love* would be a disaster. Instead, it had been an awesome climax for the play's week long run.

Alex held Simone in his arms for a moment. He gazed into her eyes – they glistened with excitement.

"Thank you, very much. That was a fabulous performance," Simone said.

And then he kissed her. A sweet, gentle, loving kiss fully on the lips. She returned his passion for a moment before she pulled away. Alex slowly lowered his arm, placing her feet on the floor.

"I have work to do," Simone said, as she headed for the stage to make her final Save The Park fundraising appeal. Just before she reached the curtain, she turned to Alex and said, "Wait for me."

She didn't have to ask.

Alex was an expert at being the recipient of fan adulation. A big part of the reason he had come here to Okoboji, heavily disguised, was to escape those clinging arms and grabby fingers that wanted to take a piece of him home for themselves. Now, as he mingled with the crowd, passing the hat for the fundraiser, they were touching, feeling, and hugging him. But, they were giving to him – giving thanks, warmth, support, friendship, and love – they weren't taking of him for themselves.

Martha hugged him tightly and brushed away several tears from her cheeks. "That was a wonderful performance by Simmy and you," she said. "It reminded me so very much of a performance by a handsome actor and his leading lady on this very stage many, many years ago." And then she hugged him again, more tightly this time, as the tears again trickled down her cheeks. Alex had all he could do to keep from joining her.

They were shouting from the dressing rooms again, "Wrap party at The Ritz." "Wrap party at The Ritz." "Wrap party at the Ritz."

This time Alex didn't have to ask. He had been to plenty of

wrap parties when the filming of a movie had ended and they had been wonderful, wild, crazy, emotional events. After working closely on location for maybe two or three months, focused on the singular goal of creating an art form known as a movie, the cast and crew forms a bond and becomes a family. Then, suddenly, it's over – the movie is finished, the family breaks up, and everyone goes their separate ways. The wrap party is a time for sharing stories and for reliving memories. It is a time for congratulating one another and for offering appreciation for each other's contributions. It is a time for releasing all of the tensions and frustrations that might have built up over the past months and for repairing any relationships that might have become strained. It is a time for fun and, it is a time for partying. And, often, it was a time for one last fling.

Most of the cast and crew were part of the theater for the entire summer, so they would wrap up this play tonight and start rehearsing for the next one tomorrow. At the end of the summer, when the ten-week season was over, they would have the mother of all wrap parties.

Alex's theater career had been a short one, consisting of three performances. Yet, he felt like a veteran of the Okoboji Lakeside Theater. He felt like a part of it, like he really belonged.

Weeks ago, the parts had been cast for the new play that the troupe would begin rehearsing tomorrow. There would be no role in it for Alex Gideon. That would be okay with him – he had played the lead tonight and had brought down the house. He had proven that he was more than a movie star – he was an actor. His work had been scrutinized by hundreds of critics this night and they had rendered their overwhelming approval. That was enough for him - for now.

He looked forward to the wrap party. It might be his last time to be a true part of this group that he had come to admire and love. Soon, he would need to return to Beverly Hills to straighten out the mess that was getting worse by the day. He knew that the tabloids would not rest until they discovered where he had been for the week of his "disappearance." Alex had not decided if he would tell the world that he had been in Okoboji or if he would make the reporters figure it out on their own. At any rate, there would come a time when it became known that he had been here, in Okoboji, and that he had performed in the Okoboji Lakeside Theater. Perhaps fifty years from now, some elderly woman would tell a young upstart that she had seen Alex Gideon, a famous movie star of the day, perform right here at the Okoboji Lakeside Theater. He wondered if it would bring tears to her eyes.

"You never asked," Big Teddy said.

"Asked what?" Alex asked.

"Asked if 'everyone' is going to the wrap party – she always does," Big Teddy said with a grin.

Alex waited on the stage for Simone. Most of the troupe had already left for The Ritz when she appeared wearing a light blue blouse with a sailboat on the front, khakis, and dark blue tennis shoes. She looked fabulous. It was impossible for her to look anything but.

"Going to the wrap party?" he asked.

"I never miss a wrap party," Simone answered. "But, I can't stay long – tomorrow's the last day of the fundraiser and we have to start early."

They walked from the theater with their arms around each other. Alex thought back to when he had first met Simone. It seemed like two or three months ago, but it had been just three days. He had made a lot of progress in that short time, but his days in Okoboji were numbered and he had a long ways to go.

The Orange Blossom Special and Simone's Mercedes were parked side by side. Before Alex could offer to give her a ride, she said "I'll meet you there," as she pulled her keys from her purse and headed for her car.

The progress that Alex was making with Simone reminded him of the oft-used phrase, "One step forward and two steps back." Perhaps after the Save The Park fundraiser was over tomorrow, she would relax and would have more time for her personal life.

Cars were parked two-deep in Alex's reserved parking spot at the Four Seasons Resort, so he ended up parking six blocks from The Ritz. By the time Alex got there, the wrap party was well underway on the outdoor deck overlooking the lake. Simone and a dozen others were sitting at a large round table and others in the troupe mingled with friends on the deck and inside the building. As Alex stepped out of The Ritz and onto the deck, the entire troupe broke into applause. It was a tradition at a movie wrap party for the cast and crew to applaud the stars when they entered, but he never expected it here. He was humbled by the experience.

The table was packed, but Big Teddy commandeered an extra plastic deck chair from a nearby table and everyone scooted around to make room for Alex next to Simone. It appeared that everyone in the troupe considered the two of them to be an item, or maybe they were just bent on helping Alex out.

It was a beautiful eighty-five-degree night and the full moon glistened on the lake. The night was still and people could be heard singing, laughing, and partying in boats that slowly motored by.

The conversation was lighthearted, rehashing the week's performances of *Sisterly Love* and catching up on the latest Okoboji gossip. This would be no time for Alex to make any moves on Simone, so he would just enjoy being next to her and being part of the group.

Alex was relieved that Sally was preoccupied with a University of Iowa football player who had come up from Iowa City to see her in the play. Hopefully, she would not be keeping an eye on the television set, waiting for late-breaking news about "the disappearance," as it had become known.

Filbert was across the table from Alex. His voice was getting better and he even croaked a feeble "Good job," to Alex.

The big blonde was nowhere in sight. Groupies were often like that – curious to see what it would be like being with a star, and then, afterwards, putting a check mark next to their name in their little book, and moving on, looking for bigger fish to fry. It is said you can't own people, but you can rent them for a while. And the big blonde had rented the semi-famous actor, Filbert Kauffman for one night.

A tall, striking brunette who was introduced to Alex as Taylor, the owner of The Ritz, delivered three large pizzas to the troupe's table. "I heard you did really good in the play tonight," she said to Alex. He had heard that word travels fast in a small town, but he wouldn't have believed how fast if he hadn't experienced it first hand. And, this was with good news. Bad news would probably travel faster than the speed of light.

The pizzas were great and they were on the house, besides. No wonder they loved coming to The Ritz for their wrap parties.

"Are you going to work the phones tomorrow?" Simone asked Alex.

"Yes, what time are we starting?" he asked.

"Seven o'clock," she said. "Well, that's when I'm starting, you can come any time you want – you're supposed to be on vacation, remember?"

Alex had planned to invite Simone to meet him at Arnolds Perk for a cup of coffee and a scotcheroo before starting work on the fundraiser – but, not if they were going to start work like this in the middle of the night.

Simone rose from her chair. "Everyone," she said, "thank you for your tremendous efforts and memorable performances in

Sisterly Love. Filbert, and Al, thank you for being my leading men. Tomorrow's our final day to save The Park, and we're starting early so I'm going to go get some sleep. Big Teddy is directing next week's play and he'll fill you in about rehearsal times. I'll drop by tomorrow afternoon and see how things are going."

Alex rose and joined her as she left the deck and walked into The Ritz.

"Nathan, Nathan," someone shouted from a table off to Alex's left. He didn't even have to turn around, he knew. He made his way over to them and was greeted with hearty handshakes and hugs from Jeff and Dougherty.

"Loved the play tonight," Dougherty said.

"You were fabulous, Nathan," Jeff said.

It took some doing, but he finally broke away from them after promising that he'd let them buy him a drink next time he saw them. Simone was easy to find – she hadn't moved more than three feet. Everybody in the place seemed to know Simone and everyone wanted to hug her or talk to her, so it took about fifteen minutes to get out of there. Simone again introduced him as "my friend," to at least two dozen people.

Alex looked forward to a slow, romantic five- or six-block walk in the moonlight to her car with Simone. However, two of Simone's friends, Scott and Cherie, own a condo at The Crossings next to The Ritz and invited her to use their guest parking spot any time she wanted. That resulted in a quick half-block hand-in-hand walk in the moonlight.

"Where would you like to have dinner tomorrow night?" Alex asked.

"You haven't given up on that idea?" she asked.

"You promised – a deal's a deal," He answered.

"Well, if you're going to insist, how about Bob's Drive-Inn?" she asked.

"I hear Bob's is great, but I was thinking about somewhere a

197

little bit more, well, formal," Alex replied.

"Well, you're buying, you decide," Simone said.

"How about dinner at six thirty?" he asked.

"Six thirty will be fine," she answered.

They reached Simone's car. She looked fabulous in the bright moonlight. As if on cue, they moved toward each other simultaneously and held each other tight as they shared their first long, passionate kiss. And then they kissed again.

"That was nice," Simone said softly, "but I must go - I'll see you in the morning."

As she drove away, Alex thought back. He could not recall a night in his entire life that was as fantastic as this one had been. And beside that, they had given him a standing ovation at the theater.

15

There were not many days in the past eight years that Alex had seen six a.m. At the end of a night sometimes, yes, but not as the start of a day - no way. But here he was, wide-awake and heading for the shower with a bounce in his step, a twinkle in his eye, and a song on his lips.

Alex was almost afraid to take a look at the Des Moines Register. He was tired of seeing stories about "the disappearance" and was sick of seeing his picture on the front page. Maybe now that Charlie and Heather had been found out, it would stop. That was the great thing about being a celebrity – no matter how bad you screwed things up, somebody would always come along in a week or two and screw things up twice as bad and become the center of attention while you drifted out of sight.

Alex had no trouble believing that Charlie had devised that ransom note scam to fan the flames of publicity, but he was surprised that he had been stupid enough to actually go through with it. Through the years, Charlie had come up with a dozen harebrained ideas to create publicity but Alex had always talked him out of them. There was the time, for instance, that Charlie wanted to announce that Alex had a mysterious disease that might be fatal, which later on would be miraculously cured by some Indian Guru. Another time he wanted to tip off the tabloids that Alex had impregnated three of the biggest female Hollywood movie stars on the same night. Another time, he wanted to wait until a small plane crashed in some remote area and then claim that Alex might have been onboard, only to have Alex appear somewhere a couple of weeks later. And still another time he wanted to pay a psychic to say that Alex had lived in a previous life and had been Marilyn Monroe's lover. Apparently, this time, he ran the idea of the ransom note past Heather, the genius, and she thought it was brilliant.

It was obvious to Alex that when he disappeared suddenly, Charlie could not resist the temptation to take it and run with it. So in a sense, Alex may have been partly to blame for Charlie's predicament.

Good news. There was no story or picture on the front page. Alex flipped through the newspaper. There it was on page four – a picture of Charlie and Heather leaving jail with their lawyers, out on bond. Predictably, Charlie's lawyers said they would sue the Beverly Hills Police Department, the LAPD, the FBI, the Governor, the television stations, Peter Jenkins, and a half dozen other people.

Charlie's story was that he was setting a trap for the people who had abducted his good friend and client, Alex Gideon, and he was about to spring it on them when the police muddled in and screwed everything up. In most cities around the country, you'd get laughed out of court with a tale like that. In Beverly Hills, though, it was a lead pipe cinch to win.

Heather Devreaux looked like Heather Devreaux again – big hair, long eyelashes, long fingernails, big boobs. Her lawyer tried to shut her up but there were reporters and cameras everywhere and they drew her like a magnet. She, too, was going to sue everyone in sight, particularly the liar who said that Alex Gideon had sent her home alone in the limo from the Academy Awards while he took a taxi home. The real story, she said, is

200

that Alex had sent a lookalike decoy off in the taxi while he hid in the trunk of the limo for the ride to Heather's home. When they got to Heather's mansion, she and Alex had made mad, passionate love for seven hours nonstop during which they had performed a somersault. She finished by saying, "Can you imagine anyone sending me home alone in a limo while they took a taxi in the other direction?"

Alex had to admit her argument made a lot of sense. One of the most important possessions a woman can have is her reputation, and Heather Devreaux was doing her best to save hers.

The story concluded by saying that the disappearance of Alex Gideon was still a mystery and that police were still investigating. Alex could sense that the story was starting to cool off. That was fine with him.

Alex arrived at the Maritime Museum at two minutes before seven and found Simone already there along with a dozen other volunteers, working the phones. She smiled when he walked in, like she was really glad to see him. She walked up to him and gave him a hug and a quick kiss on the lips, right there in front of the whole world. It was worth getting up at six o'clock.

"We're at nine million, four hundred thousand," Simone said.

"One million, six to go," Alex stated.

"It's a long shot," she said, "but we're going to try right up until the last minute."

"How about getting an extension of a week or two on your deadline?" Alex asked.

"We already tried that," Simone said. "There will be no extension."

Alex grabbed a phone that was ringing – it was a donation of $100. In the next two hours he fielded donations of $250, $50, $1,000, $500, $50, $750, $20, $10, $100, $500, and $2,500. That was a lot of money, totaling nearly six thousand dollars. Again, he did some mental mathematics – if each of the twelve phones averaged what he did, they would take in a total of about $35,000 an hour. In the ten hours today they would take in about three hundred fifty thousand dollars. That's a bundle for one day – but still over a million short. But, they were still working the outgoing calls, also. Perhaps they would find one of those angels they had been talking about – an angel with deep pockets.

"I need to run an errand," Alex said to Simone. "I'll be back in a half hour or so."

Simone patted his hand and smiled. "Hurry back," she said.

Big Teddy had said that Wellington's-on-the-Water, located next to the Central Emporium, was rated by *Food and Beverage* magazine as one of the top three restaurants in the state and nothing but the best was good enough for his Simone.

Alex decided to take a quick walk through the Central Emporium on his way to Wellington's, just to check things out. It was a quarter to eleven and the shops were buzzing. Cindy Fred and Bev waved as he walked by the Funhouse Gallery and a couple of other shop owners waved as well. He didn't know if they were just being Midwestern friendly or if they recognized him from the theater. Either way, the friendly smiles were appreciated.

Alex opened the heavy door to Wellington's and walked in. The far wall and both sidewalls were solid glass providing a panoramic view of West Lake Okoboji. He had eaten at many renowned seaside restaurants in California, Florida, and the gulf coast and this view would rival any of them. Yes, this would be the perfect place to take Simone to dinner.

A slight man, maybe five feet nine, weighing one hundred thirty pounds, approached Alex. "What can I do for you?" he asked.

I'm looking for the manager," Alex said.

"What do you want him for?" he asked quickly. He was an intense man, wound as tight as a piano wire.

"I'd like to make a dinner reservation," Alex said.

"I'm the manager; James is my name," he said as he grabbed the reservations book. "For when do you want the reservation?"

"Six thirty, tonight," Alex said.

"Absolutely impossible – out of the question," James said as he slapped shut the reservations book.

Alex had been through this routine many times before in posh restaurants all over the country. He looked James in the eyes and directed his gaze down to his hand, which held a fifty-dollar bill. "Is there any possibility you could squeeze us in, somewhere?" Alex asked.

James stared at the fifty. Alex could see that his wheels were spinning, desperately trying to come up with something. Alex had already found that these Okobojians liked cash – but this guy worshipped it.

Suddenly James said, "Can't do it."

Alex could see that this dilemma had caused James excruciating mental anguish – he would have given anything for that fifty-dollar bill, but there was, in fact, no room in the inn.

"If you want me to, I'll check with another fine restaurant on the lake, Crescent Beach, to see if they have room for tonight," James said.

"I'd appreciate that," Alex said as James dialed the number.

"And who would the reservation be for?" James asked.

"Simone Delaney and Al..."

James slammed down the phone. "Simmy? Are you taking Simmy to dinner? Doc?" he asked.

"Yes," Alex replied, "Simone from the Lakeside Theater."

"Why didn't you say so?" James asked as he grabbed his reservations book and studied the evening's reservations. "I could move the Tiefenthalers to that table, the Hirschs to that table, the Langes to that table, the McMahons to that table, the Klohs to that table, the Throwers to that table, the McHughs to that

203

table and the O'Donoghues to that table - and I could move those people down into the basement. It'll work. Be here at six thirty – your table will be ready."

"Thank you very much," Alex said as he turned to leave.

"One more thing," James said.

"Yes?" Alex asked.

He stuck his hand out, "The fifty," he said.

"Of course," Alex said as he forked it over. Yup, this was just about the way it worked at posh restaurants everywhere.

Alex could hear James talking to himself as the door closed behind him, "Guess who's coming to dinner – Simmy!"

They had raised about twenty thousand dollars in Alex's half-hour absence, including one donation of ten thousand.

The volunteers worked through the lunch hour and the numbers continued to mount on the tote board. There had been several donations of over twenty-five thousand and one of an even hundred grand. It was a fabulous outpouring of support, but as one of the volunteers had told Alex the previous day, too much money to raise in too little time.

It was four o'clock – one hour to go. The incoming calls had been reduced to a trickle and most of the volunteers were making outbound calls, trying desperately to stumble across some big donor that they had somehow overlooked. The reality of the situation was starting to set in. They had fought a valiant battle, but the odds had been too great, yet, there was still hope and they dialed feverishly.

"I need to go verify our dinner reservations – it was kind of an iffy situation," Alex said to Simone.

"Take your time," she said. She was trying her best to keep a stiff upper lip, but Alex could see that she, too, had finally come

204

face to face with the reality of the situation.

Alex hurried down the corridor of the Central Emporium, past the shops that had now become familiar to him. He stopped at the Sugar Shack and got ten dollars in quarters. He hurried down the steps to the second floor and rushed to the side entrance. He had remembered correctly, but some teenage boy was on the phone trying to impress some sweet little thing on the other end. Alex looked at him in desperation. The kid turned away and kept on talking. This could go on for hours. Alex walked up to him and held out a twenty. "I need to make a quick call," Alex said.

The kid stared at the bill and then looked into Alex's eyes. He saw nothing but desperation. "Make it forty," he said. The lad had all the makings of one day becoming a fine, upstanding Okoboji businessman.

Alex forked over the money and the kid handed over the phone. Alex deposited a fistful of quarters and dialed a number from memory.

"Winthrop Investment Services," a familiar voice said on the other end.

"I vould like to shpeek vit Missh Vinntrop," Alex said with a thick German accent that sounded more like Henry Kissinger than Kissinger did himself. Alex could talk like this all day long if he had to, for he was, after all, the star of that fabulous movie, *Bilingual Bunny*.

"I'm sorry, but Miss Winthrop is in a meeting, may I take a message?" she asked.

"Dish ish an emerrrgancy. I musht shpeek vit Missh Vinntrop immeediatchtely," Alex said.

"I'm sorry, she cannot be disturbed," she said.

If Alex had spoken in his normal voice the receptionist, Annie, would have recognized him immediately. Then she would have fainted. Then she would have recovered and would

205

have run into the street yelling "Alex Gideon is alive," and he couldn't have that – not quite yet. When this was all over, he would apologize to his good friend and number one fan – well, number two fan, behind Sally – and they would have a good laugh over it.

"Vait!" Alex exclaimed. "I haff a fiffty millyun dohlar accouwant dat I vant to placsh vit Missh Vintrop. She mayh beh verry dishappointed vit youh if youh forcsh meh to goh elshvare vit myh mohney."

"Okay, just a moment, I will interrupt her," Annie said.

Alex checked his watch. This was taking forever. Maybe she really was in a meeting.

Barbara Winthrop had been a promising actress a dozen years ago but had walked away from the business just when it looked like she was about to break out and become a major star. She simply did not want the pressures and demands of stardom. She wanted a real life rather than the type of artificial life lived by so many stars.

In addition to being fabulously beautiful, Barbara was smart and she had become a financial advisor. Since she was well connected in the entertainment industry, it was easy for her to develop a client list that resembled a Who's Who of the Rich and Famous. And, she was fiercely loyal to her clients, was discreet, and kept all transactions strictly confidential. Charlie was quick to point out that he was responsible for making Alex rich, and that was true. But, it was Barbara Winthrop who had made Alex fabulously rich. Barbara was the only woman Alex had ever met, before Simone, that he had a true romantic interest in. She was beautiful, she was smart, she was witty, she was fun. And, she was also committed to keeping her relationships with her clients strictly on a business level and was determined not to get romantically involved with anyone even remotely connected with the show business she had abandoned. Even so, she and

Alex had almost been lovers once, but had stopped before she broke her code of noninvolvement. They could laugh about it now and Barbara remained his financial advisor and one of his closest personal friends.

"Hello, this is Barbara Winthrop," she said.

"Missh Vintrop, pleash tellh youhr resheptionisht to hangh up dah phoneh," Alex said, knowing that Annie would be curious enough to eavesdrop.

"Annie, you can hang up the phone now," she yelled and Alex could hear a click.

"Nowh, siht dowhn und don't shay a vord abouwt vat I amh abouwt to shay," he said.

Barbara followed his directions. She was accustomed to dealing with eccentric celebrities and billionaires and had learned to roll with the punches.

"Doh not shay a vord or makeh ah shound - but this is an old friend of yours," Alex said, switching back to his normal voice.

"It's you! It's really you!" she screamed.

"Shhh," Alex said, "I told you to be quiet."

"Are you okay?" Barbara asked.

"I'm fine, why do you ask?" Alex asked.

"You don't know?" Barbara asked.

"Know what?" Alex asked, leading her on.

"The whole country is looking for you – the whole world – where have you been?" She asked.

"I have no idea what you're talking about," Alex said, but I have something I want you to do...."

Alex returned to the Maritime Museum at twenty to five. The volunteers were still valiantly trying to find an angel or two that would swoop down and save The Park in these dying moments of the campaign, but it was looking like a lost cause.

"Reservations are all set - six thirty," Alex said to Simone.

"Good," she said, but Alex could see that dinner was the last thing on her mind.

The phone rang, and Alex grabbed it. It was a donation of twenty thousand dollars – that brought the total up to a little over nine million eight hundred and seventy thousand – they were still well over a million short and there was less than ten minutes to go.

The volunteers were drained. They had lived the Save The Park project around the clock for the past month and had dreamed what turned out to be an impossible dream. Several were weeping softly and others were hugging one another for comfort. Simone sat with her eyes closed, dejected. Alex went to her and put his arms around her – at this rate the dinner date was going to be a real bust.

It was an ear-shattering scream that could wake the dead. It was Marjo, one of the Liberty Bank volunteers, staring at her computer screen. "A million two hundred seventy-five thousand!" she screamed. "We're over the top!"

The volunteers all jumped up at once and rushed to take a look at Marjo's computer. Was she hallucinating? Had she misread the number by a zero or two? Had she finally cracked under the pressure? Or, was there one more angel out there who had waited until the last moment to swoop down and bless them?

It was no mistake. The money had already been deposited directly into the Save The Park account in the bank. Pandemonium broke out. Everyone was laughing and crying at the same time, hugging one another, and floating on air. In a matter of seconds, the room had been transformed from one resembling a wake into one resembling the Mardi Gras.

Simone leaped on Alex, wrapping her arms around his neck and her legs around his waist as they hugged and he twirled around in circles. Alex had never witnessed a happier time. He was proud to be a small part of it. And, he was glad to see Simone so deliriously happy.

16

Simone was ravishing. She wore a tight white dress that came to just above her knees accompanied by a dazzling string of black pearls and white heels. She seemed five years younger than she had just yesterday, now that the anxiety of the Save The Park fundraiser was over.

They arrived at Wellington's-on-the-Water at six twenty – ten minutes ahead of their reservation. As they approached the Central Emporium, Simone said, "Let's stop in here, we've got a few minutes to kill."

Simone led the way into the Central Emporium and headed straight for the Funhouse Gallery. There was a new employee, probably a high school girl, behind the counter who hadn't been there when he bought up all the Alex Gideon posters, so Alex figured it wouldn't do any harm.

Simone walked straight to the counter, "Do you have any Alex Gideon posters?" she asked.

Alex almost fell through the floor. "What would you want one of *those* for?" he blurted out.

"Sally has been such a help to me this summer. I want to give her a framed poster for her apartment at college," she replied.

Alex was relieved. But on the other hand he wondered if Simone was toying with him.

"Some guy bought all the Alex Gideon posters we had the day

before he disappeared," the clerk said. "We tried to order more, but they're all sold out and there's a three-week wait on backorders. We're keeping a waiting list - if you want I'll put your name down. We have over two hundred names on the list already."

"No thanks," Simone said. "I'll stop back later in the summer."

Alex and Simone turned to leave. "Besides," the clerk said, "I don't know what all the fuss is about – he's not that hot."

Simone broke out in that half-laugh, half-giggle of hers. She looked at Alex and raised her eyebrows and giggled some more.

"I couldn't agree more," Alex said, wondering if the two of them had rehearsed that dialogue.

James himself greeted them at the door. He looked dapper in his dark blue suit with gray pinstripes, white shirt and red and gray necktie.

"Good evening, Simmy – good evening, Al," he said. "We are honored to have you dine with us this evening."

Simone gave him a gentle hug and Alex and James shook hands.

"May I escort you to your table," he said. "Please follow me."

The dining room was nearly full and all eyes were on Simone and Alex as James led them to their table. Alex had to admit that they made a striking couple. Simone not only had great beauty, but she also had that rare combination of class and presence to go with it. And, he, of course, even in disguise, was the famous movie star, Alex Gideon, that the entire world was talking about.

Alex soon discovered why all eyes were on them. James led them to the finest table in the house, in the center along the windows overlooking the lake. While all of the other tables had oil lamp candles, their table had real lighted twelve-inch candles in silver holders. James pulled the chair out for Simone to be seated and then he did the same for Alex. "I'll be back in a moment," he said.

"You have pull," Simone said.

"He wasn't going to give me a table, even after I tried to bribe him, until I told him I was bringing you," Alex said.

"I don't go out for dinner much, so when I do they treat me well," Simone explained.

That was probably true, Alex thought to himself, but it went beyond that. And, it went beyond the type of star power he enjoyed in L.A., where he could command any table he wanted any time he wanted. He had seen it in the way people looked at Simone, in how they talked to her, how they hugged her, and how they reacted to her – it was called respect.

James approached the table and held a bottle for Alex and Simone to view, "A complimentary bottle of wine," he said, "Margaux 1er Grand Cru Classe' Margaux Bordeaux, 1982."

"Very nice," Alex said. Alex preferred a bottle of beer when he drank socially, but with dinner he often drank a glass of wine. He was familiar with this particular vintage – it retailed for about three hundred seventy five dollars a bottle. When James had said he was honored to have them dine in his restaurant, he had meant it. Alex wished he had tipped him a couple of hundred for the table. But then, after being robbed by Filbert, he had been pressed for cash and was in no position to be spreading Franklins around. But, Alex appreciated this wonderful gesture by James and vowed that one day he would find a way to make it up to him.

James removed the cork from the bottle and handed it to Alex. He examined it. It was nice and moist – the bottle had been stored properly. Then he sniffed the cork – it was a pleasant bouquet. He nodded to James, who poured a small amount into Alex's glass. Alex swirled it in his glass, sniffed the wine, and took a sip. He smiled and nodded to James, "Very nice," he said.

211

"I'm glad that you approve," James said as he set the bottle on the table in front of Alex and returned to his duties as host.

Alex poured a glass for Simone, two-thirds full, and poured a glass for himself.

"I propose a toast," Alex said, raising his glass.

Simone raised her glass to within an inch of his.

"To you, for proving to me that I can act, and for renewing my faith in the decency of humanity," Alex said.

"And to you," Simone said, "for sharing your talents with Okoboji and with me, and for helping make some of my dreams come true."

They clinked their glasses lightly and took a sip, while they looked deep into each other's eyes. It was an entrancing moment for Alex and he couldn't help but believe that it was for Simone as well.

Alex ordered gulf shrimp and Simone ordered Maine lobster. It always seemed fitting to Alex to eat some type of seafood while dining in a restaurant by the water.

"What would you have done if the Save The Park fundraiser had failed?" Alex asked.

"I suppose everything would have been moved to a new location a mile or two from the lake and we would have operated from there," she said.

"It would have lost its atmosphere and charm," Alex said.

"I'm afraid attendance would have dropped off considerably and the whole thing might have folded in a couple of years," Simone said. "If that had happened I probably would have looked for a theater to perform in elsewhere in the summertime."

"And leave Okoboji?" Alex asked.

"I would never leave Okoboji completely. It is truly a magical place. But, I probably would have spent just a month here in the summer, vacationing and visiting with friends."

"Friends like Martha?" Alex asked.

"She's a dear friend – of the theater and to me personally," Simone said. "She called me last night when I got home from the wrap party and talked for an hour."

"What did she want?" Alex asked.

"Partly, she was terribly concerned about the Save The Park fundraiser – it would have broken her heart if the theater had been moved elsewhere. And, partly it was personal – she feels this need to protect me."

"From me?" Alex asked.

"No," Simone said with a chuckle, "from myself, mostly."

"That's him! That's him!" someone was shouting from two tables down.

Alex was becoming callused to such ramblings and he didn't even flinch. Three days ago he might have jumped out of the window, thinking he had been busted, but there had been so many false alarms and his disguise was working so well that he didn't even bother to glance at the table.

"I tell you, that's him, "Wild-Eyed Al, the guy with one blue eye and one brown eye."

"Oh, shit," Alex said to himself. He shot a quick glance at the table – there sat the Iowa Navy in their dress whites – the whole damn Iowa Navy, with Whitey at the head of the table.

"Shut up, you old goat," the woman next to him said. "Leave that nice young couple alone."

"But I tell you, that's him, Wild-Eyed Al."

"And I'll tell you one last time – shut up."

Saved again.

Simone was giggling. Half the people in the place were quietly giggling. Whitey was half deaf, and so was his wife, so they both had to shout to hear themselves and each other. Fortunately for Alex, Whitey's words made no sense whatsoever unless someone knew the background from whence they came.

213

"What was that all about?" Simone asked.

Alex looked mystified, "I think he got hit by one too many water balloons in the big battle Saturday."

"Could be," Simone said as she continued to laugh.

Alex could not recall a more wonderful dining experience, except for Whitey, of course. James had been a magnificent host, setting the tone for the evening. The view was splendid as the bright sunlight shined down on the lake and boats passed by creating waves that gently splashed against the shore. The meal had been excellent, including Bananas Foster for dessert. But best of all, he had been alone with this fantastic woman for well over an hour, engaged in real, bona fide, meaningful conversation. Alex had enjoyed the company of many beautiful women in Beverly Hills and around the world, to be sure, but he had longed for something more in a woman – someone with whom to share ideas, hopes, and dreams. And for that reason this dinner had been so extraordinarily special.

James was standing by the door and turned to greet them. "Thank you so much for dining with us tonight," he said as he shook hands with Alex.

"It was a wonderful evening," Alex said. "Just wonderful."

The good news had spread throughout the crowd in the Roof Garden and everyone was in a festive mood. Speculation was rampant, trying to figure out who had made the final contribution that had pushed the total over the top. Some thought it was the Waitt brothers, who had founded Gateway Computers on a farm outside of Sioux City. Some thought it was Warren Buffet, the second richest man in the world, who lived in Omaha and who had spent time in Okoboji as a youth. After all, a nephew of his had donated a share of Buffet's company's stock,

Berkshire Hathaway, America's most expensive stock valued at over sixty thousand dollars per share. It was the first time ever a Buffet family member had parted with a share of Berkshire Hathaway, but the nephew had said, "Some things are just too important." Others thought it might have been Berkley Bedell, founder of the world's largest fishing tackle company, which he started in Spirit Lake, or his son, Tom, who built the company into worldwide prominence and who was a local philanthropist. Some thought it was John and Martha Butterworth, for she loved the theater so. But everyone knew that the donation had been made anonymously and that the donor would most likely never step forth to be recognized.

"Golly, Gee," the voice said from the loudspeaker, "it's great to see everyone here for this celebration, and gosh, if there's one thing we know how to do in Okoboji, it's throw a party." The thunderous applause echoed agreement.

Someone from the Maritime Museum took the microphone, "As you probably all heard, we raised eleven million, one hundred sixty-seven thousand dollars – The Park has been saved!" Again, thunderous applause.

"We asked repeatedly during this fundraiser if there were angels among us – and yes there are," he continued. "We received donations from every state in America and from nine foreign countries. Some were for less than a dollar and some were very substantial – all of these donations were welcome – all of you who gave are the angels that we had prayed for." More wild applause.

One of the things that impressed Alex about Okoboji was that everyone was valued and appreciated. People had given what they could to the fundraiser and every donation, large or small, was equally appreciated. The wealthy were not singled out for special recognition or for a plaque on the wall, nor did they expect it, and the small donors were not looked down upon.

They were all Okobojians, and that was good enough.

Alex thought back to the time when he was a sophomore in high school and the school district decided to build a new library. The fundraising committee sent letters to all of the parents identifying how much they expected them to donate to the cause. Alex's parents had been earmarked by the committee for a thousand-dollar donation. Being told how much to give sent The Kaiser through the roof and being told that the amount was a thousand dollars sent him into orbit. Wanting to do his part, though, The Kaiser had mailed in a check for five hundred dollars. The school didn't even send him an acknowledgement, receipt, or thank you note and when they reached their goal and threw a big party, they only invited the people who had contributed five thousand dollars or more. That was the last time that The Kaiser ever gave a donation to anything. That incident had remained vivid in Alex's mind and when he became wealthy he ignored most of the hundreds of requests for donations that he received every year, choosing to give generously to a few well-chosen charities.

"We're here to celebrate," the speaker said. "There's food in the Majestic Pavilion behind the Roof Garden, the bar is open, all of the amusement park rides are running, free of charge, and the band will be playing shortly – let's party!"

The speaker didn't need to encourage them. The party was on. Mostly everyone milled around, greeting old friends and basking in the glow of the fabulous accomplishment that everyone had contributed to. Some of these people were like the tax man – they were everywhere – Deano, Jodell, Jeff, Dougherty, George, Scotty, Norm, Sparky, Bob, Barb - they were all here.

Martha approached Alex and Simone with a big smile and gave each of them a long, tight hug.

"Where's John?" Alex asked.

"Back in Des Moines," she said. "He's got a new secretary to

216

break in." She let it go at that.

"Remember what I said," Martha said to Simone as she gave her an encouraging look that seemed to say, "and *do* what I said." And then she hugged them both before she moved on.

"There you are – we've been looking for you," he said to Simone. It was the developers, Blaine and Ken.

"We got to thinking," Blaine said. "We have been so fortunate here in Okoboji and now that everything will stay here on the lake where it belongs, we'll continue to be fortunate – so here's the deed to your lot, it's yours."

"You can't do that," Simone protested.

"It's done," Ken said. "We'll consider the money we paid you for the lot to be our contribution to the Save The Park fundraiser."

"I can't accept this," Simone said.

"You have no choice – it's done," Blaine said, as the two of them walked away.

"That's Okoboji. So typically Okoboji," Simone said, on the verge of tears.

It had been years since Alex had ridden on a Tilt-A-Whirl. He had forgotten how the spinning could pin your head back, and how it could press the girl so tightly against you that she was almost sitting on your lap. How he loved riding the Tilt-A-Whirl.

The roller coaster was one of only a handful of wooden roller coasters remaining in America. Earlier in the summer The Society of Wooden Roller Coaster Riders, eighty strong, had ridden the roller coaster non-stop for three hours and had pronounced it one of the two best wooden roller coasters in America. It wasn't as long as some of the modern roller coasters, the declines may not have been as sharp or as deep, and there were no loops, but it was vintage Okoboji – quaint, but cool. Simone screamed throughout the entire ride and Alex laughed.

217

It was a great ride, but once was enough.

The view from the top of the Ferris wheel was magnificent. It was on the edge of the amusement park, lakeside, and you could see for miles. Simone pointed out landmarks every time they reached the top and started back down – West Lake in front of them and off to the left, East Lake on the right beyond Highway 71, and the town of Spirit Lake off in a distance. They rode the Ferris wheel three times before returning to the Roof Garden to rejoin the party.

The band, in typical Save The Park fashion, was made up of volunteers from a variety of bands. There was John Senn, Denny Storey, Bob Godbersen, Gary Lind, and Denny Kintzi, from Dee Jay and The Runaways, Al Klein and Shane Von Holdt from Mosquito Flats, Dean Aakhus, Steve Streit, and Christopher Jon from Daybreak, Terry Klein and Rusty Davis from Upson Downs, rising star Damon Dotson, and, of course, Maestro Horsman. They sounded like they had been playing together for years and were a great band to dance to.

Filbert was dancing with a skinny redhead a few feet from Alex and Simone. The big blonde was nowhere in sight – she was probably off seeking other conquests now that she had satisfied her curiosity about that semi-famous movie star, Filbert Kauffman. A sudden urge came over Alex – he could take Filbert out right then and there with a quick jab to the ribs or an elbow to the side of the head and everyone would think it was an accident. But, no, he would not stoop to Filbert's level. He had already reaped a good measure of revenge by dumping the big blonde on him. And, the day would come soon when he would confront Filbert Kauffman face to face, as Alex Gideon, and would ask him to repeat the vicious things he had said about the Bunny Boy – and he would watch Filbert crumble right before his eyes. And then, he would get the money back that

Filbert had stolen, with interest. He was, after all, the star of that fabulous movie, *Terminator Bunny*.

"It's not worth it," Simone said, apparently being adept at reading body language herself.

"Some day," Alex said, "but not right now. After all, this is a party."

The party broke up at about ten thirty, as people headed for the bars and for their boats.

"You don't have to get up early tomorrow morning," Alex said.

"No, I don't," she smiled. "What did you have in mind?"

"You probably wouldn't approve of what I have in mind," he said.

"Try me," Simone said.

17

Alex had been allowed to where no man in Okoboji had ever been – to the inner sanctum of Simone Delaney's existence. He drank with her in her kitchen, he laughed with her in her den, and he danced closely with her and kissed her passionately in her living room. But, he was not allowed to enter into the inner, inner sanctum of her bedroom.

And now here he was, lying alone in his bed at the Four Seasons Resort. To make things worse, the couple in the next room was really getting it on, and the damned bed squeaked to boot. She reminded him of a saying that he had once read on the condom machine in a men's restroom, "If she is a mourner, this will turn her into a screamer – if she is a screamer, this will get you arrested." The police should be arriving with guns drawn at any moment.

Alex was too hot and bothered to sleep. He reflected on the evening, especially the part in Simone's apartment. They had danced so closely that they were almost in each other's pants. They had kissed so passionately that his lips almost bled. They said sweet nothings to each other. But, then, at the point where any woman he had ever known would have ripped his clothes off, and hers, too, Simone had suddenly turned it off and had sent him packing with a goodnight kiss. On one hand, he had to admire and respect Simone – she was not a woman who gave of herself easily, either emotionally or physically. On the other hand, he had to wonder just what game she was playing here, anyway.

Alex covered his head with a pillow. He wished the police would hurry and get there.

Alex must have slept, for he was now waking up. He checked his watch - nine o'clock. He had no plans until two in the afternoon, when he was to meet Simone at the theater for an afternoon convertible ride. She wanted to show him where she planned to build her dream house and wanted to drive him past some of the beautiful lakeshore homes.

Alex turned on the television and flipped through the channels. And there he was, that damned Peter Jenkins, making another breakthrough announcement. "We have just learned that an enormous ransom payment was transferred from Alex Gideon's investment account yesterday afternoon. So far, investigators have not revealed the exact amount of the payment nor have they been able to determine where the funds were sent. For additional news in the Alex Gideon disappearance, we go to our affiliate in Beverly Hills."

Alex almost croaked. Somehow, they had found out that Barbara had transferred money from his account yesterday. No doubt they were questioning her at this very moment, and Annie, too. Annie didn't know anything, so they wouldn't learn anything from her. Barbara didn't know everything, but she knew enough to throw a clinker into his plans. But, she had a passion for her client's confidentiality and Alex knew she wouldn't talk – even if they threw her in jail. Oh, oh, he hadn't thought of that. This was serious. Two innocent friends of his had now been dragged into the investigation. He may need to do something about this very soon.

The newscast cut to a reporter who was standing on the street in front of Alex's gated mansion. Behind him was a huge crowd, all of whom were women.

"Peter, I am standing in front of Alex Gideon's forty-five room, fifty million dollar mansion in Beverly Hills."

Alex almost croaked for a second time. They had added nine rooms to his house and thirty million dollars to its value since their coverage of "the disappearance" had begun a few days ago.

"As you can see," the reporter continued, "there are literally thousands of Alex Gideon fans holding a vigil here outside his mansion. Some of them have been here day and night since the news of Mr. Gideon's disappearance broke last week. It is a grief-stricken group, weeping and hugging each other for support, holding out hope against hope that somehow, miraculously their idol will be delivered to them safe and sound."

"How did they react to the news that a ransom has been paid?" Jenkins asked.

"No one knows exactly what to think, Peter," the reporter said. "Half of them believe he may soon be released, since the ransom has been paid. The other half are fearful that the kidnappers will do away with him so he cannot identify them. It is a time of great anxiety as emotions have been swinging widely with every bit of news that breaks and with every rumor that surfaces."

"He is truly loved by his fans from all over the world," Jenkins said.

"There is one more thing I want to show our viewers," the reporter said as he walked through the crowd toward the fence. The camera panned the fence as the reporter spoke. "As you can see, Peter, there are literally thousands of cards and signs that have been piled up here and have been taped to the wrought iron fence outside the mansion. And here, as you can see..."

The reporter paused for a moment until the cameraman could move in for the proper shot. "Here are hundreds and hundreds of stuffed bunny rabbits of all sizes and colors that fans have placed here as a symbol of love and hope for Alex Gideon, the Bunny Boy."

Alex pushed the off switch on the remote. He hung his head for a moment, deep in thought. He knew his fans would take the news of his disappearance hard but he had been oblivious to the extent of their worry and grief and had been unaware of their round-the-clock vigil. And now, he sat here in a motel room in Okoboji and he grieved for them. For seven years he had brought his fans happiness and joy – now he had brought them sorrow. This was the day that he would put an end to that, but he had a few particulars to take care of first. And, for the sake of his fans, he vowed that from this day forward he would be proud to be known as Alex Gideon, the Bunny Boy.

Alex grabbed the phone on the second ring. It was Sally. "Did you hear the news?" She asked anxiously. "A huge ransom was paid for Alex Gideon's release."

"I heard," Alex said.

"I'm so afraid that the kidnappers might do him harm," she said. Alex's heart ached for her.

"Are you going to see Simmy today?" Sally asked.

"Yes, this afternoon," Alex said.

"I don't have the heart to tell her myself, but will you tell her for me – I'm going to Beverly Hills to join the vigil until Alex Gideon is home safely."

"No!" Alex shouted. "Don't go."

"I have to," she pleaded.

"Trust me," he said, now being the one who was pleading. "He will show up within twenty-four hours, safe and sound."

"Do you really think so?" Sally asked with hope in her voice.

"I haven't mislead you yet, have I?" he asked.

"No, you haven't," she replied.

"And you can trust me now, too," he said. "Besides, Simone

needs you to help with the theater, she's counting on you."

"Well, maybe you're right," she said, "but if he doesn't show up in twenty-four hours, I'm going to Beverly Hills no matter what you say."

"Fair enough," Alex said with a sigh. He had averted yet another crisis.

Alex had to move fast. He had places to go, things to do, and people to see. This would be one of the most important days of his life. No, it would be *the* most important day of his life.

Alex was entering the theater as Big Teddy was leaving. "She's not here," Big Teddy said.

Alex's heart sunk.

Big Teddy read the look on Alex's face. "She just went over to the Maritime Museum for a few minutes – she'll be back soon," he said with a grin.

The theater was empty. Alex climbed up on the stage and faced the empty seats. It had been wonderful, performing here incognito playing the parts of William and Nathan with Simone, Sally, Big Teddy, and the others. They simply knew him as Al from Rapid City and they had accepted him with open arms. It was a time he would treasure for always.

As a movie star in Hollywood and as an actor here in Okoboji, Alex had learned the value of rehearsing. He was about to make his most important delivery ever, and he had not yet been able to write the script. He imagined her standing there in front of him.

"You probably know who I am," he started as his voice echoed in the empty theater. "No, no, that's no good."

He started over, "I think you know more than I think you know," he said. He paused for a moment, frowned, and started again. "I know you think more than I know you know.

"You sound like a babbling idiot," he said to himself. "Why not just come out and tell her – she probably knows anyway."

He took a deep breath and spoke the words loud and clear. "Simone, I am Alex Gideon. I think you know I am Alex Gideon. I disguised myself and came here to Okoboji from Beverly Hills for a short vacation and I met you and fell in love with you. I, Alex Gideon, the Bunny Boy, am in love with you."

There was a crash followed by a thud behind the stage. Alex rushed to see what had happened. There, lying on the floor, unconscious, was Sally.

"Sally, Sally," Alex said as he gently slapped her face.

She opened her eyes and looked up at Alex like she was seeing the Holy Ghost. "Are you really my Bunny Boy, Alex Gideon?"

"Yes," he said. "I really am."

She passed out again. Alex slapped her face gently and she came around again. He put his arm under her shoulder and head and raised her up to a sitting position.

"You've got to stop doing that," he said.

"It's really you, here in Okoboji?"

"Don't faint again," he said.

Sally grabbed him and hugged him with all her might. He hugged her in return.

"I'm so happy you're safe," Sally said as a wave of relief washed over her.

"You're not mad at me for not telling you?" Alex asked.

"Oh, no," she said, "I could never be mad at you – I know you had your reasons and they were good ones, and that's good enough for me. I'm just so relieved. I'm just so happy."

In the back of his mind, Alex knew that this was the way his fans would react - relieved, happy, and non-judgmental. If their Bunny Boy had found it necessary to disappear for a few days while the world went nuts looking for him, that was good enough for them. They would not question it and they would fiercely defend him against anyone who did. Such is the loyalty of the Bunny Boy's fans.

"If you still want to go to Hollywood and be a movie star, I can make it happen," Alex said.

Sally thought for a moment. "No," she said, "after seeing that Charlie Waller and Heather Devreaux in action, I want nothing to do with that bunch in Hollywood. I'm going to make a career of the theater, just like Simmy did."

"That's a wise choice," Alex said.

"Speaking of Simmy, are you in love with her?" Sally asked.

"Yes, I am," Alex said. "I love her with all my heart."

"Then go after her," Sally said, "and keep me in mind for the Maid of Honor."

"I will. I will do both of those things," Alex vowed as he helped Sally to her feet.

Sally hugged him again. "I'm so glad you're safe. My prayers have been answered."

"Can I ask a favor of you?" Alex asked.

"Yes, anything," Sally replied.

"Please don't say anything to anybody – I need just a little more time to work things out."

She looked him in the eyes and made a vow, "You can count on me."

They walked to the stage, hugged again, and Sally headed for the exit with wings on her feet. "Good luck," she called back.

Simone entered the theater when Sally was a few feet from the exit, "Hello, Simmy," she said with a melody in her voice.

Simone stopped and watched her as she left the theater and started skipping down the sidewalk.

"What's with her?" Simone asked Alex.

"She's just happy to be in Okoboji," Alex said.

227

Simone joined him on the stage. He took her hands in his and leaned back so both of their arms were fully extended. They looked into each other's eyes, each waiting for the other to make a move. Slowly, they turned in a circle, counterclockwise.

"I have something to tell you," Alex said.

"I know," Simone said.

"Know what?" Alex asked, hoping that maybe she would take the lead.

"I know that you have something to tell me," she said.

"Oh," he said, still searching for the right words.

"I have to go away," he said.

"I know," she replied.

"I have other things to tell you, too," he said. God, this was hard, trying to find the way to say it.

"I know," she said.

"I'm not who people around here think I am," he said.

"Oh?" she said, not helping him out one bit.

"Do you know?" he asked. "Do you know who I am?"

"Are you trying to tell me something?" she asked.

They kept turning slowly, holding onto each other's hands as the mental gymnastics continued.

"When did you first know?" Alex asked, changing strategies to a technique known as *begging the question*, where you assume that question number one has been answered and now you're on to question number two. It's like asking someone, "Are you still beating your dog?"

"Who said I knew something?" Simone asked.

"Was it in Ruebins when Sally screamed?"

"No, I thought you had pinched her in the ass."

"I mean after that – when they said on television that – that *he* was missing?"

"No, not then," She answered.

Finally, it seemed that he was making some progress. "Then

228

when?" he asked.

Simone took a deep breath. It was time for her to come clean. "When Filbert said those terrible things about Alex Gideon, I saw the hurt in your eyes. Then, when Sally attacked him, I saw your gratitude. Then, when Filbert asked me if Alex Gideon could act, I said, 'He has potential,' and realized that those were the same words I had used to describe your acting after your audition for the part of William. Then someone said that a *guy* had bought up all of the Alex Gideon posters and pictures - before it had been announced that he was missing. That was very curious, since it is women who adore Alex Gideon and buy his posters. Shortly after that, when Bev from the Funhouse Gallery approached the table, I could see the panic in your eyes. I was pretty sure that it was you who had bought the posters - and then you acted like you'd never met her. I wasn't certain, but it all made sense. Then, when you comforted Sally, telling her that he was safe and that she had nothing to worry about – you said it like you knew it was true. And then the name – Alex – Al – well, that was the clincher. After that, I was just curious to see what you were going to do next."

"You didn't tell Sally?"

"No. This was your scene and I decided to let you play it out. If she had become despondent or if I feared she would do something rash, I would have told her," Simone said. "I was watching her pretty close."

"There were times that I thought you knew, but I was never certain," Alex said.

"There were probably some signs," Simone said, "but nothing that I did on purpose to give you a hint. Why did you come to Okoboji, anyway?"

"To get away from Charlie and Heather and the screaming fans. Believe it or not, I threw a dart at a map and it landed on Okoboji – it was divine guidance."

"Why didn't you leave and go back to Beverly Hills when the news broke?" Simone asked.

"I think you know," Alex said.

"Did you know that just a half hour ago they announced the amount of the ransom that was paid?" She asked, suddenly becoming a little testy.

"No," Alex said. He had figured that it was only a matter of time before that came out and he had hoped that Simone would not put two and two together.

"I went over to the Maritime Museum, just to double check – the ransom paid was coincidentally one million, two hundred seventy-five thousand dollars – the same as the anonymous donation that put us over the top." There was a tinge of accusation in her voice now.

"That's quite a coincidence," Alex said dryly.

"Did you think that I would fly into bed with you just because you dumped some money, pocket change for you, into the fundraiser account?" Simone said sharply.

This was not the way Alex had played out this scene in his mind. This woman could be feisty when she thought someone might be trying to compromise her.

"No, never," he said. "You're not that way."

"You're right, I'm not," she said, relaxing a bit.

"But, I did do it for you – and Martha, and Sally, and Big Teddy, and everybody in the theater troupe - and for Okoboji. I did it because I could, and I didn't think anybody would ever find out – I hoped nobody would ever find out," Alex said.

"You would never have told me?" Simone asked.

"No. I didn't want anybody to know and I didn't want anybody to question my motives," he said.

"Sorry," Simone said with a wince.

"Apology accepted," Alex said, smugly.

"Do you think I'm a good actor?" Simone asked.

"Why, yes. Very good," Alex answered.

"Has it occurred to you that since I knew who you really were and knew that you had lots of money and knew that the fundraiser would probably fall short, that I kept you around, led you on, and set you up for a big donation at the end to bail us out?" She was smiling a wicked smile.

Alex couldn't believe his ears. Had this, the woman of his dreams, been nothing but a small-time hustler who had cleverly conned him into donating more than a million dollars to some outfit he had never even heard of a week ago? If it were true, The Kaiser would not only be turning over in his grave, he'd be spinning like a pinwheel.

"No, never," Alex said. "You're not like that."

Simone looked him in the eyes for a moment and a little smile tugged at her lips. Alex was afraid that he was about to hear the words that would tear his dreams apart.

"You're right," Simone said. "I'm not."

The time was right and Alex seized the moment. "Simone, I might be out of line here, but I just have to say what I've got to say – and you might hate me forever – but I love you. I've always loved you, and I will always love you."

Simone blushed. She looked away from Alex and smiled weakly.

"You're supposed to say, "Oh Alex, I've been such a fool, I…""

"I know the words," she said, "but William and Savanna were just actors in a play – those were just words. This is real life."

"I'm not acting," Alex said.

"There would be so many complications," she protested.

"Martha talked to you about us, didn't she?" Alex asked.

"You're pretty clever," Simone answered. "She likes you – she told me."

"What else did she tell you?" Alex asked.

Simone hesitated for a moment. There are some things a lady

doesn't tell. But, if there ever was a time to tell it all, this was it.

"She and George C. Scott were in love. He begged her to go with him when he left for Hollywood, but she was afraid. She was afraid that the great actor may have been leading her on. She was afraid that she was infatuated and not truly in love. She was afraid that she would get lost in his world of movie deals and starlets. She was afraid it wouldn't last. So he left, but vowed to return and to make her his bride."

"Did she ever see him again?" Alex asked.

"Martha waited three years without hearing from him and finally gave in to John's pleas to marry him. Two years after she was married, George showed up and wanted her to go with him. Her heart told her to go but her mind told her to stay."

"Did she ever regret it?" Alex asked.

"No, not the second time. She was married and she honored that commitment. She and John have had a good life together and she has never regretted not going with George," Simone said.

"And the first time?" Alex asked.

"She has regretted it deeply her entire life. She wonders what might have been if only she had not been afraid to take a chance – to take a chance on love."

"And you?" Alex asked. "Are you afraid?"

"Yes, I'm afraid. For one thing, I'm afraid all the Bunny Boy fans would hate me," she said with a smile.

"You don't understand them – they're special. They would be truly happy for me that I finally found the love of my life - and they would be happy for you, too. Besides, it's time to put this Bunny Boy adulation to rest and for them to go on with their lives," Alex said.

"I'm afraid that..."

"What would Martha tell you to do?" Alex asked, playing his trump card.

Simone smiled as she looked at him. A tear was forming in the corner of her eye. "She would tell me to follow my heart," Simone said.

"My heart tells me that I love you and that I always want to be with you," Alex said. "What does your heart tell you?"

Simone let loose of Alex's hands and looked down for a moment, thinking. She looked up and their eyes met. She smiled weakly and turned from Alex.

His heart stopped. How could he have such power over millions of women who had never met him but not be able to win the love of his life?

And then Simone turned to Alex. She took two quick steps, jumped into his arms, and kissed him madly. Alex always liked the part best where the guy ends up getting the girl. Her lips had not said the words, but they didn't have to − her body was screaming loud and clear, "I love you! I love you, Alex Gideon!"

He would leave for Beverly Hills in an hour. He would slip through the side gate and sneak into his mansion unnoticed. He would dye his hair back to its original color, remove the brown contact lenses, take out the tooth caps, glue on a mustache and shaggy beard, and be instantly transformed into Alex Gideon, the Bunny Boy.

He would phone that reporter from the television station in Beverly Hills and cut a deal − a live interview in return for his promise to help persuade all of the Bunny Boy fans around the world to go back to their own lives and to let Alex Gideon enjoy his in peace and quiet. He would lend a hand to those two idiots, Charlie Waller and Heather Devreaux to help them out of the jam they had gotten themselves into. They belonged in a nuthouse, true, but they didn't belong in jail. And then he would be done with both of them. The question would remain − where had Alex Gideon been these days that he was missing? He would simply tell them that he had been with friends. If they needed to know more, they would need to figure it out for themselves.

They say that home is where the heart is. Alex believed that to be true. He had a few details to take care of in Beverly Hills that may take a day or two, and then he would be going home – home to Okoboji.

The End